AN INTRODUCTION TO PLEASURE

MISTRESS MATCHMAKER, BOOK 1

JESS MICHAELS

An Introduction to Pleasure

Mistress Matchmaker Book 1

Copyright © Jesse Petersen, 2012

ISBN: 978-1-947770-22-5

For more information, contact Jess Michaels

www.AuthorJessMichaels.com

To contact the author:

Email: Jess@AuthorJessMichaels.com

Twitter www.twitter.com/JessMichaelsbks

Facebook: www.facebook.com/JessMichaelsBks

Jess Michaels raffles a gift certificate EVERY month to members of her newsletter, so sign up on her website:

http://www.authorjessmichaels.com/

As always, for Michael, who knows why.

CHAPTER 1

1811

The hack was overly hot and smelled of whatever its last occupants had been eating during their travels. The seats were covered with threadbare fabric and the cushioning had long ago worn away to leave hard patches. However, all these things were not why Lysandra Keates shifted in discomfort.

Rather than her mode of transportation, it was her destination that gave her pause and made her quake. And now they were here, in front of a rather marvelous London estate that was obviously well tended but these facts gave Lysandra no comfort. In fact, she was utterly numb as she stared through the dirty carriage window to the house.

"I do not wish to do this," she whispered to herself, clutching her reticule against her chest. It was very light, thanks to its nearly empty state.

And that was why she *was* here, despite her strong misgivings.

Suddenly the door to the hack flew open and sunlight streamed into the confined space, making Lysandra lift her hand to her eyes until they adjusted and the man who had opened the door became more than shadow. The driver was fat, sweaty and scowling.

"'Ey, are you going in or what, chit?" he snapped. "I don't have all day to wait for you to make up your damn mind."

Lysandra flinched both at his harsh tone and the strong scent of uncooked onion coming from his rancid, rotting breath. She had never been spoken to in such a coarse fashion...at least not until this most recent year of her life. Now it felt all the more commonplace.

Still, this was her last chance to make this decision, to answer the question he so rudely posed to her.

"Well?" he said as he folded his arms.

She swallowed. Like it or not, this was her only choice, wasn't it? She had gone over all the others and here she was. Slowly, she nodded.

"Y-yes. I'm going in."

The driver smirked as he looked her up and down in slow, leering appraisal. With a start, Lysandra realized he knew what this place was. Who this place belonged to, and he was judging her accordingly.

Hot blood rushed to her cheeks, making her dizzy as her stomach turned ever so slightly. She forced herself to speak, though, to maintain what little dignity she had left.

"Will you wait for me while I have my meeting?" she asked.

Not that she wished to see this man ever again, but hailing another hack might be difficult.

He gave her a grin that revealed missing and rotting teeth and shrugged. "Love to, but it will cost you."

Lysandra clutched her nearly empty reticule closer. She could scarcely pay for her trip here and home, there was no way she could afford a fee for sitting, too. It was a long walk back, but once again, she had no choices.

"Very well, then be on your way," she said as she pushed past him and got down from the vehicle without his assistance. She didn't wish to touch him.

He chuckled as he slammed the hack door behind her and swung back up into the driver's seat. As he pulled away, his laughter echoed and she shivered, feeling as dirty as if she had allowed his hand to take hers.

Once he was gone, that feeling faded, but it left another in its wake:

Doom.

There was no going back now.

With a sigh, she smoothed her gown, which was two seasons out of style and at least a size too big, and then forced herself to move up the marble staircase and to the very tall, very official-looking black door. With shaking hands, she knocked and in a few moments, it opened to reveal a butler dressed in a smart livery that spoke of the homeowner's wealth and taste.

Lysandra drew back in surprise.

"Good afternoon, miss," the butler said, his tone bland, though not unfriendly. "May I help you?"

Lysandra blinked a few times, still taken aback by how very sophisticated the servant seemed to be. She had expected many things, but not this.

The butler tilted his head. "Miss?"

She shook her head. "I'm so sorry, my mind wandered. M-my name is Lysandra Keates and I'm here to see Miss Manning."

The servant's brow wrinkled ever so slightly and his gaze flitted over her, not in the leering fashion of the driver, but judging nonetheless. Lysandra forced herself not to shift under his appraisal and prayed her cheeks weren't flushed with embarrassment.

"And do you have an appointment?" he finally asked, not unkindly.

Lysandra pursed her lips. She hadn't even thought to make one. "I... No, I do not. But I assure you, I do not wish to trouble her, nor take up too much of her time. But this is a matter of great importance and I really must see her if she is at home."

She swallowed hard as she awaited the servant's decision whether to even allow her entry into the foyer, let alone to have an audience with the woman she had come to see. If he wouldn't...

Well, she had no idea what she would do. Her options were few and very unpleasant at that.

"Do you have a card?" he asked.

Lysandra sucked in a breath. A card. Of course that was what someone who mattered would present.

"No," she whispered and couldn't help it when her gaze slipped down to her feet.

There was a moment's hesitation, and Lysandra waited for the inevitable excuse that Miss Manning was not at home at present, but that the servant would certainly pass along a message. Which, of course, he wouldn't. Why would he trouble his mistress with such a trivial person who she did not even know?

"If you will follow me to the west parlor, I will ascertain if Miss Manning is currently at home," the butler said.

Lysandra jerked her gaze to his face. Although his expression was still bland, his eyes were kind and filled with understanding, which actually made her want to weep. But she pushed that reaction aside and simply nodded.

"Oh, thank you so much," she whispered and followed him down a short hallway and into a small, elegant parlor.

"I will be but a moment. Please help yourself to tea and cakes on the sideboard if you would like." He gave her a short bow and then backed from the room, shutting the door behind him.

Lysandra covered her mouth as she sank into a chair before the low fire. Somehow she had made it past the first challenge in meeting Miss Manning. There was no guarantee the woman would see her, of course, but this was far closer than Lysandra had ever dared to believe she could come.

Her gaze slipped to the cakes the butler had so kindly offered, and her stomach growled faintly. She had eaten no breakfast and her lunch had consisted of only a hunk of dry bread with a ridiculously thin wedge of cheese.

She got to her feet and slipped to the table. With a quick glance at the door, she yanked her handkerchief from her reticule and quickly folded a cake into the fabric before she returned it to her bag. She was too nervous to eat now, but tonight this would supplement whatever meager supper, or lack thereof, awaited her.

The door behind her opened and Lysandra spun around, guilty and embarrassed that she had nearly been caught stealing cakes like a child. But those feelings faded as a woman swept into the room.

She was utterly beautiful, with honey-blonde hair twisted into an intricate fashion. Her pale blue gown was of the finest quality silk and had hand-stitched pink rosettes that cascaded over the fall of the skirt. Lysandra had never been of the *ton*, even before her life had changed, but she had worked for her betters. This woman put them all to shame.

"Good afternoon, my dear," the lady said as she closed the door behind her. "I am Vivien Manning."

Lysandra sucked in a breath. Of course, this had to be true, but...

"But you don't look like a—"

With a gasp, Lysandra covered her mouth with a trembling hand. Dear God, had she almost voiced that statement aloud? Insulted this woman who held her fate in her perfectly manicured fingers?

But Miss Manning did not look insulted. In fact, her expression didn't even falter as she said, "A whore?"

Lysandra flinched both at the harsh word and the fact that Miss Manning knew that the word had been her intent.

"There, there, Miss Keates," the other woman said with a smile. "I have been called far worse. Now please, do sit down. Have some tea. You look very pale."

Lysandra took a step backward and managed to take the seat she had abandoned just moments before. She watched silently as Miss Manning poured her a cup of tea, adding a generous amount of sugar to the cup and placing one of those delectable cakes on a plate. Once she had handed everything over to Lysandra, she took her own place in a chair across from hers and smiled.

"Now, I do not believe we have ever met before this afternoon, have we?" She shrugged. "I meet a great many people, of course, but I normally do remember faces, if not names."

Lysandra took a cautious bite of her cake and a sip of tea before she responded. "No, we have never met."

Miss Manning pursed her lips. "I did not think so. I must ask you, then, why have you come to my home? My servant gave me the impression that it seemed to be of great import for you to meet with me."

Any appetite Lysandra had possessed fled in an instant. She set her half eaten cake aside and stared at the woman who held her future without even knowing it.

"Miss Manning—" she began.

"Vivien," the other woman said softly.

Lysandra blinked. She had never called a woman who had rank or power over her by her first name. But Vivien seemed to offer the privilege without thought or ulterior motive.

"Vivien," she corrected herself with discomfort. "I apologize for intruding upon your home and your time without invitation, but I find myself in a quite dire situation that I fear you may be the only person to solve."

Vivien tilted her head. "I'm listening."

Lysandra sucked in her breath before she continued. "You see, ma'am, I-I have heard of what you...are. What you...do."

"Ah." Vivien stared at her evenly. "And what is that? Just so that we do not misunderstand each other as this conversation continues."

Lysandra hesitated. She had never said out loud the kind of words that would be required to describe Vivien Manning's life and profession. Dear Lord, it was embarrassing enough to think them in her head.

But here she was, and this was the lady's demand.

"I— Well—"

Vivien leaned back in her chair and smiled at her, kind and patient. "Take your time, Lysandra."

It was the use of her first name that put Lysandra at ease. She had been so far removed from anyone of an intimate enough acquaintance to use her given name, except for her mother, that it sounded sweet to her ears.

"I know you are, or have been, a mistress to many men in the *ton*," she managed to croak out with a powerful and hot blush burning her cheeks.

Vivien smiled, wan. "Several, though I wouldn't categorize it as *many*."

The other woman tilted her head, and Lysandra realized Vivien expected her to continue. She gathered her strength, cleared her thick throat and did so.

"I have also heard rumor that you...well, that you have matched ladies who wish to become mistresses to gentleman of rank."

Vivien's eyes grew wide with surprise. "I did not realize that was such common knowledge outside of my own circle."

Lysandra shook her head. "I do not think it is. I simply heard someone speaking of it in a house I once served."

A house of horrors, though at least it had given her the name of this woman. *If* Vivien would help her, perhaps there was some value to the end of her time as a servant.

"And *that* is why you've come here," Vivien said softly.

Lysandra dipped her head. She had never spoken her next words out loud, either. And they were much harder to push past her lips, for once they were said, they could never be taken back. They would change not only how she saw herself but who she was.

"Yes," she finally whispered. "I have come here to ask to be matched with a gentleman. A protector. If it would not be too much trouble for you."

CHAPTER 2

*N*ow that the shocking request had been spoken out loud, Lysandra was surprised to find she actually felt better. She had been dreading this moment for days, ever since she realized this was the only course of action left for her, but now that it was out, an unexpected peace came over her like a warm blanket after a very cold winter.

A peace that was quickly replaced by anxiety when she realized that Vivien Manning was staring at her. Simply *staring*, almost like Lysandra had sprouted a second head or danced a lively jig on the table before the Queen.

"I have offended you," Lysandra said softly, almost more to herself than because she expected an answer from Vivien.

The other woman blinked a few times, but then a slow smile lifted the corners of her lips.

"No, not offended. You *have* surprised me, and no one has done that in an age."

Lysandra covered her face with her hands. "I'm sorry."

Vivien laughed. "Don't be. I find I rather enjoy the sensation.

Slowly, Lysandra let her hands fall away and she looked at Vivien. The other woman had no malice in her expression, nor mocking. In fact, she had a kindness to her face that once again surprised Lysandra. She had not been raised to think that women of Vivien's kind could be so...nuanced.

Or that she could like one as she was beginning to like Vivien.

"But, my dear, what you are asking...it is quite a lot."

Lysandra tried to ignore the tightening in her chest and the tickle of tears that stung her eyes.

"I do understand that," she said.

But Vivien shook her head slowly. "I'm almost certain you do not. You see, while I *have* matched certain ladies as mistresses to certain gentlemen, I don't just match up any woman with any man. There is nothing willy-nilly about it."

Lysandra clasped her hands together tightly. She almost felt like a schoolgirl in the face of Vivien's wise attitude. "No, of course not. You would not have the success that is whispered about you if you did that."

Vivien smiled as she continued, "You and I have only just met. How would I know your disposition? Your values?"

Lysandra could sense the final refusal hovering in Vivien's next sentence. To head that inevitability off, she jumped to her feet.

"I could tell you! I *would* tell you anything you wished to know, I assure you!"

Vivien's smile fell, replaced with concern. "Lysandra—"

Without thinking, Lysandra fell to her knees in front of the other woman and clasped both her hands. "Please, please do not refuse me."

"You are trembling," Vivien whispered.

"This is my only choice," Lysandra said, just as softly. "Please, if there is anything I can do or say, any way I can convince you to be my savior, I will do it."

It was only then that she realized the tears had begun to fall, trailing down her cheeks.

Vivien clucked her tongue and pulled one of her hands free from Lysandra's to grab a handkerchief from the pocket of her pelisse.

"Here, take this," she said as she handed it over.

Lysandra retook her seat and dabbed away the tears. "I'm sorry. I did not intend to come here and deposit my difficulties onto your doorstep."

Vivien shook her head. "Clearly you are in a most difficult position and though I do not know the details, I do understand. I've been there myself. But I am not certain you truly know what you are asking me to do for you. And I hesitate to introduce you to this life if you aren't ready for all it entails."

Lysandra squeezed her eyes shut. She had been trying very hard not to think of what "this life" would entail. Foggy images clouded her brain, but she shoved them aside. In this, she could not waver.

"Miss Manning, I assure you that while I may not be as experienced as some of the women in your acquaintance, I do know what I'm asking of you. And I can only hope that you will help, for my alternatives are far more unpleasant."

Vivien's eyes shut, and she sat like that for almost a full minute before she sighed. "I suppose if you are in such dire straits then those alternatives would be quite terrible. I would hate to be the one to place you in their path. So yes, if you insist on this course of action, I will help you."

Lysandra was seated, but she gripped the arms of the chair as dizzy relief washed over her in an almost uncontrollable wave.

"Thank God," she breathed.

Vivien smiled again, but this time there was a sadness to the expression. "I will need to ask you a few questions in order to best help you."

Lysandra refocused and bit her lip. "Of course."

"This is delicate, but what kind of experience *do* you have?"

Lysandra tried to focus over the increased throbbing of her heart. Here was the difficulty. If she told Vivien the truth, she could easily lose the opportunity she had finally won. If she lied, she could end up far over her head. But better the second than the first.

"Not much, as I said," she finally answered. "But I am aware of the expectations placed upon a mistress."

Once again, Vivien was quiet for a very long time, simply watching Lysandra through a hooded and nearly unreadable gaze. To Lysandra's surprise and relief, she did not press the issue, but instead said, "And what do you ask for in a protector?"

Now it was Lysandra who was silenced by surprise. She hadn't thought much about that subject, mostly because she had never thought a mistress could demand anything of her protector. Wasn't it he who held all the power, along with the purse?

But when it came down to it, wouldn't she ask for the same qualities in a lover that she had once hoped for in a husband?

"A kind man," she said, almost beneath her breath. "One who would not be cruel. One who would take care of me and not mind if I had other...responsibilities."

Vivien's expression grew softer. "A child?"

She shook her head. "M-my mother. She is quite ill."

Slowly, Vivien nodded. "I see."

There was one more silence between the two women. Lysandra couldn't help thinking of her mother, and she had a suspicion Vivien's thoughts were also of people she loved and had sacrificed for.

Finally, the other woman shook her head as if clearing her thoughts and said, "I can make you no promises, Lysandra. Leave your information with Nettle, the butler who showed you the room, and I will call you back to meet with me within a week at most."

Lysandra clutched her reticule with both hands and pushed to her feet. A week was so long to wait, especially considering her current situation, but she could ask for no more from Vivien.

"Thank you," she whispered. "I so appreciate your assistance."

Vivien waved her hand as if her help mattered little, but as Lysandra slipped from the room, the swell of emotion that filled her was not to be minimized. This woman, if she could truly help Lysandra, could save her life.

And for that, she would never be able to repay her debt to Vivien.

. . .

*A*ndrew sighed as his carriage pulled up to the London estate he had taken almost five years ago. There was nothing wrong with the beautiful home, per se. In fact, many complimented it and envied him its posh situation near St. James's Park. But regardless, he did not look forward to these quarterly trips to Town. If it were up to him, he would let the place out and stay in the country permanently.

But his father requested his visits. And he respected the man too much to refuse him, even for very good reason.

The carriage stopped, and he stepped out to find the main members of his staff lined up and awaiting him. With a forced smile, he greeted each one by name and asked a personal yet empty question about family or illness or whatever else came to mind.

And as always, he saw the pity and worry flash in their stares before they could cover the reactions. Once those things had made him angry. Now they were just embarrassing and tiresome.

The last servant in the line was his butler, Pruett. Unlike the others, he was able to keep any emotion from his face, thanks to a great many more years of experience in service. He had been with Andrew's family for years.

"Welcome home, Viscount Callis," the older man said with a shallow bow at the waist.

"Thank you, Pruett," Andrew said as he led the way inside. The other servants dispersed back to their duties, leaving him alone with the butler in the foyer.

"And are there any messages?" he asked.

It was habit to request them when he arrived, when in truth he expected only something from his father. His old friends no longer tried to coax him back into their wicked lives and he hadn't tried to make many new friends since...well, in a long time.

"Yes, sir, there are," Pruett said, and to Andrew's surprise he handed over two missives.

Andrew wrinkled his brow in confusion. Two?

"Thank you," he said. "I will take these to my chamber. That will be all for the time being."

He wandered up the stairs, barely hearing Pruett's response. The letter on top was the expected one from his father, of course, but as he flipped to the second, it was in a hand he didn't recognize. It was feminine and the paper smelled faintly of lightly perfumed waters.

He waited until he was alone in his chamber to break the seal and open it. As he scanned over the words within, he couldn't help but sit down beside the fire with a thump.

The message was from Vivien Manning.

It wasn't that he didn't know the notorious former courtesan. The woman had been mistress to at least two friends from his youth, and he had always liked her.

But he hadn't seen her in almost three years, let alone spoken to her in a way that would encourage correspondence.

And yet here she was, asking him to visit her home at his earliest convenience.

He stared at the request over and over again, trying to decipher the meaning behind the simple, one-sentence request. There was no reason she should ask to see him. They had no relationship beyond a vague acquaintance, nor had he ever expressed a desire to expand that. Everyone knew he lived a monastic life, by his own choice. He had made that abundantly clear to the few friends who dared to question his lifestyle.

But how could he refuse her request? He had no desire to be rude to Vivien, even if he had long ago divorced himself from the lifestyle she represented. Perhaps it was best to simply visit her, kindly make it clear that he had no interest in an affair with her, and be done with it.

He did not look forward to that refusal, for he doubted Vivien heard the word "no" very often. She was a beautiful and powerful woman. One he couldn't help but respect.

With a sigh, he pulled a sheet of paper from the table beside his bed and scrawled a quick note indicating he would call on her for afternoon tea the next day. But as he called for a servant to take the note and arrange delivery, Andrew stifled the curiosity and thrill of excitement that filled his chest.

He had let go of that life long ago. He had no intention of ever going back.

CHAPTER 3

*A*ndrew sat in Vivien's parlor, staring at the delicate wallpaper. The dark red and pink pattern depicted something most people would never notice: naughty scenes of men and women entangled. He remembered coming to a party here once many years ago and trying to find all the hidden images.

A lifetime ago. Before he had married Rebecca. Before everything in his life had changed. He could hardly recall the man he was back then. He didn't *want* to recall it. In retrospect, it seemed like such a frivolous, empty existence.

The door behind him opened, and he rose to his feet and turned as Vivien entered. She was undeniably one of the most beautiful women he had ever met, and that beauty had always been complemented by her quick sense of humor and sharp intelligence. There was no wonder she was so sought after by the men in his circles.

Hell, a decade ago, he had lusted over her himself. But not now. Now she did nothing for him, not even a quickening of his blood.

Even if she had, any desire would have been squashed when she smiled at him and the pity she felt toward him was as clear and obvious as her hair or eye color.

How tiresome it was to always see that damned expression.

He forced himself to return the smile, though it was just as false.

"Good afternoon, my lord," she said as she closed the door behind herself and crossed to him, hands outstretched.

"Good afternoon, Vivien." He took them, and she pressed a kiss to each cheek before she stepped back and looked him up and down.

"I have not seen you in so long; I'm so pleased to have you here," she said, motioning to the two chairs before the fire. "Please, sit. May I get you tea or other refreshment? You were always a fan of bourbon, were you not?"

Andrew tilted his head. Damn, but she was good.

"A bit too early for bourbon for me, I am afraid."

She laughed. "I suppose so. I am simply pleased you are here at all. I must admit, I was a little surprised when you answered my missive, let alone so quickly. I half expected you to ignore me. Or at least refuse my request for a call."

Andrew arched a brow. Vivien had always been direct, that was certain.

"Who could refuse you?" he asked.

Her smile grew more wry. "I hear told that you refuse many, if not all, of your old friends nowadays."

Andrew pursed his lips. He knew what those in his former circles said about him. He had received at least two accusatory letters from old friends who called him all manner of names because he had turned them away again and again. But he didn't want to get into a long discussion about those facts with Vivien. In the end, he hardly knew the woman and he refused to discuss his personal life with his own family; why would he drag it out for her to see?

He shrugged. "Perhaps I simply like you more."

She tilted her head. "If that is true, than I am flattered."

"*But*," he stressed, "my time today is short. There must be some reason you called me here beyond wishing to press me about why I no longer see our mutual friends."

Vivien nodded as she got to her feet. "There is. Would you follow me out onto my terrace and I will clarify my reasons?"

Andrew wrinkled his brow. The terrace? What an odd request. Odd and somewhat intriguing. He got to his feet and followed her to the double doors that led out onto a sunny terrace. There was a table and chairs there, but Vivien passed those by and moved to the terrace wall. She leaned there and looked out over her gardens.

Slowly, Andrew joined her. He had no idea what this was all about, but it felt just a little like an ambush to him. Though what Vivien could hope to ensnare him into, he couldn't say. Entrapment had never been her personality; in fact it was just the opposite: Vivien caught with honey, not vinegar.

"What is this all about?" he asked, perhaps a bit more peevishly than he had intended to sound.

She didn't react to his sharper tone.

"How much do you hear about your old circles now that you have divorced yourself from the life you once led?"

Andrew faltered. The woman was shrewd and had just summed up exactly what he'd done. "Not much," he finally admitted softly.

"Then perhaps you do not know that I am no longer the mistress to any man in Society." She smiled and he saw a flicker of relief to her expression that he had not expected. Vivien had always seemed contented in her role in the world. "But I continue to keep myself in that world. I have recently begun matching young women with protectors."

Andrew nodded. "Er, yes, I believe I might have heard such a thing in passing."

For the life of him, he couldn't remember who had said that, but he did not think it was new information.

"But what does that have to do with me?"

Vivien motioned to the gardens below. "Do you see the girl in my rose maze below?"

Andrew followed the direction of her elegant hand and was surprised to see that there was, indeed, a woman in the garden below.

"Yes?"

He turned toward Vivien and found she was holding out a spyglass for him.

"Look a little closer, you could hardly see any detail of her from all the way up here."

He tilted his head in increasing confusion. "Vivien—"

"Please," she insisted, her tone firm.

With a grunt, Andrew took the glass from her hand and peered through the viewer to the young woman below. As he focused on her face, his breath caught.

She was utterly lovely. Chestnut locks framed a face with high cheekbones and full lips, not to mention china-blue eyes that lit up with delight as she paused to sniff this flower or that. Her clothing was well-worn, but when she twisted to observe her surroundings, it accentuated soft curves.

Andrew shifted as a most unfamiliar feeling began to stir his loins. Desire, hot and powerful, pumped through his veins, and he lowered the spyglass in shock. He hadn't had such a strong reaction to a woman in years.

"I assume you like what you see," Vivien said softly.

Andrew clenched his teeth. There was no hiding the swelling of his cock through the tight breeches he wore, and Vivien was too aware of such things not to notice.

"She is, obviously, very pretty," he said coolly as he handed the glass back to Vivien and turned away.

He tried to think of anything, *anyone*, that might force the inconvenient blood upward.

"She is looking for a protector," Vivien said from behind him. "I thought you might be the right match for her."

Andrew spun around, no longer caring if his erection was obvious. "I beg your pardon?" he barked.

In the face of his outrage, he expected Vivien to step away or flinch. Instead, she maintained her ground and kept her gaze focused firmly upon him.

"Her name is Lysandra Keates, and she arrived uninvited on my doorstep a few days ago. I do not know the particulars of her situation as of yet, but my impression is that she is in dire straits. She has begged me to match her with a man."

"I am not looking for a mistress!" Andrew snapped, but he couldn't help a brief, powerful image of the girl in the garden...in his bed, her legs wrapped around him as he drove into her.

"So I assumed," Vivien said. "But I fear this young woman perhaps has had limited experience with the physical aspects of passion. Perhaps a tumble with a man who promised her a life and then abandoned her. She may even have been forced. She believes she can handle whatever being a mistress would entail, but I have my doubts. The men in my circles expect their mistresses to be bold, daring, passionate. Lysandra could get swallowed up by them."

Andrew had been staring, mesmerized as Vivien recounted the details of Lysandra's request, but now he shook off his interest. "And again, what does this have to do with me?"

"I need a man who would be willing to gently introduce her to pleasure. One who would be patient with her fears and yet experienced enough to turn her into a mistress any man would desire."

Andrew opened his mouth, but found he could say nothing for a moment. Once again, images bombarded his mind. Illicit. And much more befitting the man he had once been many years before.

"No!" he barked, more to himself than to her. "No. I appreciate you are trying to help this young woman in your own way, but I am *not* the one to take her under my wing."

Vivien moved closer, and Andrew groaned. The woman was a sorceress. She knew how to look at a man and sway him. He was not entirely immune to that ability, despite not wishing to have her in his bed.

The other woman, though...*Lysandra*...that was another story.

"My lord," she said softly. "Andrew, I knew you before..." She paused. "...before everything changed. I know the desires you pursued and the lust you then had for women and for life. I hate to see you as you are now: isolated and in obvious pain."

Andrew turned his face, desire gone in an instant. He did *not* speak of these things to anyone. Ever.

"Nonsense," he snapped.

Vivien hesitated a moment, then stepped back with her hands lifted. "Very well, I may be wrong. But this would be a favor for me and for Lysandra. And it might even help you."

Andrew moved to the edge of the terrace and looked down over the gardens again. Lysandra had taken a seat on a bench in the middle of the garden and now had a rose in her hand. She brushed it over her own cheek absently, and the desire that had been quashed rushed back over Andrew in a dizzying wave.

He had spent years wallowing in his own pain and guilt, knowing he deserved both. Now the idea that the pain could disappear for a moment... It was bewitching. So tempting to think that a person could make him forget, even briefly.

"There would be no expectation that this...*situation* would be permanent?" he asked softly.

He could hear the smile in Vivien's tone as she said, "No. Lysandra would learn under your tutelage, nothing more. You could send her back to me at any time. Although if you end up liking her and wish to make her your mistress more permanently, then I would, of course, leave the details of that arrangement up to the two of you."

Andrew shook his head without taking his eyes off Lysandra. "No. I will take no permanent mistress. A month, that is all. Just a month with this woman and I will ensure she is ready for a man with loftier expectations in his bed."

Vivien hesitated before she said, "Very well."

Andrew turned away from Lysandra and straightened his jacket. "You may send her to my London home tomorrow at two. Tell her not to be late."

Vivien nodded. "I will do so. Thank you, my lord."

Andrew wanted to look at Lysandra one final time, but he forced himself not to do so. Instead, he strode to the doors that led back into the house.

"I must excuse myself, I have another appointment."

Vivien followed him into the parlor. "Of course. It was good to see you again, my lord."

Andrew said some kind of pleasantry, he wasn't sure what and headed into the foyer and back out onto the street where his rig was waiting for him. But as he got into the phaeton and urged his horses toward home, he couldn't help but flash back to the images of Lysandra in the garden.

She was utterly desirable, but he wondered if he would come to regret his choice to surrender to these baser instincts. After all, the first man had also given in to his desires in a garden.

And it hadn't ended well for him.

*L*ysandra followed Vivien's butler, Nettle, back into the parlor where she had first met the woman a few days before. It had been a long morning, one where she had been called here only to be sent into the garden to await her fate. And while she could appreciate the beauty of that place…well, there was still a lump in her chest. One of fear that Vivien had reconsidered helping her and that was why she'd been forced to wait so long.

As she entered the room, she was surprised to see Vivien already there. There was an unreadable expression on the other woman's face, but it wasn't unpleasant.

"Good afternoon, Lysandra."

Lysandra shook off her fears and forced herself into the room. "Good afternoon. Thank you for seeing me again."

Vivien first motioned the servant away and then waved to the same chairs where Lysandra had first confessed her embarrassing secret. She flushed as she took one.

"I have news," Vivien said with a smile that looked like a cat gotten into cream.

Lysandra shifted, uncertain if she could trust Vivien's smug satisfaction. "Y-yes?" she squeaked.

"A few moments ago, a man left my home. You may know his name. Viscount Andrew Callis?"

Lysandra shook her head with a heavy dose of hesitation. "No, I'm afraid it isn't familiar to me. I wasn't of the *ton*, you see."

Both Vivien's eyebrows lifted delicately. "My dear, a good mistress must know of men of rank and power. But never mind, it will all be part of your tutelage. I will be certain to send you a copy of *Debrett's* once you are settled."

"Tutelage?" Lysandra repeated weakly.

"Yes. You see, what a man expects from his mistress is beyond, I think, what you may be ready for." Vivien smiled at her kindly to soften the words. "But this man, the viscount, is a man of vast experience in pleasure. And he has agreed to tutor you for a month and ready you for a more permanent protector. You are to meet with him in his home tomorrow."

Lysandra gripped the armrests of her chair with both hands, hard enough that her knuckles whitened and pain shot up to her elbows.

"Oh."

Vivien tilted her head. "Is this not what you wanted?"

Lysandra swallowed hard. "It is, of course. As I said, I have no alternatives."

Vivien leaned forward and covered Lysandra's hand with hers. "Please don't worry yourself. This man will take care of you as a man would his mistress. You will not have to worry about money or a place to stay or clothing while you are under his care. And he will be gentle with you."

Lysandra nodded. The idea of having the burden of her financial woes lifted from her was comforting, at least. The rest...well, it was what she had asked for.

"And," Vivien continued, "you will be helping him, as well."

Lysandra stared at her. She could not have understood that statement correctly. "Helping him? How?"

Vivien's expression softened with sadness. "The viscount has a sad history. He may not realize it, but he needs you as much as you need him."

Lysandra pursed her lips. "I'm not certain I understand."

"You will. Someday. Now, why don't we share in some tea and I will see if one of my gowns might be a good fit for you for tomorrow."

Lysandra smiled as Vivien bustled out of the room to call for tea and make other arrangements. She wasn't certain she believed Vivien when she said Lysandra would one day understand. But the idea that she might help someone else during this trying time actually helped her.

And she was so nervous that she needed all the assistance she could get.

CHAPTER 4

*L*ysandra's hands shook as she followed the expensively liveried butler to a parlor that was far bigger than the entire set of rooms she let at present. And dear God, the furnishings! She was almost afraid to sit on them, for they clearly cost a fortune and were meant for important guests, not utterly common women attempting to become mistresses.

"May I offer you any kind of refreshment?" the butler asked her, his tone cool but polite and not revealing any of his thoughts about her being in a place she so clearly did not belong.

"N-no, thank you." Lysandra shook her head.

In truth she wasn't certain she could keep down anything she ate at present. Her nerves had kept her from taking a bite for most of the day.

"Very good. Lord Callis will be with you shortly."

With that, the servant left her. Lysandra paced the beautiful room, trying very hard not to look at all the expensive items around her. The sale of one could probably help pay for both her mother's rent and her own for half a year.

Not that she had sunk so far to consider theft as a possible solution to her problem. Humiliating herself, of course, but theft...no.

Behind her, the door opened and Lysandra spun to face her

temporary protector. What she saw had her catching her breath and stepping backward until she almost tumbled into the fire.

He was the most beautiful man she had ever seen. Blond and tall like Adonis from the Greek myths her father had told her as a child, with a chiseled, hard and rather tanned face, despite the fact that he was titled and probably never saw the sun but for a few visits to the countryside each year. And then there were his eyes.

They were the brightest green she had ever seen and they were focused on her, running up and down her body, though they reflected no answer as to what *he* thought of her.

But what could he think? She was a woman far below him, dressed in the gown of a fallen woman that she had been forced to *borrow* and she was here to beg him to take sex in trade for money and training. There was little good to come from those facts.

"Lysandra Keates, I presume?" he said, and his rough voice seemed to weave its way into her chest. She felt peculiar as she stared at him, hot and odd and out of sorts, but none of the sensations were unpleasant, just unexpected.

He tilted his head when she didn't answer right away. "I assume you can speak."

Hot blood rushed to Lysandra's cheeks and she nodded swiftly. "Oh yes, I'm sorry. A-are you Lord Callis?"

His lips thinned, once again drawing her attention to the line of them. Assuming he didn't kick her out of his parlor out of sheer disappointment in her appearance, he was going to kiss her with that mouth. She found it rather thrilled her to wonder when and how he would do so.

"Andrew," he said softly. "Under our rather unusual circumstances, I believe it would be better to limit formality. In public, a mistress would address her protector by his title, of course, but in private his given name or an agreed upon nickname would be proper."

Lysandra nodded. Ah yes, so this was to be the training Vivien had promised she would receive from this man. At least, part of it.

"Andrew, then," she said softly.

He reached back to close the door behind himself and then took a long step closer.

"You don't belong here," he said, almost on a whisper.

Lysandra squeezed her eyes shut. So it was obvious and now there would be the inevitable rejection.

"Please don't turn me away," she said, humiliated to have to beg as her voice cracked with high emotion.

When she opened her eyes, she was surprised to find that Andrew had moved closer again. Now only a sliver of distance separated them. She could smell the warm, woodsy scent of his skin, feel his body heat as it reached out for her and made her want to move closer.

"I am not turning you away," he said and his hand reached out to curl around her shoulder. "I only meant that you are too beautiful to be here. You should be protected, but not the way Vivien arranges. What in the world would make you turn to this?"

Lysandra stared up at him, shocked that he would ask such a thing, that he would care about those details of her rather small life.

"A great many complicated things have brought me to your parlor," she answered.

She would tell him more if he pressed, but she was hesitant to do so. There was a heated spell being woven in the room, shrinking the world down to just the two of them. If she told him all the sad details of her life, she feared that bewitching enchantment would be broken and she would never see where it might lead.

And to her surprise, her curiosity had nothing to do with the duties and desperation that brought her here. It was born from her own forbidden thoughts.

His hand slid down from her shoulder to her collarbone. Lysandra shifted. He was not wearing gloves, and the neckline of the dress she had borrowed from Vivien was shockingly low, at least for her. His bare skin seemed too hot against hers, yet her back arched ever so slightly and her breath expelled in a sigh.

Andrew's gaze flitted to her face and for the first time emotion existed in those captivating green eyes. Something heated and dark and passionate that she couldn't name, mostly because she had never seen such an expression before.

"You are very responsive," he said quietly. "That will serve you well."

"Responsive?" Lysandra repeated, focusing on the training he was meant to be giving her so that she wouldn't be dizzied by her own body.

He nodded before his hand glided lower and he cupped her breast.

Lysandra's knees nearly buckled at the intimate touch. Her whole body ached, but it was anything but an unpleasant sensation. She felt on fire, alive, and she wanted more. More of what, she couldn't have expressed.

"Your nipple is already hard," he explained further and strummed his thumb over that same nipple as he spoke.

Lysandra's eyes shut again, this time not out of embarrassment, but from utter pleasure. There had never been any kind of sensation like this before. This feeling of being hot and shivery at once, of being so out of control over her body that she arched her back and moaned softly without meaning to do either.

"I think your tutelage will be smooth," he said and took a step closer, forcing Lysandra back up a step in response.

She bumped against the settee and staggered into a seated position. He dropped down next to her.

"But testing that is my duty," he continued, his rough voice as seductive as his hands were.

Lysandra couldn't formulate words. She couldn't even think of any words as she watched those hands, those magical hands, return to her body. He cupped both breasts now, lifting and massaging her with exquisite gentleness.

Lightning bursts of pleasure and desire struck her, and she shivered with the sensations this man was awakening in her. She had always pictured this arrangement in its most unpleasant aspects, but this...*this* was heavenly.

She watched, her lips parted, as he removed one warm hand

from her breast and glided it lower, down to the apex of her body. Her heart rate was doubled, for she knew that he was moving toward the most secret places on her body. Her most private treasures that she had always been taught were forbidden except to a husband.

But despite being trained to reject these kinds of caresses, especially from a near stranger, Lysandra felt no fear, but only giddy anticipation. An emotion that only intensified when Andrew bunched a handful of skirt into his fist and began gliding the entire skirt of her gown upward. The hem crested over her knee and halfway up her thigh before he slipped one hand beneath.

"Andrew," she gasped as his hot flesh met her equally hot flesh. She wouldn't have been surprised to look later and find he had branded her with his hand, marking her as his forever.

More surprising was that she did not dread that concept. To be his. To be marked. To surrender fully to what this affair, what this decision to be a mistress entailed.

And then all thoughts fled because he slipped his hand higher until his fingers met the spot where her legs met.

"Wet," he whispered, almost more to himself than to her. "Ready already."

Lysandra rested her head back on the armrest of the settee and gripped at the closest pillow with her fist as he stroked her through the thin fabric of her drawers. He was right that she was wet, a fact that both titillated and embarrassed her. She wanted to ask him if that was normal, but she didn't want to reveal too much about her inexperience in these matters. She just wanted more from him.

And he gave it. Without warning, he pulled her drawers open at the slit and his fingers moved inside to touch her in the most intimate way possible.

Lysandra couldn't hold back her cry of surprise and pleasure as his fingertips stroked the folds of her womanly center, coaxing her to open her legs wider and surrender to his wicked ministrations.

And she did. She spread her legs shamelessly and shut her eyes as he explored her. He was so gentle in his examination, just barely skimming his hands over the outer regions of her core, but every touch inspired lightning bursts of heavenly sensation. She found herself lifting and straining toward him, aching for more, though she still had no clear idea of what that more entailed.

"I want to see you come," he murmured.

Her eyes flew open, and she whispered, "Come?"

He stared at her for a long moment and then said, "No one has ever made you come?"

Slowly, she shook her head.

"You have never touched yourself and brought on that reaction?" he asked.

A heated blush flooded her cheeks. "N-no."

He gave her a slow smile. "Then it will be my pleasure to give you this first experience. Lie back and relax, Lysandra. Let me pleasure you in this way."

She worried her lip with her teeth for a brief moment and then settled back once more. She didn't know what he meant, but found herself wildly curious.

A feeling that fled when he settled himself away from the settee and onto his knees on the floor before her. He caught her hips and dragged her forward, until she was positioned just before him. Lysandra stared down. He was eye-level with her half-naked body and the pleasure she felt earlier was muted by utter humiliation at this new position.

She shifted, but he held her steady with a hand on her thighs.

"Don't. Don't," he said. "This is part of your tutelage. You have nothing to be embarrassed by."

"You shouldn't be...seeing me this way," she protested, though her voice was weakened by the touch of his hands on her skin.

He smiled up at her. "If I am to be your lover, this is exactly how I should be seeing you. This is a gift you will give me, something you won't share with anyone else, at least while we are together. Give yourself over to me and let me give you something in return."

She was silent, unable to speak, unable to think of how to respond, but that didn't seem to bother Andrew. He continued to look her in the eyes, but lowered his head, closer and closer to her. Then, to her utter shock, he pressed his mouth to the apex of her thighs.

She cried out in surprise, but also in pleasure. His mouth was even hotter than his hands.

"Shh," he whispered as those same hands massaged her open thighs in a soothing rhythm.

She flopped back on the settee and stared up at the ceiling as he continued to nuzzle and kiss her nether lips. His hands moved and she gasped again as he delicately spread her open to reveal the slick opening to her sex.

He made a rumbling sound of pleasure deep in his throat and then returned his mouth to her. But this time he was less gentle, more insistent. He licked her like she was a sweet treat, and her back arched with an explosion of sensation she had never even imagined.

Her reaction didn't slow him, if anything, his tongue became more insistent, his mouth more demanding. He tongued her opening, tasting every inch of her exposed flesh from the rosette of her bottom to the top of her slit.

And there he hesitated.

"Do you know what this is?" he asked, looking up at her as he pressed his thumb against her.

She cried out, for the pressure of his touch sent an electric shock of intense pleasure through her.

"N-no," she gasped.

He smiled. "Your clitoris, Lysandra. And it is the key to your pleasure. I'm going to touch it, to suck it, until you scream my name."

Her eyes widened, but he gave her no chance to reply, only lowered his mouth back to her. True to his word, he sucked the hidden bundle of nerves between his lips and began to work it with his wicked tongue. He stroked, he sucked, he scraped her gently with his teeth. And Lysandra soon realized that she had begun to lift her hips in time to his touch.

Then, without warning, the pleasure she had been experiencing multiplied out of control. Her hips jerked as wondrous, amazing feelings mobbed her, taking her away from all her worries, from all her fears and leaving her weightless and quivering as she did exactly as Andrew had predicted:

She screamed out his name in the quiet parlor.

She had no idea how long she lay sprawled across Andrew's settee, spent and satiated, but slowly she began to realize he was no longer positioned between her legs. At some point, he had stood and moved to the fireplace where he watched her with a hooded, unreadable expression.

She moved to smooth her dress back over her exposed body but found he had already done so. With a heated blush, she struggled into a seated position and stared at him.

He smiled, but the expression held no warmth or genuine happiness. Instead, it was tight and false.

"I think that is enough tutelage for today," he said, his voice strained.

Lysandra blinked. That was all? All that passion had built to a crescendo, yes, but he had not taken her, claimed her, in the ultimate way. In fact, she realized now, he hadn't even kissed her... at least not properly on the mouth.

"I—" she began, but then stopped.

What was she going to say? Beg for something she couldn't properly express? Demand he take this strange, erotic afternoon to its expected end? She was not daring enough to do so.

"I shall arrange for a place for us to meet. You will stay there throughout the course of our...training," he said.

His voice was cool and distant, as if he were arranging a luncheon meeting, not a tryst.

She blinked as she looked around the parlor. "We will not meet here?"

He jerked his eyes to her in surprise. "No."

Lysandra turned away. What a foolish notion. Of course a

gentleman didn't keep his mistress in his main house. She must look like an idiot of the highest order.

With a shake of her head, she said, "Well, then I will leave my direction with your servant at the door so you may reach me with the address and when you would like me to move there."

"No, my driver will take you to your current address, then he can deliver my message to you," he said.

She shook her head. "Oh no, I wouldn't trouble your servant. I can take a hack."

His lips thinned. "If I am to be your protector, for however short a time, you must allow me to protect you, Lysandra. No more hacks. You will allow my driver to be at your service today and I'll arrange for one of your own as soon as possible."

She opened her mouth, but he arched a brow and silenced her with just that pointed look. She nodded.

"Very well. Thank you for the…er, protection."

From the way he shifted, she could see he felt as awkward in this exchange as she did. Had she done something wrong? Was her passion too muted? Too powerful? Or was a man with experience and power like this simply unmoved by a girl of her ilk?

Whatever the reason for his sudden coolness, it could not bode well.

She gathered her reticule and tilted her head toward him. "Good afternoon, my lord."

"Good afternoon, Lysandra," he said softly as she slipped from the room.

Once in the hall, she rubbed a hand over her face. She had never felt so confused and ill at ease in her life. But she had also never felt so alive and passionate. And it was very clear to her that whatever happened next with Andrew, she would never again be the same person she was when she entered his parlor.

. . .

*A*s soon as the door closed behind Lysandra, Andrew began to pace. His world felt like it was spinning out of control, pushed off its axis by the slight frame of a woman he had only just met.

Since Rebecca's death three years ago, he had been sleeping. That was his choice, to live in a way that left him happily numb and dead to the world. His wife deserved that after what he had done, what he had not done.

But now, in the span of an hour with Lysandra, it was like he had been shocked awake. His emotions boiled inside of him, raw and so pleasurable that they bordered on pain.

Worse, he wanted more with this woman. He craved her body in a way he hadn't done since...God, since before he was married. Since he was a rake of the highest order and had thought only of the pleasures of this world.

He had no idea why this woman would inspire such strong reactions in him, except that there seemed to be something so complicated to her. Something so troubling.

Yes, she was exquisitely responsive, but there was also an innocence about her. He had taken mistresses before his marriage, and they had all been worldly, not wide-eyed and shivering with pleasure. He feared Lysandra might be eaten alive in that world those kinds of women inhabited.

A strong urge to protect her swelled up in him and he sank into the closest chair to ponder it. Vivien had asked him to tutor Lysandra in the ways of pleasure in order to prepare her for the life of a mistress. But perhaps in the process of that tutelage, he could shock Lysandra into reality with his touch, his kiss, his passion.

Perhaps he could convince her that this path was not the right one for her. And in the process, slake these unwanted desires and feelings.

Either way, the next few weeks promised to be heady with pleasures. And he had never looked forward to, nor dreaded, something more.

CHAPTER 5

*L*ysandra jerked her head up at the knock on her door. She had been waiting for this knock for two days, and now the moment had come. Only one person knew where she lived; even her mother wasn't truly aware of her circumstances, and that was by Lysandra's choice. That left only one man with a reason to contact her here.

The knock sounded again, this time louder, and Lysandra stood up from the threadbare bed that was shoved into the tiny corner of the room in the boarding house and hurried to the door.

Her landlady, a nasty woman with a wart on her nose the size of a large pebble, stood outside, a letter clutched in her dirty fingers.

"Miss Hoity Toity has a missive," the woman spat.

Lysandra flinched. "Thank you, Mrs. Cringle."

She reached for the note, but the woman held it out of her reach. "Paper looks expensive, lovey."

Normally, Lysandra was intimidated by the woman. After all, she could throw Lysandra into the street without a cause or a care at any moment. But today she was in no mood for the woman's nastiness and a strength she often kept in check rose in her.

Her eyes narrowed. "Give me my letter, Mrs. Cringle."

With a throaty chuckle, the landlady gave over the missive. "Rich men, they're hard to keep, chit."

Lysandra slammed the door in the woman's face and spun around to lean on the doorframe. The horrible wretch had actually come closer to the truth than she knew. But Lysandra's duty wasn't to keep Andrew. It was to learn from him in the hopes she could secure a future for herself and for her mother.

She paced to the bed and sat down to open the seal that held the pages together. The message was brief at best, only an address where she was to come at once and the instruction that she could give up the rooms she was letting, for this home would be considered hers for the duration of their affair.

Lysandra set the note aside and let out a sigh she felt like she'd been holding in forever. Part of her was relieved. She could leave this horrible place and, if her life went as planned, never look back.

But there was a stronger part of her that dreaded what Andrew's curt missive required.

For two days, she had been able to think only of him. Of his touch, his mouth so hot on her flesh that she lost all control of her body, and his dismissal when their first encounter was over. She didn't know much about the requirements of a mistress, but she had a sneaking suspicion that she wasn't supposed to think of her protector night and day.

"Perhaps there is still another way to make money," she said as she folded the note and put it in the pocket of her pelisse.

But how? She had already racked her mind in the months before she gathered enough nerve to speak to Vivien in the first place and thought of nothing but this end. She just hadn't counted on this man who would make her feel so shivery and weak.

"Mama," she whispered under her breath as she shoved those unwanted thoughts of Andrew away once again.

No, she couldn't tell her mother the details of what she was doing, but sometimes just being around her mother helped Lysandra see life more clearly.

She gathered her reticule and a wrap and slipped from her

room and out of the nasty boarding house. She had one last chance to turn away from this path, and she could only hope that a moment with the person she loved most would help her clarify her choices.

*W*hen Lysandra had asked her cousins August and Marta Ingram to take in her mother, she had known they did it with reluctance and an eye for the money that Lysandra scraped together each month to pay for her board and care. Still, she had always prayed that what they gave in return was a loving home for her mother.

Now, as she stood in their parlor with its ridiculously overdone furniture and knickknacks that could only wish to be as sophisticated as Andrew's fine parlor, she worried her lip. The servant who had allowed her entry was as chilly as a north wind and seemed perturbed to have to fetch Lysandra's mother.

But the door finally opened and Lysandra stepped forward to greet the woman who had raised and loved her. Her heart dropped as she did so.

Regina Keates had never fully recovered from the death of her beloved husband over eight years ago. The first few, she had tried to carry on, but illness and the pain of slow and creeping poverty had stricken her, and she had succumbed to the affects of both.

Now her mother was pale, with dark circles beneath her once vibrant blue eyes, and her frame was so thin that Lysandra had to blink back tears at the sight of her. It was always so much of a shock to see her this way.

"Mama," she said, covering the reaction as best as she could and moving to offer her mother an arm of assistance. She pressed a kiss to her mother's thin cheek and helped her to a chair.

"My dearest," her mother said with a smile that was still the same as Lysandra remembered from her childhood, even if nothing else was. "I didn't expect you today."

Lysandra would have poured her mother tea at this juncture, but none had been provided by the servants. Instead, she tilted her head with a smile of her own.

"I simply wished to see you."

"That's so nice." Her mother rested back on her chair and shut her eyes briefly, as if the exertion of the visit was already affecting her. "Your employer is kind to give you a day off. How is your life as a ladies maid? Any gossip to share about the lives of the Earl and Countess of Culpepper?"

In that moment, Lysandra was happy her mother's eyes were shut so she wouldn't look at Lysandra as she formulated the best lie. She hadn't told her mother that she'd been let go by the Earl of Culpepper over six months before. She certainly hadn't told her why.

What that one lie had resulted in was a dangerous maze of other lies that she was forced to twist and turn through each time she called on her mother.

"Oh, nothing too interesting," Lysandra said past suddenly dry lips. "Just the usual parties and soirees to ready the Countess for."

Her mother looked at her. "Ah, well it all seems very glamorous. I do wish you hadn't been forced to enter a life of service, but since you have, I do take comfort in that you seem to be happy doing it."

Tears stung Lysandra's eyes, but she had become expert at hiding them from her mother and instead forced a weak smile.

"And what of you, Mama? Are you still happy here? Do August and Marta treat you well?"

There was a moment's hesitation where Lysandra swore she saw a flicker of fear in her mother's gaze, but then it was gone. But the idea that it had ever been there was troubling in the highest way, and she stared as her mother talked.

"They are kind to take me in," she said softly. "Family or not, I realize I am a burden in my current state."

Lysandra pursed her lips. When she had asked her cousins to bring her mother into their home, she had believed they would welcome her. Her cousin August did well with his store and his wife and brats never seemed to want to anything.

Yet there had always been a tension in the home. A feeling that her mother wasn't wanted there, even though she was kind, ate very little and caused no one trouble.

Lysandra fisted her hands at her sides. "Mama, you couldn't be a burden—"

She stopped before she could finish the sentence and stared. When her mother shifted, the sleeve of her worn-out gown slid up her arm and revealed a bruise beneath the fabric. A bruise in the shape of fingers, as if someone had grabbed her there and wrenched her body.

Lysandra got to her feet. "How did you receive that mark?" she demanded.

Her mother reached up and pulled her gown sleeve down as hot color flooded her cheeks and made them bright with embarrassment.

"I was so silly," her mother said, ducking her gaze. "I bumped myself getting out of the tub."

Lysandra clenched her teeth. "Are you certain?"

Slowly, her mother lifted her gaze to Lysandra and held it there with whatever dignity she had left. "Of course."

Lysandra wanted to confront her, to tell her mother that she knew she hadn't received that mark from a tub. To demand that she tell her the truth. But what could she do about it even if she knew? She had no funds to remove her mother from this place. Soon she wouldn't even have enough to keep her mother here.

And *that* was why she was doing this. *That* was why she had turned to Vivien Manning and Lord Andrew Callis. Because with the income she could make as a mistress, she could save her mother. She could save herself.

"Lysandra, my dear, are you all right?" her mother said, interrupting her thoughts. "You have gotten very quiet and faraway."

Lysandra shook away the thoughts and focused on her mother again. "I'm sorry, Mama. I was just thinking of a duty I must perform. I wasn't certain I could do it, but now I have realized that I must and I will, no matter what."

Her mother smiled. "You've always been so determined, my dear. I've admired that about you. When your father died, I seemed to have lost my strength, but you found yours."

Lysandra blinked at the tears she could usually control. Found her strength? Dear God, she hadn't felt that way over the last eight hellish years. She had never felt weaker.

The door behind them opened and both women turned. Her cousin August stood framed in the doorway, his face red and angry, as usual. Lysandra stood, but from the corner of her eye, she caught a glimpse of her mother and the expression on her face was one of fear.

"I was told you were here," her cousin grunted. "I want to talk to you. Come with me."

Lysandra sighed. So much for a visit with her mother. "Let me say goodbye and I'll join you, of course."

He waved at her dismissively and stepped into the hallway to wait, though he left the door open and stole any privacy she might have had for her farewell.

"Mama," she said softly. "I will do anything I can to...to make this better for you."

Her mother's expression darkened, and she lowered her chin in something so close to defeat that it broke Lysandra's heart.

"It isn't so bad," her mother whispered. "I don't want you to worry yourself."

"But I do." Lysandra pulled her close for a hug and was once again struck by how thin and frail her mother had become. "And I always will. Go upstairs and rest. I'll call on you again when I can."

Her mother nodded, and Lysandra squeezed her hand one last time before she moved into the hallway where her cousin was waiting. He motioned her to follow him and went to his office a few doors down.

He did not offer Lysandra a seat nor tea as he glared at her across his big oak desk.

"You know, when we took your mother in, we did not realize

what a burden we had taken on," he began with no preamble. "Nor that her presence would last so long."

Lysandra wrinkled her brow. "What do you mean, August? You knew fullwell that I had taken a job as a servant and I wouldn't be able to offer her a home myself. How could you not know that she would be here for more than half a year?"

"We thought she would likely die," her cousin said, cold as ice.

Lysandra sank into the seat he hadn't offered and stared at him in a mixture of horror and anger. "How could you say that?" she managed to ask after a long pause to find her voice.

Her cousin shrugged. "She is frail and clearly unwell."

Lysandra bit back all the things she wanted to say as she thought of the bruise on her mother's arm and the fear in her eyes. She could do nothing at this point to bring her mother to a safer place, so all she could do was not make this place even worse.

"I pay you, don't I? Every month, without fail. That money is to cover your expenses and to ensure she is *safe*." Lysandra emphasized the last word so that her cousin would understand she felt her mother might not be safe in this house anymore.

He smirked in response. "What do you give me, a few pounds for all our care and trouble? That was actually why I wished to speak to you today, Lysandra. I believe you and your mother are taking advantage of my family's kindness."

Lysandra's thoughts kept returning to those finger-shaped bruises on her mother's arm as she stared at her cousin in silence.

He didn't seem to care about her lack of response and continued, "And her staying here has become a financial burden to us."

Lysandra fought to keep her voice calm. "What are you saying?"

"We need more money in order to continue to take care of her," he said, blunt and sharp.

"How much?" she whispered.

He folded his arms and smiled. In that moment, Lysandra realized he was *enjoying* this exchange. "Double what you pay at present."

Lysandra lowered her head. All her money was tied up between her own meager expenses and paying what she already sent for her mother's care.

Only when she moved to Andrew's home, she would not have her boarding to worry about. That wouldn't cover double the price she paid for her mother's care now, but it would be close.

"Now we can work this out in several ways," her cousin said as he leaned closer. "For example, in trade. You've always had a few things I've admired."

Lysandra blinked at him in confusion and then followed the line of his sight to her breasts. She leapt to her feet with a cry. "You are married!"

He shrugged. "Most men are. I'm merely offering you a way to cover your expenses, my dear."

Lysandra folded her arms over her breasts and shook her head. "No, I will find another way to cover the expense. Now if you will excuse me, I have other business to attend to."

She spun on her heel and left the room with her cousin's ugly laughter following her. Once she was out of the room, down the hallway, she began to run. She burst from the doors and down the stairs without looking around her. She just wanted to get away. Away from her fears about her mother's welfare that she had no way to address. Away from her disgust over her cousin's advances.

And away from the realization that she was well and truly trapped by her circumstances. Her arrangement with Andrew was her only hope to escape this life and the life that had been thrust upon her mother.

From this point forward, there was no looking back.

CHAPTER 6

*T*he carriage Andrew had sent for her pulled to a stop, and Lysandra finally dared to pull back the curtain and peek out at the home she would live in, albeit briefly. What she saw made her catch her breath.

It was a little home in a row of other little homes, but it was so pretty. The front gardens were well-tended so that bright roses and white trim stood out against the brick walls. The neighborhood was one Lysandra had heard of before. Bikenbottom Court was just west of the more stylish neighborhoods in London and boasted of merchants who were rich and second sons of lords who lived on inheritance and their father's names.

And apparently...mistresses.

The carriage door opened, and the driver reached out his hand to help her down. Lysandra drew a deep breath and then allowed his assistance.

"We'll unload your bags, miss, and have them taken to your rooms," the driver said after she said stood staring at the house for far too long. "Please go in. You'll find Carlsworth waiting for you. And let me know if you would like to go anywhere else today."

Lysandra spun on him with a shake of her head. "Oh, I couldn't ask you to stay, Mr. Wilkes. I'm sure Lord Callis would miss your service and his carriage."

The driver blinked. "Just Wilkes, miss. And…I'm *your* driver, miss. This is your rig."

Lysandra stared at the man dressed in a fine livery and the lovely carriage he had come in.

"My driver?" she repeated before she realized how foolish the words made her sound.

He smiled, a very kind expression. "Yes, miss. I'm so sorry I didn't make that clear."

Lysandra swallowed hard and then smiled back at him. "Thank you, Wilkes. I appreciate your assistance. Good day."

"Good day, miss." He tipped his hat at her and then went to work unloading the very few bags she had packed for her move.

Lysandra stepped forward but before she could knock the door opened and revealed another servant.

"Good afternoon, Miss Keates. I'm Carlsworth, your butler."

Lysandra's head was spinning. She hadn't had the advantage of servants for…well, she could scarce remember how long. And even in her father's house, it hadn't been a butler! There had been a cook, a maid she and her mother had shared and a man her father used for all kinds of duties, but that was all.

"Are you quite all right, Miss Keates?" Carlsworth asked as he took a step toward her. "You are very pale."

"I'm sorry, Carlsworth," she said, breathless. "I didn't mean to alarm you. I find I am a bit overwhelmed."

"Of course," he said, his tone as kind as could be. "You must be quite tired. Lord Callis has sent word that he will be calling within the half hour. Would you like to wait for him in the parlor while we ready your room? I'll call for your tea."

Lysandra blinked. So she was to be waited on like a princess?

"Miss?" he asked.

She shook her head. The servants would think her a daft princess, indeed, if she continued to stare at them like a fool.

"Thank you, that sounds very nice." She followed his indication of one of the open doors in the hallway and stepped into a parlor.

Immediately, she fell in love. The parlor wasn't imposing like Andrew's was or ridiculous and showy like her cousin's, but it fit her perfectly. It had been painted in warm greys and blues, with fine furniture that seemed as comfortable as it was pretty. There were very few decorations beyond a handful of paintings and a clock on the mantel, but the lack of décor didn't bother Lysandra. She was too busy being utterly mesmerized by the fact that, at least for a little while, this home was hers to enjoy.

Behind her, there was the clearing of a throat, and she turned to watch a maid come inside with a serving plate of tea and a few sandwiches.

"Cook wasn't certain what you liked," the girl explained as she set the entire platter on the sideboard. "So she gave you a few selections. When you meet with her, you'll have to tell her your favorites."

Lysandra blinked in disbelief and stared at the girl. "H-hello."

She smiled. "I'm Candace, miss. I'm your downstairs maid."

"M-my downstairs maid?" she repeated, once again daft in her confusion and disbelief.

The girl nodded. "I do the cleaning and tidying. Your ladies maid is Faith, and she is upstairs readying your room. Cook is Eliza, but we all just call her Cook because it makes her laugh. You've already met Carlsworth and Wilkes, of course."

Lysandra continued to nod, regardless of the fact that her eyes were beginning to hurt from being so wide.

"We're all at your service, Miss Keates," the girl pressed. "Ring for any of us any time."

"Thank you," Lysandra breathed. "I shall do so."

She said the words, but she could scarcely picture herself doing so. Ringing for assistance like the lady of a manor! When just that morning she had woken in the uncomfortable confines of one of the worst rooming houses in London.

"I'll go now. Lord Callis will be here shortly."

Lysandra forced both her attention back to the girl and a smile as Candace stepped from the room. Once she was gone, Lysandra sank into the closest chair and let her breath out all at once.

"Dear God, I am a ninny," she said to herself. "They are going to talk and laugh about me below stairs."

That she knew for a fact. After all, she had done the same in her former employer's home. Right before he...

Well, there was no use thinking about that. Not right now. Right now she had to prepare for Andrew's arrival. She looked down at herself. Her worn gown didn't really fit in this pretty home, but it was what she had and there was no use feeling badly about that.

She caught a glimpse of a mirror hanging above the fireplace and moved in front of it. She grimaced. But for the faint circles beneath her eyes that seemed to be a permanent fixture anymore, she looked well enough, she supposed. But would "well enough" be *good* enough? Wasn't a mistress supposed to be outrageously beautiful and alluring? Seductive and sophisticated like Vivien was?

She pinched her cheeks until they had a bit of color and smoothed her dress. She was checking the status of her teeth when the door behind her opened and in the reflection of the mirror, she watched Andrew walk into the parlor.

She spun from the looking glass with a dark blush and shoved her hands to her sides. Wonderful, now she had been caught examining her teeth like she was a horse.

If he noticed, he made no mention of it. He only reached behind himself and shut the door to the parlor with a loud click. They stared at each other for a long moment, long enough that Lysandra shifted. Perhaps she was supposed to say something. To begin the seduction. But what?

"Hello," she managed and then sighed.

Hello? *That* was the best she could do.

But as silly as it was, it seemed to break the spell. Andrew took a long step toward her.

"Hello, Lysandra. Carlsworth tells me you only just arrived yourself, but I hope what you have seen of your home thus far is satisfactory to you."

Lysandra blinked. "You cannot be serious in that question. It is a beautiful home, no one could find fault with it."

He tilted his head and there was a flash of something in his stare that she couldn't properly read. "I ask because the home is a bit smaller than some mistresses require. I only thought that since we would only share an affair for a short time—"

He trailed off, and Lysandra wrinkled her brow. "Of course you wouldn't invest in a large mansion for me. And if you had, I wouldn't know what to do with it. Having so many servants and such a beautiful home to myself is almost too much as it is. Thank you, my lord, for providing it for me."

He stared at her, but finally nodded. "You are welcome, but I would say that you shouldn't be overly grateful when you take on a protector. You want them to pursue you, to be driven to give you more."

Lysandra stared at him. "But if I'm provided for, that should be all I require. I wouldn't be able to demand something from a person as you suggest. Why would I?"

"The chase, my dear," Andrew said softly as he took another step toward her. "You must provide these men with a chase, otherwise they will lose interest. And since the chase will not involve the pleasures of your body, it must involve something else. Your comfort. Your company. Your approval."

Lysandra shook her head. "I understand what you're saying, but I have a hard time picturing being so demanding."

One corner of Andrew's lip lifted in a half-smile. "Then there will be much to teach. But first..."

He trailed off and moved closer, closer, close enough that Lysandra could smell the masculine fragrance of his skin and feel its heat. Close enough that when he reached out he could take her hand. Slowly, he drew her toward him and then against him.

Lysandra shivered as her mind flashed to the intimate kisses he had rained down on her quivering body just a few days before. The body that continued to react with both his touch and the memories, tingling as the area between her thighs grew wet and hot in anticipation.

"I didn't kiss you the last time we met," he said and his rough voice was even rougher. "At least, not this way."

He gave her a wicked glance and then his mouth lowered to hers.

Lysandra stood stock-still in shock as his lips pressed against her own. She had been kissed before, but they had been clumsy and often highly unpleasant attempts at the activity. Andrew's mouth, however, was firm and warm on hers. She relaxed at the pressure of his lips, the way they fit so perfectly against her own.

And then he parted them and traced the crease of her mouth with his tongue, rather in the same way he had done with her womanly lips the last time they met. Her mouth opened with the sensation, and he let his tongue touch hers.

She moaned against his lips as she lifted her arms around his neck and returned the kiss out of pure instinct. Their tongues collided and danced, stroking and tasting as Andrew pulled her closer, closer, closer with every touch. His hands drifted down her back and he cupped her backside, lifting her against him.

Lysandra gasped, first at the intimacy and passion of the touch and then at the feel of something hard and hot against her belly when he smashed her against him.

"The servants assured me that your rooms would be ready for us," Andrew whispered as he pulled away and stared down at her with a heated, heavy expression. "Let's go there now."

Lysandra swallowed as he took her hand. She allowed him to lead her up to the second floor of the home. There were a few shut doors, but she couldn't be curious about them. Not when she was being taken to a bedroom with a huge, pillared bed against the wall. It was a gorgeous room, fit for the princess she had earlier compared herself to, but she couldn't look at it or enjoy it.

Because Andrew shut the door behind them and promptly pressed her against the hard surface of it, lifting her against him once more as he kissed her and kissed her and kissed her into dizzy submission. She clung to him, helpless in the face of the storm, unable and unwilling to pull away and break the spell he weaved with his hot touch.

His fingers caught the buttons along the front of her gown and he tore at them, popping them free even as he sent two of them skittering free across the floor thanks to their cheap thread. He didn't seem to notice, though. He stopped kissing her long enough to part her gown in the front.

Her chemise was just as cheap as her gown, with no decoration, just scratchy cotton fabric against her bare skin. He slipped his hands beneath the shoulders of her gown and the thin straps of the undergarment beneath and shoved them both down her arms, baring her from the waist up.

Lysandra shook with need and lifted her hands to cover herself out of pure instinct. Andrew touched her hands and lowered them as he finally looked at her face.

"In the past, perhaps this was a humiliation for you," he whispered, his tone hypnotic in the quiet room. "It will never be again. Enjoy the fact that when I look at you, it makes me mad with desire. When *any* man looks at you in this way, you could have anything you wish for. *That* will be the power you wield as a mistress."

Lysandra blinked. She felt anything but powerful at this moment. She was weak with desire, mixed with a heavy dose of anxiety for what she knew was about to happen and embarrassment at her current state of undress. And yet the idea that she could drive a sophisticated and experienced man like Andrew wild with just a glimpse of her naked breasts...it was a heady thought.

"And now I am going to remove the rest of your gown," he said, even as he hooked his fingers into the fabric and began to tug it over her hips. "Don't turn away. Don't cover yourself."

She shut her eyes as the gown fell away, but even then she could feel his stare burning into her almost as hot as a touch on her flesh. The touch that came next. He reached his hands out and gently cupped each breast, massaging the flesh there with the perfect amount of pressure.

"Andrew," she gasped and he smiled.

"Crying out my name already? We've only just begun."

She couldn't find the breath to respond, but it didn't seem to matter. He guided her backward across the room until her backside hit the bed. There he lifted her and set her on the edge of the high mattress. He pushed her legs open, splaying her naked body just as it had been when he had licked her to completion a few days before, and stepped into the space between them.

He kissed her again and all thoughts, all embarrassment, all anxiety fled as he tasted her, stroked her tongue with his, seduced her senses with his mouth.

He caught her hands as he kissed her, and she yanked away as he lowered them to the buttons that fastened his trousers.

They stared at each other for a long moment, her panting breaths echoing in the quiet room.

"Open them," he ordered.

Her fingers trembled as she hesitated, staring at him in entreaty. It wasn't that she didn't understand the words, but she was so overwhelmed by everything happening that she couldn't seem to move.

"Lysandra," he said and held her gaze evenly. "Open them."

She nodded, a jerking movement that brought her back to reality. The buttons were tight, and she discovered why as she opened a few of them. His member pushed against them, as hard as granite. When the fly was open, it sprung free, swiping her hand with its silken steel fire as she pulled away.

"Touch me," he groaned.

She stared at the length of him and had no idea how to proceed.

"Have you never seen your lover's cock before?" he asked when she made no move to touch him.

She shook her head. Slowly, he touched her chin and lifted her face to look at him.

"I'll teach you." Without another word, he caught her hand and closed her fingers around his length. With a groan, he stroked her palm down the length of him once, twice. When he released her, she continued the rhythmic stroking, mesmerized by how he flexed his hips toward her with each stoke, how his eyes rolled in the back of his head.

In that moment, she recognized that *this* was what he had meant when he told her she had power as a mistress. She quickened her pace and found that she was squeezing and relaxing the inner muscles of her body in time to her strokes. The feeling was quite pleasurable, and she sighed out her breath.

He stared at her.

"Enough," he said, his voice rough as he snatched her hand away.

She flinched. "Have I done it wrong?"

"No, but any more and I shall spend. And I want to have you, Lysandra. To claim you."

She opened her mouth to respond, but he didn't allow that. He crushed his mouth to her, dragging her forward on the bed and cupping her hips. She felt the hard head of his...what had he called it? Cock. She felt his cock at her entrance and then he slid inside of her. The first few seconds were heavenly, a full stretching of her body that made her quake.

And then a raging burst of pain made her cry out.

CHAPTER 7

*A*ndrew froze as Lysandra cried out not in pleasure, but in pain. Her face contorted in surprise and agony as her fingertips dug into his shoulders.

With great effort, he pulled from her clinging, warm body and looked down to see the telltale streak of blood on his cock. Virgin's blood.

With a roar of frustration and guilt, he flung himself away from her. He was on fire with desire, and it took everything in him to back three steps away. Despite what he now knew, he still wanted her. To finish what they'd started.

But he couldn't.

For a long moment, they simply stared at each other. Lysandra was blinking, clearly trying to control her tears. And Andrew was too upset to formulate words in that moment.

"Wh-why did you stop?" she finally asked, her voice twisted with emotion.

"Are you truly asking me that ridiculous question?" he snapped. She flinched, and he shook his head. "Virgin's blood, Lysandra? Virgin's pain?"

She squeezed her eyes shut, but not before he saw a pain far deeper than her virgin's pain. Slowly, she reached behind her, her hand sliding along the bed until she found a pillow. She covered her nakedness with it and shook her head.

"Of course not. I don't know what you're talking about."

Andrew took a step closer and lifted a trembling finger. "Don't you lie to me, Lysandra. Whatever else you do, don't lie."

She struggled for a long moment, but then finally shrugged. "Very well. I won't lie."

He stared at her. "You are...*were* an innocent! How could you keep that from me? How could Vivien?"

She jerked her gaze to his. "Vivien didn't know. I think she assumed I must have some experience when I showed up and asked her to find a protector for me. After all, what kind of virgin would be so bold? I didn't correct that misconception, just as I didn't correct yours."

He ran a hand over his face. He could think of no words to express how angry and guilty he felt. Two emotions he didn't want to associate with this kind of pleasurable endeavor. He had enough of both in his everyday life.

"God damn it, Lysandra!" he finally burst out.

She drew in a few long breaths to calm herself and then looked him in the face. He could see what a struggle it was for her to do so and how much she wanted to look away. But she remained calm and collected.

"Rail at me all you like, but now that the truth is out, I still need this training. Perhaps even more than ever. Will you not give it to me?" she asked, her voice as steady as her stare.

He blinked. "You cannot seriously expect me to carry on with you now that I know you are an innocent."

She tilted her head. "As you said a moment ago, I *was* an innocent. I may not know much, but I am perfectly aware that I cannot give twice what you just took. So the problem of my virginity, as you seem to see it, is now gone. How is this any different than when you believed I had already been used and discarded?"

"It *is* different," he insisted, but he could hardly think of any reasons why.

The woman was intelligent, he had to give her that. She could argue a good case. Not that he wasn't biased. Even now, he still wanted to bury himself inside of her and finish what they started. Deflowering of virgins be damned.

"Why?"

He gripped his hands at his sides. "You are not some woman of the streets. You were clearly gently bred and educated. A woman like that, with nothing to mar her character, shouldn't turn to a life of a mistress. There are other options."

Her lips thinned and he saw a flash of both sadness and unexpected anger in her stare.

Her voice was faraway when she said, "No. This is the only way for me."

"That cannot be true," he insisted with a sigh. "There are other ways."

She glared at him and her chin lifted stubbornly. "And what would you know about it, *my lord*? You have lived a life of privilege since the day you first drew breath. You have never seen your family's money vanish, you've never been forced to become a servant in someone's home only to have them want more from you...demand more."

She flinched and the words of rebuttal on Andrew's lips evaporated. He stared at her.

"That is what happened to you?"

She nodded, just once. "I worked for a very influential man in Society and I thought, I hoped, that it would be a way for me to support myself and those I loved. But when he demanded I service more than the house..." She shivered. "I-I refused him."

"But isn't that what you are doing by becoming a mistress?" he asked.

She shook her head. "No. If I become the mistress of a man, it will be by my choice. And there are benefits that come along with that title, aren't there? Ones far better than to be a maid whom the master toffs behind his wife's back. I can already see that in this arrangement, I would have some control...some power."

Andrew swallowed. Staring at her, her curves only barely covered by the bed pillow, her face flushed as she spoke of wielding her own kind of sensual power…his cock began to ease to attention. Fuck if she wasn't right. She had the power. At least some of it.

"This man who I served, he was enraged when I said no. He put me on the street that very day and refused to give me a good reference. In fact, he went beyond that. His poisonous words have guaranteed I'll never work in a good house again. And for a servant, that is the death of a career."

"I see," Andrew said softly.

He so rarely considered those in his service. He treated them well, he offered them money and a home, as well as help if they required it. He sometimes forgot that others did not treat their staff as well. And he never reflected on the consequences of what might happen to those put out on the street.

"I'm not certain you do see," she continued. "If you won't teach me how to be a mistress, I'll simply be forced to go about this another way. With another man if need be." She shivered at the thought. "I'll be on the street if I don't and so will—"

She cut herself off and shook her head as if she hadn't meant to say so much. Andrew stared at her.

"So will who?" he asked.

She shook her head. "It doesn't matter. I'm not asking for your pity. Just your assistance."

"Who?" he asked again, his voice low and even.

She swallowed. "My mother," she admitted.

He drew back in surprise. "Your mother?"

She flinched and then dropped off the bed to snatch at her gown. "Yes. I have one you know. Those in the class below yours are still human, my lord."

He reached for her as she fumbled with her gown. When he touched her, her skin burned his, stoking the fire he had extinguished when he discovered her secret.

"I didn't mean to offend you, Lysandra," he said softly. "Whatever you think of me or my 'class', I do understand about family responsibility. My own family is…complicated."

She stopped trying to pull away from him and instead looked up at him. "If you understand, then does it follow that you will help me, despite your misgivings?"

"You will truly continue down this course if I don't?" he asked.

He wasn't certain what answer he wished for as he asked the question. The idea of her being with another man…well, that was torture. He wanted a taste first. A moment. And he wanted to be certain she would be "trained" by someone who would understand her drive and be gentle in his instruction.

"I will," she said without hesitation. "I must."

"Then I'll help you," he whispered.

She almost buckled and he could see it was from relief. For the first time, he saw her desperation and it frightened him a little. He caught her elbow and pulled her closer.

"But you must understand that if I do this, I will do it all the way. I will teach you what a man desires…*everything* a man desires. It may be too intense for you."

She swallowed, and he could see that his warning both frightened and titillated her. Once again, he was rock hard with just a nibble of her lip and the light of curiosity in her eyes.

"It would be best for me to know every aspect of a man's desire," she finally said. "So I welcome anything you can teach me."

"We'll see," he whispered and then surrendered to the desire that had begun to course through him again. He dropped his mouth to hers, driving his tongue between her lips as he molded her still-naked curves to his body.

The dress in her hands fell away, and she let out a tiny moan into his lips as she tangled her fingers into his hair and lifted herself closer.

Andrew gasped for breath as she stole it. She might be an innocent, but she was utterly responsive and fantastically erotic. With just a touch, she arched and moaned, and she had come so fast and hard the first time he touched her that it had only added to his belief that she was experienced in some way with sex.

But now she would be his to tutor. To please. To train. And he intended to enjoy every moment of it, even as he taught her to do the same.

He didn't have to think about the fact that she would take those erotic lessons to a relationship with another man, a more permanent protector. Those were thoughts for another day.

Today was just about this.

He maneuvered her back toward the bed and immediately they were back where they'd left off before he discovered the truth. She perched on the edge of the bed, panting as she looked at him.

"Did you like how this felt before..." He hesitated and pushed at the guilt. "Before the pain?"

She nodded. "I-I did."

"The pain is temporary," he explained as he laid her back. "Something that happens the first time a man breaches you, but never again with him or any other man. Had I known you were a virgin, I would have been gentler, more careful. I would have treated that taking as the gift it is." He smoothed a lock of chestnut hair away from her face. "But now that I know...well, I promise you that I will make this first time a memorable one for you."

She blinked up at him. "I think I can safely say that has already been done."

He chuckled. "That seems like a challenge."

He didn't wait for her to reply, but dropped his mouth to hers. Her words died on his lips and he kissed her, tasted and exploring her mouth until she was relaxed on the bed. Then he began to move lower. He nuzzled her neck, sucking her flesh there with little nips and scrapes of his teeth. She arched beneath them, gripping at his shoulders as her breath rasped in and out of her lungs in a broken, heavy rhythm.

A rhythm that all but stopped when he sucked one hard nipple between his lips.

"God!" she cried out, and her hips jerked upward.

He sucked harder in response and she whimpered, clutching at him, begging him for something he knew she didn't fully understand. But he was going to show her. Right now.

He eased her backward on the bed and positioned himself over her. Since he had broken her hymen, the worst of her pain was over now, but she likely remained tender. He opened her legs as he continued to suckle and tease her nipple, then pressed his cock to her.

He swelled at the feel of her nether lips welcoming him, hot and slick, into her waiting pussy. He glanced at her face and she had her eyes closed, groaning and whimpering at the feel of his tongue against her nipple. He could take her now, quick and hot, so that she would have no time to tense and make the sensation unpleasant.

He glided inside to the hilt and her eyes came open in shock at the sensation, though she didn't recoil or cry out with pain this time. For a long moment he held still inside of her, even though the tight, hot pulsing of her pussy walls made him want to slam inside of her with little finesse or thought.

"Are you all right?" he panted.

She nodded. "Yes. The pain is minimal," she said.

"I want to take it away," he growled. "I want to make you come. To make you feel as good as I did when I licked you."

She shivered, and her body flexed, probably without her even knowing it. It was too much. Andrew stroked into her with one long thrust and grunted with the pleasure of it.

"God, you are like heaven," he moaned against her neck. "Hold tight to me, Lysandra."

She did as he asked, clutching her hands around his back as he rotated his hips a second time. He flexed and drove, fighting to remain steady, calm, gentle, but his long-neglected cock wanted more. More of her weeping slit. He hadn't lost himself for so long.

"It feels..." she gasped from beneath him and he tensed.

If she said painful, he would stop, though he had no idea how he would do such a thing now. Not when he was on the edge.

"...good," she moaned. "So good."

Those words shot him over the edge he'd been balanced on, and Andrew lost control. He drove into her, taking, claiming, stroking until he felt nothing but the oblivion of pleasure.

And just as he thought he could no longer control himself, Lysandra tensed beneath him, her face contorting in a mask of wonder and pleasure and she shuddered with release, crying out his name as she held him tighter.

He exploded, barely able to withdraw from her hot body to milk his seed against the sheets instead of deep inside her. Then he collapsed back onto the pillows and dragged her against his chest.

It was done. She was his in a way she would never be another man's. And though the idea had originally given him pause, now he felt triumphant in the thought that he would be the only one to first take her, first give her pleasure.

Whatever else happened, that fact would always belong to him. And she would always remember it. As would he.

CHAPTER 8

*L*ysandra hadn't bathed in front of another person in years. And she'd *never* bathed in front of a man. But now she was seated in a big tub in the middle of her new bedroom and Andrew sat beside it, watching her soak. The only protection for her naked flesh was the soapy water, and that was small coverage, indeed.

A fact Andrew seemed to be enjoying. He had positioned himself so that he could look down at her, watch her. She wasn't certain whether to squirm with embarrassment or blush with the surprising and intense desire he inspired. She couldn't help but think of the passion they had shared just an hour before and she dropped her gaze.

"Don't look away from me," he said softly.

She gave him a questioning glance. "I beg your pardon?"

"This is your training."

She wrinkled her brow. "Was our...our..."

"Fucking?" he finished for her.

She had never heard that term before, but she knew instinctively that it wasn't a proper or appropriate term to use in mixed company.

When she flinched, he said, "Or you could call it making love if the other term is too vulgar."

She bit her lip. Making love seemed too intimate a label for what they had done. Love was not part of this equation in any sense. In truth, she hardly knew this man, let alone had any feelings for him. But when she had to choose between the two terms…

"Was our making love not part of my training?" she asked.

He nodded slowly. "Oh yes. A most pleasurable part that will be a cornerstone of everything we share from this moment until we part. But now that you are no longer a virgin, we must move on to more strenuous lessons about expectations, desires and the future you insist you must have."

Lysandra's eyes narrowed. Was he trying to frighten her in order to force her to alter her course? He had so passionately argued against her decision to be a mistress before he finished…*making love* to her that she couldn't be mistaken about his feelings on the subject.

But she wouldn't be deterred. So she lifted her chin and looked him straight in the eye. "Why shouldn't I look away?"

He held her gaze evenly. "As a mistress, you mustn't simper or play coy. A gentleman encounters enough of that in ballrooms and parlors as he pursues women to be his wife. A mistress must offer something different. Something exciting and new to brighten a gentleman's drab life."

Lysandra shifted in the water. Could she do such a thing? Be exciting and new to men who had far more power and experience than she did?

"But all men do not want the same thing, do they?" she asked.

He arched a brow. "In some ways they do. All men want the sweetness of your body. But in some ways, no. They all have different desires."

"Then perhaps I shall end up mistress to a man with a harridan of a lady in his wife." She shrugged. "Perhaps *he* would prefer a demure mistress."

Andrew stared at her for a long moment and then he began to

laugh. It was a pleasant sound, though a bit rough, almost as if he hadn't used it in a long time.

"My dear, if you can use that wit with whatever man you end up with, you will find it serves you as well as your body," he said when he could again speak.

Lysandra blushed with pleasure. She had not been complimented on her wit since her eighteenth year. Her father had been dead a year then, and she and her mother had clung to the hopes that she would find a proper husband to save them from their mounting troubles. She had briefly made a foray into the middle class Society in London. The gentlemen had all claimed to enjoy her company, but ended up marrying dull girls with large dowries.

And perhaps that was the point Andrew was trying to make.

"So you are saying that men are often forced into matches that they would not choose if they didn't have to breed proper heirs for their titles or fill their coffers with the dowries of their wives. When they seek a mistress, they look for someone quite different from the woman they have at home or the woman they know they must court down the road," she said with wonder.

He nodded. "Exactly."

"How sad for all of them," Lysandra said with a shake of her head. "How sad for the men to marry someone they could never love and how sad for the women who cannot ever be good enough to keep the attention of their husbands."

Andrew pursed his lips. "It isn't all so bleak. There are love marriages amongst the *ton*, as I'm sure there are in the middle class. They are simply rarer."

He turned his face away, and Lysandra stared. There had been a brief moment of pain on his face that was unmistakable. She recalled Vivien had said something about his "sad history", but could it have something to do with a marriage? Dear God, she didn't even know if he *was* married. She had assumed not when he took her into his home, but she could be utterly wrong.

"Do you have a wife?" she blurted out.

He jerked his gaze to her and held it there a long moment. Then he slowly shook his head. "No. My wife died three years ago."

Lysandra swallowed hard. At least she wouldn't be the "other woman" aiding in the painful deterioration of a marriage, but she could feel no glee about the reason. A death of a spouse, she knew how that had broken her poor mother.

"I'm sorry," she said softly.

He rose to his feet. "This is exactly what I'm speaking of, Lysandra. Your duty is to keep these painful thoughts, these proofs of reality, away from your protector's mind. Create a world of fantasy and pleasure, nothing more. That is what he will desire."

She stared at him. He was angry. Angry with her or angry with himself, she wasn't certain. But before she could ask him, he spun on her.

"Stand up," he ordered.

She flinched at the rough tone but did as he asked, shoving to her feet from the steaming water. She still felt a desire to cover herself, but it was beginning to fade. Andrew had already seen her in every intimate way, after all.

"Have you ever touched yourself?" he asked.

"Touched myself?" she repeated.

He stared at her. "As I touched you. Touched yourself intimately."

She drew a few long breaths before she answered, so he wouldn't hear the tremble in her voice.

"No," she admitted.

He frowned. "Never? Not even in the dark of your room?"

She bit her lip. "No."

"Hmmm, well then, your first lesson shall be one you carry with you the rest of your life. Know your body." He smiled, but it was wicked. "To create pleasure in others, you must experience it yourself. Take the towel from the table beside the tub, dry off and lay down on the divan."

Lysandra shivered, but she did as she had been told. Once she was dry, she moved to the divan, a fainting couch that was positioned in front of the blazing fire. Once she was lying across it, staring at him with anticipation heating her blood, he moved to kneel at the end of the couch.

"Open your legs, Lysandra and touch yourself."

She sat up a fraction and stared at him. "Touch myself with you watching?"

He growled out his answer, "Normally, I would simply tell you to do so in the privacy of your chamber, but our time together is limited. I will be your guide in helping you find ways to give yourself release and then you must do this every night, whether I visit you or not. Keep your body at the ready and you will more enjoy your duties as my mistress." He stopped and shook his head. "A mistress."

Lysandra bit her lip. She had no idea how to proceed in touching herself intimately. But as Andrew tilted his head in encouragement, she realized that he wasn't about to release her from his order.

She crooked her knees and spread her legs a fraction. He shook his head.

"No. All the way."

"Splay myself out in an entirely unladylike fashion?" Lysandra burst out in horror.

He smiled. "You may be a lady in the parlor all you like—in fact, that is what you should do, no matter what your position in life ends up being. But in the bedroom, in private or with your lover, you must be willing to go further. To forget conventions which tell you not to look, not to touch, not to *feel*. Otherwise you will have very short and unsatisfying affairs, indeed."

He reached forward and grasped her knees, then shoved them apart until she was sprawled across the couch in a most revealing position.

"Now place your hands on yourself and think of what has given you pleasure," he continued, though his voice was becoming rougher and rougher with each order.

"Andrew," she whispered, mostly because she was afraid.

Afraid of what fully surrendering to this life would entail, and worse, how it might change her. Already, she longed for his touch, for more of him, did that not make her a wanton?

"Stop thinking about everything that frightens you and do this," Andrew said, breaking into her thoughts like he had a window into her tormented soul.

"How do you know what I was thinking?" she asked.

He laughed. "You have an expressive face, Lysandra. Now stop dallying and do as I say."

Lysandra lifted her hand from her side. It trembled as she placed it flat on her belly and let it rest there. Her fingers had never felt so heavy or so hot to her before. She stared down at them, almost as if they belonged to some unwelcomed stranger.

"Slide upward and touch your breasts," he said, staring at her hand as intently as she was.

Lysandra sucked in a breath and slowly, unsteadily, glided her hand up the apex of her body until her right palm covered her right breast lightly. Once again, she was struck by how foreign the sensation was. Of course she had touched herself innocently before, in the bath or while getting dressed...but this was something else. Now she noticed just how heavy and soft her breast was. How hard her nipple felt as her palm brushed it and how just that grazing touch could make a little frisson of pleasure jolt through her.

She gasped and jerked her hand away.

"No," he urged, so soft and seductive. "Don't stop."

She shivered and then rested her fingers back against her flesh. They were beginning to feel less foreign now, which allowed her to revel in the brush of her skin, the heat that increased as she first rested her hand back in its original position and then began to gently knead the flesh there.

She thought of Andrew and what he had done to her both times he touched her this way. She thumbed at her own nipple and gasped when the pleasure her grazing touch had caused doubled, tripled.

"You see how much more aware you become of your body when you surrender to its desires?" Andrew asked.

His voice was so low and seductive that it seemed to dance along her spine and through her nerves to tingle at the tips of her breasts and in the area between her legs that she hadn't even begun to explore.

"Tell me how it feels," he encouraged her.

"Hot," she admitted in panting breaths. "Tingling."

"Good, that is exactly how your pleasure should feel. Now lower. Move your hand between your legs and touch yourself there."

She was too mesmerized by her own actions now to refuse his request. She glided her hand down her body, noting how the touch felt, how her body reacted. Finally, she hesitated just above the triangle of hair that marked the beginning of her mound.

"Think of how good it felt when I was tasting you," he said, sliding closer. "And when I was inside you. Wouldn't you like to have that kind of pleasure at your own command, whenever you would like it?"

She shut her eyes. He was like a seductive devil, daring her to be more than she was. And she had no resistance to him. She covered her sex with her hand and caught her breath.

"I don't know how to...to touch myself here," she admitted.

He leaned along the bottom of the settee until his face was mere inches from her sex. He parted her fingers to reveal her to him and smiled. Then he covered her fingers with his own, spreading her lower lips gently and gliding her fingers against the wetness they concealed.

"Feel how you are already aroused?" he asked, stroking her hand up and down the length of her entrance. The tingles she had felt when she touched her breasts returned with even greater intensity.

She swallowed hard. "The wetness, you mean?"

"Yes. It is how your body readies itself for a lover's intrusion. And it is most pleasurable to feel that heated wetness around my cock, I assure you." He removed his fingers and Lysandra continued the work he had started, rubbing the outside of her own sex in a rhythmic, repetitive fashion.

"Now press a finger inside your sheath," he said. "As if it were my cock inside of you."

She whimpered, but did as he ordered. Her index finger slipped inside with no resistance and she felt the wet walls flex around her hard.

"Oh God," she whispered, tensing against the building wave of passion. "And then?"

He reached out and flicked at her clitoris with his finger. "Do you remember when I told you about this nub? When I licked it and made you come the first time?"

She jerked out a nod. "Yes."

"Touch it like I am."

She pressed her thumb to the bundle of nerves and began to grind against it. Her body lifted and her hips turned in time to this new wicked pleasure, almost as if it knew what to do, even if she didn't. She cried out, pushing harder, driver her finger deeper into her sheath and the wall of release burst suddenly and powerfully.

She cried out as she came, shaking and lifting her hips, trembling as wave after wave of pleasure crashed over her, carrying her away until she was spent on the fainting couch and panting.

Before she could catch her breath or say a word, he rose up like a god, stripped off the trousers and shirt he had put back on when he called for her bath and stared down at her. Her eyes went wide as she stared at him. He was utterly beautiful and now his hard cock, jutting up against his belly, no longer worried her. She ached for it.

He obliged without her asking. He lowered himself over her and took advantage of her already spread legs. In an easy thrust he was buried inside her to the hilt. She gasped at the feeling, still shocked by how full and womanly and utterly wild his taking could make her feel.

He dropped his mouth down and began to take her with his tongue and his cock. Unlike the last time, there was no gentleness to his touch, he was demanding, driving into her hard and sucking her tongue, tasting her mouth with as much command. She surrendered to the domination without hesitating. She lifted her hips to meet his driving thrusts, arching and mewling as he claimed her hard and fast.

The pleasure she had experienced at her own hand was still tingling in her loins and within a few hard thrusts he stoked the fires inside of her anew. She pulled her mouth from his to cry out against his shoulder and he roared in response, then withdrew to spend away from her.

Lysandra collapsed against the settee once more, slick with sweat, the scent of sex in the air around her. But she had never been more satisfied in her entire life. And if *this* was what being a mistress would entail, she was beginning to think it might not be such a bad life after all.

CHAPTER 9

*A*ndrew sat on the same fainting couch where he had taken Lysandra not three hours before. She was curled up in the bed, sheets tangled around her waist, sleeping peacefully.

He hadn't intended to take her after she pleasured herself. Nor had he intended to take her a third time after they shared a decadent supper in her chamber. Nor a fourth. He was no longer the libertine that could fuck a woman until they were both spent.

Except that was exactly what he had done tonight. Without thought, without hesitation.

Now, regret…well, that was another story entirely.

He stared at her. She wasn't anything like his late wife, Rebecca. For that, he found he was glad. They didn't even look alike. Rebecca had been fair and Lysandra was dark.

But there was something about Lysandra that drew him like a moth to her seductive flame. There was her beauty, of course, her sensuality that he was able to coax and demand because of the tutelage he was giving. But there was something more. A kind of sweet innocence that she maintained even as she opened her body to him with increasing fervor.

And there was a sadness that lingered in her eyes that he wanted to…heal.

He jerked his head away and stood up.

Heal her? That was ridiculous. Not possible. This agreement between them was for sex and nothing more. He could either help her to become a valued mistress to a long-term protector or help her see that she wasn't equipped for this life. But that was all. He had no intention of creating more between them than that.

He turned on his heel and stalked from the room silently. He said nothing to the servants as he walked to his waiting carriage and gave his driver the order to go to his father's home. It was late, but not too late to see the old man, and it would set him to rights. Make him remember who he was and why he had come to London in the first place. And it wasn't to begin an affair with Lysandra Keates.

He would do well to recall that fact.

After a long while of twisting through streets crowded with carriages heading for the theatre or soirees around town, his rig came to a stop before his father's London home.

As he stepped down, he stared up at the large, imposing home, so different from the modest escape he had just slipped away from. He had never liked the brashness of this home or even his own homes here in London and in the country. But they came with the title and his wife had wanted them to be impressive, so he had done what was expected of him.

Still, there was something friendlier, more *real* about Lysandra's new home.

The door opened and his father's servant greeted him. He was shown immediately to his father's office. As he opened the door, the earl looked up from his desk and his eyes widened. He got to his feet while Andrew closed the door behind himself.

"Callis, I didn't expect to see you tonight."

Andrew flinched. His father always called him by his current title, Callis, just as his peers did. Never Andrew. It put a distance between them that had always stung him a fraction.

"Good evening, my lord," he said, just as formal. "I'm sorry if I intruded upon your plans for the evening by not sending word of my arrival."

"Of course not," his father said as he sat down and grabbed for a cigar to offer Andrew. Andrew shook his head. He didn't smoke, though his father never seemed to recall that. As he lit his own cigar, his father said, "What brings you here?"

Andrew blinked. He didn't really know the answer to that question. "I-I was just driving by."

His father's brow wrinkled. "I see. Well, I'm pleased you made my home a stop on your way to wherever you were going. To a soiree?"

Andrew pursed his lips. His father had made it no secret that he thought Andrew should return to Society in full. Perhaps should even marry again so that he could create the heir the earl so desperately required, despite the fact that Andrew had a younger brother who could very well fulfill that role if Andrew didn't.

"No." He looked away. "Home. I was going home."

"Hmph." His father chewed on the cigar restlessly. "Have you seen your brother since your arrival in London?"

Andrew looked at him. "Sam? No."

"He's serious about some girl. Pretty thing, I think her name is Adela. Daughter of the Duke of Wimberly. They could marry this year. And when they breed a son, he could become the next in line if you refuse to do your duty."

Andrew stared at his father. Here he had just dropped a huge bombshell that his younger brother could soon marry, and all his father could do was try to stoke some kind of competition to create an heir.

"What does Sam think of her?" he asked quietly.

His father shrugged. "Who knows? He goes on about her often enough; I suppose he thinks himself in love with her. She's suitable, though. That's what matters to me. If they married, it would link us to yet another important family."

"Well, I haven't seen him," Andrew said with a slight sigh. "But I should go to him soon to offer him congratulations. If he is happy, I will be happy."

"You two." His father waved his hand restlessly. "Too much like your mother. The woman had many admirable qualities, but she was a ridiculous romantic. Bred bad habits about marriage into you both. It is a business arrangement, my boy. Nothing to moon over for three years."

Andrew flinched. "I realize you think I have mourned far past my rightful time. But it is my right to decide how my wife should be honored and for how long."

His father stared at him and Andrew saw a brief flash of concern on his face. For all his bluster and ramblings about propriety and business mergers, Andrew knew the old man cared for him. Perhaps not with the obvious affection his late mother had shown to her sons, but their father loved them as much as he could love anyone.

And his gruffness and bluntness was often based as much as on concern as it was on propriety or a desire for heirs or whatever else he said.

He shook his head. "Please, let us not rehash this same argument over and again. I know what your expectations are of me."

His father puffed out a circle of smoke. "You ought not to lock yourself away, boy. It isn't healthy."

Andrew nodded. "Yes, I realize you believe that. But I do come here at your request, every time you request my presence. Don't ask me for more."

His father opened his mouth, but then shook his head as if he had thought better of it. Abruptly he changed the subject to the estate Andrew lorded over in Huntington. As the earl spoke, Andrew's thoughts turned to Lysandra, asleep in the bed he had provided for her. More was what he had already unexpectedly gotten on this latest trip to London. And it was utterly confusing.

*L*ysandra stared out the window as the carriage rattled through London, but she hardly noticed the passing buildings and people. She couldn't even appreciate the comfort of the vehicle, so different from the last time she'd made this trip.

No, the only thing she could focus on was Andrew. For the

second day in a row, she had woken alone in the pretty little house he had given to her. There had been no word from him and she was too timid to send word of her own. She didn't know if mistresses even did such a thing as contact a protector in his home.

Actually, that was only one of a thousand questions she didn't know the answer to, which was why she was in her carriage. And why that carriage was stopping in front of Vivien Manning's home.

Wilkes soon opened the door and helped her down. He smiled at her. "I'll wait around the back, miss. Send for me when you are ready."

Lysandra barely contained a nervous giggle. How different this trip was than her last to this place.

"Thank you, Wilkes," she finally managed to say with some dignity.

He nodded and she swept up the stairs. The butler Nettle greeted her with much more warmth than he had during their first encounter and led her to the same parlor where she had waited for Vivien before. She paced the room, wringing her hands as she waited for her savior's arrival.

But as she moved along the back wall of the chamber, something caught her eye. She hadn't noticed the red wallpaper before, except to be aware of its bold color. But now she saw that hidden within the pattern were...

She gasped, and at the same moment, the door behind her opened and Vivien stepped in. Lysandra spun on her with a dark red blush and found the other woman smiling at her knowingly.

"Admiring my wallpaper?" Vivien said as she moved to stand next to Lysandra. "I designed it myself. It cost a fortune, but it is quite the conversation piece, is it not?"

They both stared. Lysandra could hardly breathe at the faint, artistic images of men driving into their partners from behind, women with their lover's cocks between their lips, two men with one woman...her head spun.

"My favorite is this one," Vivien said as she motioned to an image of a man and woman giving each other oral pleasure at the same time.

Lysandra's eyes grew wide. She already knew the way Andrew's mouth felt on her, but she hadn't fully considered taking his cock into her mouth. Especially at the same time that he pleasured her. Would he like such a thing?

She could add that to her questions, a list growing by the second.

"But I doubt you came here to examine my wallpaper," Vivien said with a laugh. "Not that it couldn't give you excellent ideas of how to give to and receive pleasure from a man. Is everything well?"

Lysandra forced herself to stop looking at the naughty wallpaper and return her attention to Vivien.

"I— Well…"

Vivien tilted her head when Lysandra struggled to continue. She kindly filled the awkward silence.

"My sources tell me that Andrew has given you a home to live in during your tutelage. I assume that means you have begun your affair."

Lysandra blushed. "Yes. He came to me two nights ago and we… uh, mmade love for the first time. But he hasn't returned since. I fear I must have done something wrong."

Vivien stared at her. "I see. What was his mood when he left you?"

Lysandra shifted. He had been so angry with her when he uncovered her secret, but then that emotion had seemed to fade. They had shared her bed over and over again with no mention of his being upset.

"I wasn't entirely honest with you or with him," she explained slowly. "So he was, for a time, very angry at me that night."

"Not entirely honest…what does that mean?" Vivien asked, her tone filled with caution.

"Before he came to me, I-I was an innocent," Lysandra admitted with another hot blush. These were not topics she had ever thought to talk about so freely, but here she was, discussing them for a second time in as many days.

Vivien was on her feet in an instant, and she covered her mouth with her hand. "Oh God. Andrew must have been furious."

Lysandra nodded. "He was less than pleased to find out the truth."

"And he left then?" Vivien pressed.

"No." Lysandra turned away. "We talked and then he made love to me. And again. And again."

Vivien's eyebrows shot up and a small smile tilted her lips. "I see. But if he made love to you three times—"

"Four," Lysandra choked.

The other woman blinked. "*Four* times even after he discovered your secret, why do you believe you did something wrong?"

Lysandra shifted. "He is clearly very experienced. I am obviously not. The fact that he hasn't returned or even sent me word makes me think that he has lost interest in me."

Vivien shook her head. "Or that he is just as surprised by his reaction to you as you were."

"His reaction?" Lysandra repeated.

Vivien laughed. "Of course, clearly he did have one."

Lysandra worried her lip. She had been so wrapped up in her own emotions, the sensations he awoke in her and her reactions that she hadn't actually thought much about his.

"Occasionally I felt I had some little amount of power," she admitted. "But otherwise, I am not experienced enough to know what his reaction to me could be."

Vivien leaned back in her seat with a soft sigh. "Being a mistress means more than just using your body as an instrument for plea-sure," she began. "Over time, the best mistresses begin to know things about people. They are told things. And I have been told something about Callis that you should understand."

Lysandra leaned forward. "Yes?"

"Do you know his wife died?"

She nodded. "He told me."

Both Vivien's eyebrows lifted. "That in itself is very interesting. You see, he does not speak of that to very many people. Likewise, the time he spends in London is limited. He normally hides away on his estate in the countryside, Rutholm Park. The rumor is that he has not had a lover since the death of his wife, or if he has it has been a one-night affair that did not bear repeating."

Lysandra blinked. He had said his wife died three years before. It was hard to picture such a sensual man as celibate for that long.

"But if he prefers to keep himself away from others, why did he agree to- to—"

Vivien shrugged. "To enter into this affair with you? I have no idea. Except that when I brought him here, when I showed you to him while you walked in the gardens, there was something that lit up in his eyes. He was attracted to you from the start, and I think the intensity of that attraction must be worrisome to him. It reminds him of the man he once was and everyone knows he shies away from that with all his might."

"What he once was?" Lysandra asked.

"A libertine, my dear. Filled with frivolity and lust." Vivien grinned. "He was a great deal of fun back then, though he was never my lover. We did run in the same wild circles, though, and I watched him play the role of rake to the hilt. The fact that he would make love to you four times in one passionate night makes me think perhaps you reawaken some of that rake in him."

Lysandra swallowed hard. She wasn't certain if these things Vivien was saying were compliments or damnations.

"But if he doesn't want that part of him to live again..." she began.

Vivien waved off her concern with one elegant hand. "Posh. One cannot deny what he is, no matter how he tries. His problem was that he didn't believe he could be a decent man *and* a man of plea-sures. If you could show him that he could be both, then you will help him."

"And how do I do that?" Lysandra asked with a shake of her head.

"Force him to surrender to those desires he fights so hard." Vivien smiled. "Drag him headlong into pleasure."

"I don't think I could force that man to do anything," Lysandra muttered as she thought of Andrew's bold personality and strong will.

"You'd be surprised," Vivien said. "You already said you feel you have some power over him, do you not? Minor or brief as it is, you can build on it. But you must develop some faith in your own powers as a woman."

"How?" Lysandra asked as she got to her feet. "That is why I came here. To determine what I could have done wrong and get answers on how to proceed."

Vivien tilted her head as she looked at Lysandra long and hard. "I wonder if you are ready...but how does one become ready?"

She was talking to herself, clearly, but Lysandra couldn't allow such an intriguing statement to pass unanswered.

"Ready? For what?"

"I believe the best way to learn any new skill is by observation... and practice," Vivien said as she got to her feet and motioned Lysandra to join her. "So I am going to take you somewhere that you can do the first. The second will be up to you."

Lysandra wrinkled her brow as she followed Vivien from the room and toward the hallway.

"I'm not certain I understand," she said as she trailed after the other woman, heart rate increasing with every step.

"You will." Vivien took her upstairs and withdrew a key ring from her pelisse pocket. She unlocked a chamber and motioned Lysandra inside.

It was a small room with just a few chairs scattered about. She wouldn't even describe it as a parlor, really, for there didn't seem to be any purpose to the room. The chairs all faced one wall, for one thing, and weren't tilted toward each other for talk.

"Sit down," Vivien said softly.

As Lysandra did so, the other woman approached the wall. As Lysandra stared, Vivien removed a portrait hanging there and revealed a hole in the wall that allowed a person in one room to see into the other.

"What—?" Lysandra began, but before she could continue, the door in the opposite chamber opened. A woman came through first, dressed in an utterly revealing dress that swooped down over the curves of her breasts and had a slit to reveal the length of her leg. Behind her a gentleman followed. He had a pronounced limp and a scar across his face that was still red and sore, as if it was from a recent injury.

Vivien leaned closer. "This is a friend of mine, Annalisa. She was a very popular courtesan, but she has taken her money and no longer indulges in that lifestyle. The man she is with is Major Gabriel Crook. He was injured in the war last year. They met here at one of my parties and they enjoy revisiting the room where they first...*met*."

As Lysandra stared, the Major reached back to shut the chamber door. Annalisa sashayed forward and leaned against him, pressing her mouth to his with passionate fervor as they fell against the door together.

Lysandra turned away. "What is this?"

"By making love to him, she is helping him heal. Reminding him a little about how good life can be." Vivien smiled. "They are utterly passionate...and they don't mind being watched. *You* are going to watch them."

CHAPTER 10

*L*ysandra's mouth dropped open. Watch these people as they made love? But before she could protest, Vivien called out, "Annalisa, Major, we are in the next chamber."

The two, who had continued to kiss wildly, stopped, and Annalisa turned toward the chamber. Lysandra stepped back, blushing as the other woman sought her out like a teacher seeking a naughty schoolgirl.

"Oh, most excellent," she said, her accent Spanish. She was utterly beautiful, with bright, dark eyes and a full, red mouth. "Major, we are to have an audience."

He grinned, and Lysandra was surprised that although he was scarred, he was also still very handsome. And as he wrapped his arms around Annalisa from behind and began gently kneading her breasts through the miniscule fabric of her gown, there was no denying he was a sensual man.

"Does this person wish to join us?" Annalisa asked, her breath short as her nipples began to harden at the Major's ministrations.

Lysandra stared at Vivien in horror. "No!" she burst out. "I must go, I cannot—"

Vivien turned on her. "My dear, trust me, there are no two people more passionate than these two. Watching them will help you learn the answers to many of the questions you asked me today. Annalisa is bold where you are timid. Watch her. Watch the way she pleases this man and how intense and moving an experience that can be for them both. Do it and take what you see back to Andrew. You won't regret it."

She turned away from Lysandra and called out, "This little mouse isn't quite ready to play with the cats, Annalisa. But do put on a good show for her. She is trying to learn."

Lysandra stared through the window between the two chambers, shocked as the Major began to kiss Annalisa's neck. She laughed and said something Lysandra couldn't hear. There was no denying that watching them was mesmerizing. Their passion was so effortless.

"I'll step away," Vivien said softly. "To allow you your privacy in your reactions. Come find me when you're finished. I would greatly like to hear your thoughts on what you see."

Lysandra swallowed hard and tried to squeak out one final protest, but Vivien ignored her and stepped from the room, closing the chamber door behind her with a click that rang in Lysandra's ears with finality.

She shifted her focus back to the couple in the opposite chamber. They knew she was here, watching them, yet it didn't seem to slow their passion even a fraction. Annalisa turned back toward him, rubbing her body and up and down his as she kissed him with fervor and increasing passion.

He grunted and sighed as he drove his tongue between her lips and cupped her backside to keep her firmly against him. They parted, and Annalisa smiled at him, wicked and knowing.

She drew back a fraction and began to undress her lover. His hands flexed at his sides, like he wanted to participate in the act, but he allowed her to take control. She stripped his jacket away, then his shirt.

Lysandra gasped. The scar on his face was mirrored by a series of them on his body. He had been through hell, for certain. And yet there was something about his rough damaged body, being stroked and loved by this beautiful woman, that was utterly arousing. Even though she didn't want it to happen, Lysandra's own breasts began to tingle with pleasure, her sex grew wet and she wanted, quite desperately, to touch herself.

She leaned closer on the chair instead and watched as Annalisa stripped away her lover's trousers. Lysandra couldn't help but whimper. She had spent her entire life being sheltered from the vision of a naked, aroused man. Now she had seen two in less than a week. She preferred Andrew's thick thrust, but the major was a specimen in his own right.

Annalisa smiled. "Oh, your cock. I have been dreaming of it for days, Gabriel."

He rubbed against her, stroking himself against her leg as he kissed her again. "And I've been dreaming of all the wicked things you do to that cock, my love."

"Then allow me to bring those dreams to life," Annalisa said softly. She kissed him one last time as she cupped his member and began to stroke.

Lysandra's suddenly dry lips parted. The other woman was mimicking a rhythm of sex in her slow, even strokes and the Major's head dipped back over his shoulders as he hissed out a low, "Yesssss."

But that wasn't enough for Annalisa. She dragged her mouth down his throat, his chest, his stomach and finally dropped to her knees before him. Lysandra had a perfect view as Annalisa looked up at him, eyes sparkling. He stared as she darted out her tongue and slowly licked the head of his cock.

Lysandra jolted. This was like those pictures hidden in Vivien's wallpaper in her parlor. Annalisa traced her lover's cock with her tongue, then wrapped her lips around him and drew him deeply into her mouth.

He tangled his fingers in her hair with a garbled cry and drove his hips forward even farther, thrusting like he was taking her body. But Annalisa didn't seem to be bothered by this. She moaned low in her throat and stroked her free hand up and down the side of his thigh as she began to take him with long, wet strokes of her mouth and tongue.

Lysandra hadn't known how to feel about the act when she thought of it or saw the wallpaper images, but now her body reacted to the passionate way Annalisa gave to her lover and the way he groaned and strained in turn. This was pure pleasure for him and her mind couldn't help but stray to Andrew and what he would do if she took him into her mouth the same way. She shivered at the thought of his hot, velvety member between her lips, of tasting him.

She jolted as she realized she had begun to touch her own leg, massaging and stroking her thigh. No, she wasn't going to do that, not with two other people just feet away, knowing she was there.

She refocused on them. Annalisa was driving with her mouth now, taking and taking with increased speed. The major cried out and suddenly he lifted her away.

"Inside of you," he gasped and pulled at her gown. The fabric tugged open with little encouragement and he threw it aside. She was naked beneath and arched her back almost like she was proud of what he was seeing.

Lysandra bit her lip. This was the mark of an experienced woman, wasn't it? She didn't simper or try to cover herself. She enjoyed it when her lover looked at her. She enjoyed everything about this.

And truth be told, once the initial confusion and pain had faded...so did Lysandra. She quivered every time she thought of Andrew's body on her, in her, his mouth tasting her.

Once again her fingers moved, this time to the area between her thighs. And she didn't stop herself. Absently, she stroked there as she continued to watch the couple in the other room.

The Major spun Annalisa around so that they were both facing the window between the rooms. He smiled, and Lysandra jolted. Could he see her in the shadows? That question should have made her yank her hand away from herself, but instead her fingers quickened. The touch was dulled through her dress, but still she felt pleasure building in her.

"Do it," Annalisa gasped as he positioned himself behind her. She gripped the back of a chair that was before her and braced herself there, face twisted with pleasure and tense with anticipation.

She didn't have to ask twice. Without preamble, he drove into her. She buckled against the chair, her knuckles whitening as he drove into her, hard and fast, from behind.

Lysandra could see her release building on her face. It contorted with pleasure, with the peaking of sensation deep within her. At the same moment, Lysandra's own body reacted much the same way. As she worked her hand, her fingers over her clit, there was a burst of pleasure, and she bit back a cry just as Annalisa screamed out her own.

A cry that merged with the Major's. He drove harder, faster and then arched into her, calling out her name, clinging to her bare hips as he experienced release with her.

For a long moment, the only sounds in either room were pants of pleasure. The couple's and the ones from Lysandra's own lips. She blushed at the thought that she had taken such pleasure in another couple's joining, but watching had done that.

And it had also taught her a great many things.

She stared as the couple sank down together onto the floor. They wrapped themselves into each other, embracing with an intimacy that rivaled the intensity of their coupling.

"I love you," Annalisa whispered.

Lysandra flinched. Now she *was* intruding.

"I'm not a whole man," he said in return, but he held her closer.

Lysandra got to her feet. They might have remembered she was in the room while having sex, but this exchange was not meant for a stranger. She slipped to the door just as she heard Annalisa say, "You have proven that isn't true time and again. I only wish you believed it."

She closed the door behind her and leaned against it, her breath coming short. What she had seen was an education…what she had heard…well, it was one too. It was too easy to allow emotions to merge with the physical aspects of an affair. They seemed to go hand in hand, didn't they? Passion with love.

Only they couldn't. Not for her.

She pushed away from the door and weaved her way unsteadily downstairs. Nettle stood there, almost as if he was waiting, but if he knew what she had been doing, he gave no indication. He merely bowed slightly and said, "Miss Manning is in her study. The third door on the left. She said for you to see her before you depart."

"Th-thank you," she said, still too unsteady not to stammer. "Would you tell my driver to ready himself for our departure? I'll be going once I finish talking to Miss Manning."

He nodded and left her to find the study. She hesitated before she knocked and heard Vivien's voice on the other side of the door.

"Come in, Lysandra."

She opened the door and found Vivien at a large desk, much like the ones she'd seen in a man's home. She was looking over a ledger but set it aside as Lysandra entered.

"Hello again. I trust this means it is over?"

Lysandra blushed. "Yes."

"And did you take anything away from your voyeuristic activities?" Vivien smiled. "Aside from that flush to your cheeks that tells me you enjoyed what you saw?"

Lysandra lifted her hands to cover her face and looked away. "Is it so obvious?"

Vivien shrugged one shoulder. "It is to me, but why should you be embarrassed? Did you not see how much both Annalisa and her major enjoyed their joining? How much it gave them pleasure? And how active and willing she was?"

"Yes." Lysandra sat down across from Vivien. "I could see how bold she was and how much he enjoyed that boldness. It is a lesson I must take with me as I continue my training with Andrew."

Vivien nodded. "Good. And did you see how their passion could be restorative to them both. Healing?"

Lysandra hesitated. "Yes. I think it was...but I also saw another pitfall in this arrangement."

Vivien tilted her head. "Pitfall?"

"Emotion," Lysandra whispered. "There is something deeper between them than mere sex. And it is a source of pain and strife for them both. I could see how easy it would be to fall in love with a man who was a protector or lover."

Vivien stood up and there was a moment where pain registered on her normally controlled and lovely face.

"Yes, what you say is true. Emotion is a great enemy of women in our position. Love is easy to grow, but hard to keep alive. And most men don't want it from their mistresses, as it causes no end to inconvenience."

Lysandra nodded. It was just as she thought. A mistress could offer everything but her heart to her lover. And she would do well not to forget that in the heat of passion and pleasure.

"Thank you for showing me this today," she said with a shrug. "I resisted doing something so shocking, but in the end, I believe it has given me a great education."

"And an assignment," Vivien laughed and her darker emotions were gone.

Lysandra looked at her in confusion. "An assignment?"

Her friend nodded. "Seduce Andrew. Draw passion from him, give him your own. The sooner you are a full participant when you make love, the sooner you will enjoy your training and become a good mistress to him...or to whomever else you end up with in the long run."

Lysandra swallowed. It was one thing to watch a woman who possessed such boldness, but to become one, herself?

"I don't know—" she began.

Vivien moved closer. "Don't say that. Don't cut yourself down before you even try. I would wager you've been doing that your whole life. It must stop now. You *are* capable of passion and desire and whatever else you want to achieve. Believe that and he will be forced to do the same."

Lysandra nodded. Faith in herself was a difficult gift, but Vivien was correct. It had to be done to succeed.

"I will," she said softly as she got to her feet. "Thank you, Vivien."

"Of course," the other woman said as she walked Lysandra down the hall and to the foyer. "I am pleased to assist you in any way. Call on me again if you have questions. Or perhaps we will see each other out in Town. I would think Andrew will begin to take you out soon and show you what a mistress does when she is on the arm of her protector in public."

Lysandra flashed to an image of what she had just watched Annalisa and the major do, but shoved it aside. That *couldn't* be correct. Not for a proper gentleman.

Although, as she left the house and allowed Wilkes to help her into her carriage, she couldn't help but shiver at the idea of she and Andrew being so carried away by passion that they didn't care who watched.

CHAPTER 11

*a*ndrew shifted in his seat and stared at the door once more. He had arrived at Lysandra's home half an hour ago, only to be told that the lady was out. Out calling on Vivien, of all people!

He had no idea what to think of it. Part of him worried that perhaps she had changed her mind about her affair with him, their training. It might be best for her in the long run, but the idea that what they shared might be over...

Well, it was far more disturbing a thought than it should have been. He frowned as he heard the door open in the hallway and the muffled tones of Lysandra's voice as she spoke to her butler, Carlsworth. He got to his feet, listening at how her muted words were first generic and then filled with surprise, as he assumed the servant had told her of his presence in her home.

He smoothed his jacket and straightened his shoulders as the door opened and Lysandra stepped inside. Without meaning to do so, he caught his breath. By God, but she was prettier than he remembered...and his memory had been of one of the most beautiful women he'd ever met. Her chestnut hair was drawn up in a style that had probably involved the help of one of the servants he had given her. She still wore an older, out of fashion gown, which he frowned at, but she was better than the gown. Better than anything he'd ever seen.

"Hello," she said softly. "I apologize for your wait, I had no idea you intended to call today or I wouldn't have gone out."

Andrew looked at her more closely. Her cheeks were slightly flushed and her breath was short with...was it excitement? He had never seen her look this way before and he liked it.

"I sent no word," he said with a shrug. "There was no reason for you to know my intentions."

In truth, he hadn't known them himself. Somehow his horse had just...*steered* himself here, ending days of debate with himself about whether he could afford to continue this affair when it caused him such confusion and unwanted self reflection.

Lysandra held his gaze for a long moment, then she reached behind her and shut the parlor door. Andrew arched a brow. That was unexpected.

"Do you want to know where I went?" she asked, stepping closer.

"I do now that you are looking at me like I'm cream and you are the cat," he said, keeping his voice soft so it wouldn't reflect as much of his interest and desire as he felt.

The corner of her lip lifted slightly in a knowing, sensual smile. "That is actually quite fitting," she said. "A cat licks the cream, doesn't it?"

Her voice was trembling, and Andrew smiled despite his growing arousal at her boldness. She might pretend, but she was still the same shy woman who wished to cover her naked body so he wouldn't look at her. He liked that woman.

He liked this new woman too.

"Is that what you were doing? Learning how to lick?" he asked.

Her cheeks flamed, but she stepped toward him and reached up to grab the lapels of his jacket. She drew him down to her and nodded.

"I was, indeed." She lifted her lips to his and kissed him with heat and passion...and just a hint of desperation that he recognized far too well. When she drew back, she was even more out of breath. "I want to please you, Andrew. So very much."

He arched a brow as the meaning of her words became clear. She had been alone for two days, waiting for him to come to her. And she had thought she disappointed him. The very opposite was true, but how could she know that? She wasn't an experienced mistress, but more like an innocent girl he was courting. He had to treat her with the care he would give a potential bride, not a temporary bedmate, or he would leave her feeling rejected and confused.

And though he shouldn't care, he didn't want to do that to her. He wanted her to leave their affair better off, not worse.

He cupped her chin and tilted it upward so that she was forced to look into his eyes.

"Lysandra, I assure you, I have been nothing but pleased since I first touched you."

Relief flickered in her gaze, proving everything he already knew, but then it was gone, replaced once more by the more daring Lysandra. She was on a mission and would not be deterred.

"I can please you more, though, I think," she murmured as she slipped her hands beneath the shoulders of his jacket. She stripped it off without much finesse and tossed it aside.

He arched a brow. "What *did* you do at Vivien's home?" he asked.

She jerked her gaze away from the shirt buttons she was opening and back to his face. "How did you know I went to Vivien's?"

"Your servants," he explained, and pushed her clumsy fingers aside to go to work on the shirt himself. He stripped it away and smiled as she stared at his naked chest.

It made him happy that he spent a lot of time outside in the countryside, doing physical labor on his estate that his father called menial and he called lifesaving. It made him stop thinking, at least. And if the results showed on his body and made Lysandra lick her lips like that...well, it was another reason to do what he did and damn societal expectations.

Lysandra blinked. "My servants told you?"

He nodded. "When I arrived and you weren't here, I asked."

She pursed her lips. "And since *you* pay their wages, they are really your servants and report to you in whatever way you choose."

He arched a brow. "Does that trouble you?"

"No," she said, stepping back. "Only I might have wanted to tell you myself. As a surprise. Now I'm sure you've guessed why I went there."

"I have not," Andrew said, catching her hand and slowly drawing her forward. He placed each of her palms on his chest and hissed out a breath of pleasure. "But I like the result."

She opened her mouth as if to say more, but he kissed her instead. He didn't think he could take more "descriptions" of what she had done that afternoon without exploding. And he wanted to have something much more pleasurable than a chat before he did that.

And he had a sneaking suspicion that Lysandra needed the same. To ease whatever tension remained in her body after her visit with Vivien...and to repair any damage he'd done by making her believe he had rejected her.

She kissed him with fervor and passion, lifting up to her tiptoes to get closer as she glided her fingers into his hair and angled her mouth for better access. She tasted like honey and desire, a heady combination that made Andrew's knees weak and cock as hard as granite in the uncomfortable confines of his trousers.

He released her from his embrace to slide his hands down to his waistband and give himself some relief, but she caught his fingers. With a smile, she whispered, "Let me."

He stared down at her as she opened each fastening carefully and parted the fly of his pants. His cock was so ready that it popped from the opening she had created. She licked her lips as she pushed the last vestiges of his clothing away and he stood before her, naked.

"I can see why you had me undress while you stayed clothed," she said with a laugh. "It is quite invigorating to stand here, still entirely proper, while you are naked."

He smiled slightly. This teasing, this lightness was exactly what would serve her well as a mistress, and he was pleased to see it.

He might have said something to her, used the opportunity to impart some kind of lesson in their training, but before he could do so, she dropped down to her knees before him and took his cock in hand.

"Lysandra," he burst out on a breath of shock and pleasure as she stroked him once, twice.

"Yes?" She looked up, all innocence, but in her dark blue eyes he saw a wickedness, a perfect understanding of what she was doing to him.

And she liked it.

"A cat in the cream, eh?" she murmured, referring back to what he'd said when she first entered the room. "I think if I were, I would lick you like this…"

She darted out her tongue and gently stroked the head of his cock with it. Stars exploded in front of Andrew's eyes and he groaned out of pleasure. He hadn't had a woman taste him in… years. And it was better than he remembered.

"Or would this be better?" she asked, entirely seriously. "I'm still learning, you know."

She swirled her tongue around the tip of his cock, wetting it with heated strokes and licks.

"Lysandra," he growled.

"Does that mean you like it or that I'm not doing it right?" she asked.

He glared at her, uncertain if she was being genuine or simply teasing him. "Don't play too many games, my dear. Or you may end up begging in the end."

She shrugged as she stroked him once more. "I'm not playing games. You're to train me, aren't you? I want to know. Watching and doing are two very different things."

He held back another strangled moan at the idea that she had been *watching* others perform this act and focused. "Teasing the tip is a good way to start," he panted. "But think of how I take you, I fully enter your body. I feel you from the head of my cock to the base."

"So every inch feels the touch," she said, staring at him like she was studying some tome in school. "And this touch—" She darted out her tongue and licked the head again. "Feels as good as this one."

She flattened her tongue on the underside of his cock and stroked the length.

Andrew reached behind him to steady himself on the closest chair. "Yes," he managed to groan out. "Yes."

She nodded. "And then there's this."

Without warning, she drew him into her mouth, taking him deep into her throat.

"Oh my God," Andrew gasped. "Yes. Yes, just like that. Now stroke. Take me with your mouth like you would with your pussy."

Her eyes lit up like she fully understood the connection between whatever she had seen and what she was doing now. Slowly, she began to stroke as he had ordered, taking him in and out as she gripped his cock at the base.

Andrew shut his eyes and surrendered to her touch. Everything in his mind emptied as he thought only of this woman and her mouth on him. Of her soft mewls of pleasure as she brought him pleasure.

He looked down to see that she too, had shut her eyes and was working his cock with abandon and utter pleasure. She *liked* performing this act, and with a little practice, she would be a master at it. Already he was at the edge of coming.

But he didn't want to do that. Not until he had taken her. Proven to her that he wanted her, that she had never disappointed him.

He caught her shoulders and lifted her, dragging her away from his cock. She made a moan of displeasure.

"Was I doing it wrong?" she asked, eyes sparkling as he stared at her, panting and trying everything in his power to keep from exploding right then and there.

"No," he said, his tone taut with tension. "But if I do not have you now, I will regret it."

He tugged at her ugly dress, pulling the fabric without thought to any damage he might do. She needed new gowns at any rate and the idea of tearing this one to shreds to get to her body was suddenly a very appealing one.

She gasped as a few buttons popped away, a sleeve made a rending sound at the seams. But she didn't protest as he shoved her gown around her waist and lowered his head to her exposed breasts.

*L*ysandra didn't know how this quick reversal had occurred. One moment she had been putting her lessons from earlier in the day to good use. She liked taking Andrew into her mouth, for it was obvious that the act gave him great pleasure. More surprising was how much it aroused *her*. Giving pleasure was almost as intense as receiving it.

But now, as Andrew sucked her nipples with a pressure that stayed just on the correct side of the pleasure-pain border, her back arched and her mind emptied. It was amazing how this touch, so far away from her sex, could make her body tingle and her legs shake as she teetered on the edge of orgasm.

He tugged her dress to the floor and then lifted her, wrapping her legs around his back as he strode across the room, kissing her with each step. She suddenly found her back against the chamber door.

She gasped as he lifted his hips and speared her with his cock in one slick stroke.

"Already ready for me," he growled as he nuzzled her throat. "Just as I like it."

He thrust and pressed her against the door even harder, closing any bit of distance between them. Lysandra gasped of the sensation of being so filled, so possessed. There was no space between them, no air between them beyond the breath they shared. Her face was even with his and their eyes met. For a moment he stopped moving and just stared at her, almost as if he was seeing her for the first time.

He tilted his head and kissed her, but there was little harsh possession in the kiss. This was gentle, like a bride's first kiss. He brushed his lips butterfly-wing soft and then let his thrusts join that gentle touch. He moved slowly within her, cupping her hips gently, holding her steady as he slipped within her hot sheath.

The pleasure of his touch, of the intimacy of his kiss, built suddenly, rapidly and burst within her body without warning. Lysandra arched against the door with a strangled cry that no doubt made its way to the hallway and the ears of the servants, but at the moment she couldn't care about that. Her body was out of her control, jolting with pleasure that seemed to start at her core and spread outward with warm fingers, making every part of her ache deliciously.

And Andrew gave her no respite from the sensations. He continued to drive into her body, his thrusts once again increasing in intensity. Lysandra thought of the major's face earlier in the day when he had come. How lost to sensation he had looked. She stared at Andrew, his eyes squeezed shut, his face taut with tension and pleasure and saw that he too, was as tangled in desire as she was.

She cupped his cheeks and kissed him, driving her tongue into his mouth as another burst of orgasmic bliss made her hips jerk out of control.

Andrew cried out against her lips and set her down, steadying her even as he withdrew and his hot seed splashed between their bodies. He rested his forehead against hers, their bodies flush, and they stood there for a long series of moments.

Their breathing matched and merged and Lysandra let out a long sigh of pleasure. This closeness...she had never felt anything like it. There was a warmth between them that rivaled the pleasure of release.

She wrapped her arms around his neck and smiled. "Oh, Andrew —" she began.

But she got no further, for Andrew jerked from her embrace and spun away from her, taking his warmth, taking her happy feelings with little more than a backward glance.

CHAPTER 12

*A*ndrew snatched his trousers and walked across the room to the fire where he began to put them on. He could feel Lysandra staring at him from across the room, and her hurt was palpable. He had, once again, pulled away from her.

But he had no choice. That moment against the door was supposed to have been one of pure sex, passion. It had become something else. There had been a connection between them. And he could scarce afford to make that connection.

More to the point, he didn't want to.

He finished buttoning his pants and turned to find Lysandra collecting her dress from the wrinkled pile on the floor. She held it as a shield in front of her as she examined the torn arm and the missing buttons.

"I shall mend this," she said, more to herself than to him.

He stepped forward with a shake of his head. "Don't bother, Lysandra."

Her gaze jerked to his, and she parted her lips. With her hair mussed and her face red, the action was utterly sensual. God damn, but he wanted to put her back against the door again and have her a second time. And they had scarcely been parted for five minutes.

What was wrong with him? He hadn't felt this kind of an urge to rut with a woman since he was a young man first discovering plea-sure. That was supposed to be Lysandra's role, not his.

"Are you saying you no longer want me here?" she asked, and her trembling words returned his attention to her.

"What?" he asked and shook his head. "No, of course not. I meant don't bother repairing the gown. You need new ones. I should have arranged for a dressmaker straight away, but I hadn't thought of it."

Lysandra blinked up at him. "New gowns? No, I cannot afford that."

His eyes went wide. "Do you think I was suggesting you would pay? Dear Lord, you *are* innocent when it comes to the ways of the protector/mistress bond. Your protector does a great many things, Lysandra. He pays for your home, your food, your servants, and he ensures that you have all the gowns and jewelry you need."

She folded her arms. "The necessities I understand, my lord. But gowns? That is pure frivolity. I could not allow for you to pay—"

He cut her off by lifting his hand. "You cannot be seen out with me or any other man in the *ton* dressed in a gown that is three seasons or more out of date, a size too large and designed for a middle-class merchant's daughter."

She sucked in a breath and turned her face as if he had slapped her. For a long moment, she was silent and stared at the floor. Then she nodded.

"Very well. I will see your dressmaker. I wouldn't want to embar-rass you."

He shut his eyes. Once again, he had hurt her when he was trying to give her something as a gift. And he shouldn't have cared, but he did.

He softened his tone. "You have a household account, Lysandra. So that you don't have to ask me for things that you need. And your pin money is also available to you. You only need to write to the solicitor, whose name and direction I will leave with your butler. That money is for things like clothing, shoes, hats, lunches with friends, whatever you choose to do with it. I'll make sure extra funds are deposited for the gowns."

Lysandra shifted, utterly naked, but he could see her discomfort stemmed more from the idea that he would provide her with money rather than her nudity. He supposed that was a step forward in her training.

"Andrew, you are only meant to be my 'protector' for a few weeks, aren't you? You didn't want more than that. How could I ever repay you for giving me so much money?"

He wrinkled his brow. "I am not asking you to repay me beyond your company and your desire. That is the point of the protector/mistress bond. As brief or as long as it lasts, there is parity in the roles, I assure you."

She shook her head as she stepped into her gown and covered her lush curves with the ugly fabric. She buttoned the dress as best she could with a shake of her head that told Andrew she didn't fully trust his account of their relationship.

He sighed. "We shall not speak of this again, Lysandra. The money is yours and I expect you to spend it accordingly."

He could see she wanted to argue further, but she pressed her lips together with a brief nod instead. "Very well. Thank you."

He nodded. Good, that was resolved. At least there was something in this complicated relationship that was.

"I would like to take you to the opera in a few days," he said as he shrugged into his shirt. "And I'll be certain the dressmaker I'm sending over knows that she should focus on that dress so that it will be ready before we are to attend."

Lysandra swallowed and any remnants of the boldness she had shown him earlier vanished in a flash. "The opera? Vivien said you would begin to take me out, but…"

She trailed off and Andrew stared at her. "You seem truly worried by this, Lysandra, but you must know that going out is part of a mistress's duty. And you will love the opera. Many go only to gossip, but there is a singer with a beautiful voice at the current showing who I am certain you will enjoy."

She nodded, but he could still see her hesitation, her lack of faith that she would belong in such a place, alongside the cream of Society. And he wanted to comfort her. To reassure her. To protect her, beyond what the role of "protector" entailed.

He shook his head. That was enough of this. He had to get away from her and the spell she apparently weaved on him. Before he lost himself and his own goals entirely.

"I will pick you up Saturday night. Your servants will have the particulars later in the week. Until then, I—" He stopped, for he could think of nothing better to say. "Goodbye."

She nodded and accepted the brief kiss he pressed to her cheek as he passed her by and left the room, but as he called for his horse, Andrew knew he had, once again, hurt her. And in the process, he seemed to hurt himself.

*L*ysandra had expected the dressmaker, of course, but not within two hours of Andrew's departure from her home. And yet here she was, standing on a stool in her dressing room, with the woman, Madame Bertrande, measuring her for gowns and chatting away pleasantly in the prettiest French accent Lysandra had ever heard. If the seamstress knew she was Andrew's mistress, Madame Bertrande treated her no differently and was polite and kind in every way.

"You have a very nice figure," the woman said as she measured around the circumference of Lysandra's chest. "Built exactly as a man likes it, without being too showy."

Lysandra blushed. That comment answered her unasked question about the *mantua*-maker knowing she was a mistress. She somehow doubted she said such a thing to men's wives or daughters as she measured them for gowns.

"That is all, my dear," she said as she offered Lysandra a hand to come down from the stool. "Your ballgown will be made first, as per Lord Callis's instructions. I will call on you for a second fitting in two days and will deliver the dress before four on the day of the opera."

"It must put you out to do something so quickly," Lysandra said with a blush.

Madame Bertrande laughed. "I suppose it does, but Lord Callis pays exceedingly well for that privilege."

Lysandra stifled a sigh. Once again, it came down to money. Andrew showered her with it, even though she was but a temporary mistress at best. Not to mention the fact that he could scarce be in the same room with her once he had made love to her.

"He has chosen a beautiful fabric for that dress, as well," Madame Bertrande continued, oblivious to Lysandra's thoughts. "It will suit you very well. But for the other five gowns, I will need you to choose what fabric to make them in. I brought samples."

Lysandra staggered. She couldn't have heard that correctly. "Five gowns? Did you say *five*?"

The dressmaker nodded, her gaze reflecting confusion. "Yes. His lordship said you need a full wardrobe. This will be a start to that and will get you through most events. It will take me a fortnight to complete them all, but I will do it."

Lysandra shook her head as the world swam before her eyes. She had seen a glimpse of a ledger sheet when Madame Bertrande was measuring her and the cost for each gown was so high. For the price of just one, she could pay her cousin's demands for the care of her mother for two months, perhaps even three!

"I *do* appreciate your and Lord Callis's desire to see me well-dressed," she said, treading carefully as she didn't want to offend when Madame Bertrande had been so kind to her. "But I cannot demand five gowns. Six when you count the ball gown."

The other woman tilted her head and looked her up and down. "My dear, you clearly need the clothes."

Lysandra fought the urge to huff out her breath. That was twice her clothing had been maligned in the span of a few hours. She knew she wasn't ready to meet the Queen, but for heaven's sake, it wasn't as if she was running around in a sackcloth.

"Yes, apparently I do," she said through gritted teeth. "But why don't we start with the ball gown—" she thought of the dress Andrew had torn "—and one other that I can wear for everyday use. And once those are finished, we can talk again."

Madame Bertrande looked at her evenly, but then shrugged as she gathered her things. "Very well. If that is your wish. It was a great pleasure meeting you, Miss Keates. You are a very interesting woman. I'll send word to make an appointment when I'm ready to do the next fitting."

Lysandra nodded and walked her to the door of the chamber. "Thank you. I do look forward to seeing the gowns. Your own dress is so beautiful, I know I shall feel just like a princess in a story in my own."

That made the other woman's expression soften, and she smiled as she slipped into the hallway.

Lysandra shut the door behind her and leaned against it briefly. What a day. Between her spying on Vivien's friends to her erotic encounter with Andrew and now the dresses... it was almost too much.

But thoughts of her mother had brought her back to earth. She could not spend the money Andrew was providing her so frivolously. She had no idea if she would ever find another protector...or one so generous...once her time with Andrew was done. She had to be certain she protected her mother before she swung into a hollow life where her biggest questions were what gown to wear to what ridiculous soiree.

She sat down at the little desk in her dressing area and withdrew a heavy, expensive sheet of paper. On it, she scribbled a request to the solicitor and gave the direction for her cousin's home, along with instructions for him on its use. She let out a sigh as she folded the paper and rang for a servant to fetch it.

At the very least, she would leave this arrangement with her mother's future safe for a few months. If that was all she obtained, then she would have to be happy with that. After all, she already knew she could ask for nothing more.

CHAPTER 13

*L*ysandra shifted nervously and looked at herself in the mirror one last time. The ballgown Madame Bertrande had made for her fit perfectly and was made of a beautiful scarlet satin trimmed in a dusty rose. The neckline swooped, not too low, but low enough that there was a hint of her bosom for Andrew to enjoy. Her hair had been curled and twisted and maneuvered into a beautiful style and her cheeks rouged ever so slightly to give her pale skin a hint of color.

She felt...beautiful. Alluring. She felt like a stranger had somehow forced her way into the mirror and was staring back at her.

There was a light knock at her door, and Lysandra jumped. As her maid peeked inside, she smiled. "Lord Callis is here for you, miss. He's in the parlor."

Lysandra managed a nod of acknowledgment and stared at herself again. Would he like what he saw or be disappointed? Would he even care? It seemed when they were not tangled up in sex, he was able to completely divorce himself from any interest in her.

"Oh, stop dallying and go downstairs, you foolish girl," she admonished herself in the mirror before she turned on her heel and stalked to the stairs.

She was down the first three when Andrew stepped from the parlor and moved toward the staircase. He looked up at her, and their eyes met.

Lysandra kept moving, though she had no idea how with Andrew's stare boring into her like fire. He said nothing, yet she knew that he *did* like the way she looked in her new attire. Desire lit in his stare...and a smidge of pride. Both caused her heart to swell unexpectedly.

"Good evening," she said as she stepped into the hallway.

He offered her a hand and, when he took it, stepped back. "Dear God, you are a vision."

Lysandra blushed and dipped her head. "Thank you. The dress is divine."

"The dress is a few scraps of fabric bound together by a talented seamstress." Andrew slipped her hand into the crook of his arm. "*You* are divine."

Lysandra hoped he wouldn't see how his compliment made her quiver like a schoolgirl. It had been so long since anyone told her she was pretty, at least not in a lurid, unpleasant way, she could scarce recall it. And certainly the last man to do so had been no Andrew Callis.

"Shall we go?" he asked, snapping her from her reverie.

She nodded. "Of course."

He escorted her from the house toward his carriage. It was larger than the one she rode in and much finer, with its crest on the door and expensively liveried servants to assist them into place on either side of the interior.

Once the door shut and the vehicle jolted forward, Andrew slid across to sit beside her. He tilted her chin up. The light was dim, but she saw his eyes sparkle as he examined her face. And when his lips moved down to hers, she needed no light, no air, no sustenance of any kind except for his kiss.

After a moment, though, he drew back. "More of that and I shall be forced to turn the carriage around and make love to you all night instead."

"Why don't you?" Lysandra breathed, her body trembling at the thought.

He laughed. "I would normally, but we are meant to meet someone at the opera and he would come looking for me."

She straightened up. "Oh? Who?"

He shifted back to his own seat and the wall of distance that so often crashed between them did so again, quietly.

"My younger brother, Samuel Callis." His tone reflected no emotion on that subject.

Lysandra shifted as a sudden thought gripped her. "But I... How will you explain... I mean, will he know that..."

"That you are my mistress?" Andrew finished for her. "I told him I was bringing you along tonight, so yes."

Lysandra lifted her hand to her lips and blinked at the sting of humiliated tears behind her eyes. It wasn't as if she hadn't known this moment would come, but now that it was here, it was more difficult than she would have guessed.

"Lysandra, you have nothing to be ashamed of," Andrew said softly. "My brother will not judge you on your...position in life. He has had mistresses in the past, just as most men of rank and power have had."

Lysandra shifted. She hadn't thought of that. "And will he bring his mistress with him tonight?"

Andrew hesitated. "No. My brother isn't currently connected with a mistress. He is recently engaged."

"His fiancée, then?" she asked.

He was quiet for a long moment, and Lysandra thought of the question she had just asked. Of course there would be no fiancée at the opera tonight. No man would bring his innocent future bride to an event where his brother's lover would be. She was a lady. Lysandra was not. The two worlds did not, could not, collide.

She shook her head. "I'm sorry. That was a foolish question."

"No," he said. "It wasn't. Under normal circumstances, though, a man wouldn't—"

Lysandra raised her hand. "Of course. There is no need to

explain." When Andrew said nothing, she shrugged. "You must understand, I am still adjusting to my new place in the world. But I realize that it is unlikely I would have met your brother's fiancée if I were still a servant. Why would I ever meet her as a mistress, a far more shocking position?"

Andrew shifted. "If it helps, I have not yet met Adela either."

Lysandra drew back. "Your brother's future bride?"

He nodded. "I am more often out of town than in it, and since my return I've been most busy with my own business concerns... and you." He sighed and turned his face to look out the window at the city lights rushing past. "And I fear my brother may be hiding her away from me."

Lysandra stared for a moment. Was Andrew actually offering her a little glimpse into his life that went beyond his lusts?

"Why would he do that?" she asked. "Do you not get along?"

"Sam and I?" he asked, and true surprise was in his voice at the concept. "No. I adore my brother and I know he loves me. But that is why he might hide the girl. To protect me. To keep me from being hurt by her existence. Because of Rebecca's death."

Lysandra sucked in a breath. "Your wife."

Andrew jerked his face toward hers. He hesitated and then said, "I'm sorry, I shouldn't have brought up such a thing."

She worried her lip. "Is that not part of my duties as your mistress? To offer you some kind of comfort in your...difficulties?"

"No." His tone was even and not to be argued with. "Perhaps some men would like that, but I wouldn't."

Lysandra flopped back against the carriage seat, deflated. She knew so little about Andrew beyond their connection in bed. What she did know intrigued her, but he kept her locked out, a continual reminder that she was a bedmate, not a life mate.

The carriage came to a stop and Andrew smiled at her as if their exchange had never occurred.

"And we are here. Are you ready?"

Lysandra forced a smile and nodded as the footman opened the door and helped her out. Once she stepped down, her worries about

Andrew faded. She looked up at the big, beautiful lit-up opera house with its Grecian pillars and marble stairs. Impeccably dressed people milled about on the stairs and in the entryway above, talking and laughing until the sound was nothing more than a din in the air.

"It is…amazing," she breathed.

Andrew smiled as he took her hand and led her up the staircase. "Wait until you get inside," he said.

She tensed as they neared the top of the stairs. People were beginning to look at them. Their conversations slowed as their eyes followed first Andrew, then her. The ladies lifted their fans and whispered behind them and even the gentlemen arched brows and muttered softly to each other.

Her tension was mirrored in Andrew. His lips thinned as they neared the groups of people.

"They're talking about us," Lysandra whispered.

He nodded. "Indeed they are. About me, more likely than you. I rarely come out in Society anymore."

She might have pressed more on that subject, but before she could, a man's voice boomed from behind them.

"Callis!"

Andrew turned, maneuvering her with him, and his face lit up with a wide, true smile. Lysandra couldn't help but stare. He was always beautiful, of course, an Adonis sent from the gods themselves to tempt her. But when he smiled… it was incredible how much his stern face changed. There was lightness there, laughter, a glimpse of a whole other man.

"Sam," he said, extending his hand as he released Lysandra.

The other man, apparently Andrew's brother Sam, bypassed the hand and enveloped his brother in a hard hug. He clapped him on the back a few times and then drew away.

"Drew, Drew, how I've missed seeing your ugly face." Sam laughed. "You should come to London more often."

Lysandra sucked in a breath. Drew. Sam. These were childhood nicknames, taken from a much more innocent time. She could hardly picture Andrew as a freckled boy, racing around with his brother. But when she did, it made her smile.

"London has its attractions, yes," Andrew said, awkward as he shifted. "But coming here brings me little pleasure other than seeing you."

Sam's jovial face fell a fraction, and for a brief moment Lysandra saw all his grief for his brother on his face. And worry and... surprisingly, *fear*, but not of him...for him. She jerked her attention to Andrew. Why would his brother exhibit fear when he looked at him?

"But enough about you," Sam teased. "Your lovely companion seems like a much more interesting subject. Unless you intend to keep her to yourself all night."

Andrew smiled and touched Lysandra's elbow. "Mr. Samuel Callis, may I present my friend Miss Lysandra Keates."

Sam took her fingers and leaned over them, pressing a kiss to the top of her gloved hand. "Miss Keates, a pleasure to meet you."

She smiled, and the expression wasn't forced. There was something about Sam that made her feel utterly at ease. He had a friendliness that wasn't in any way false. And although Andrew said he knew she was a mistress, he treated her no differently than he would any other person.

"The pleasure is mine, I assure you," Lysandra said. "I was so pleased to hear you were joining us tonight. And I hear congratulations are in order for your recent engagement?"

Sam blinked, and Lysandra tensed. Was that a subject she wasn't supposed to bring up? It was one that touched on the other world, the proper world that these men inhabited, while she was on its fringes.

"Thank you," Sam said. "I am most happy."

Andrew stepped closer. "Truly?"

Sam turned his attention on his brother, and Lysandra saw the worry and fear again. "Yes, Drew. Very happy."

"Good," Andrew said with a breath of relief. "I would like to meet her, you know."

Sam swallowed. "Would you? I worried it might be...difficult for you."

Andrew's smile faltered. "You needn't protect me, Sam. I'm the older brother, aren't I? Meant to fuss over you? If you take my duties then I'll have nothing to fill my time."

Sam's gaze flitted to Lysandra. "I'm sure you'll think of something. But yes, I would love for you to meet Adela. We'll make the arrangements tonight. But now I see the lights are being flickered. We should go in and take our seats."

He motioned for Andrew and Lysandra to lead. Andrew took her arm and they moved into the bright foyer. Slowly, the crowd was taking its places, ducking behind curtains that protected the boxes and into the aisles of the main audience chamber. Of course Andrew had a box and he pulled the curtain aside to allow the others to enter.

Lysandra stared. The box was private, with three comfortable, cushioned seats already set up to face the stage. A bottle of champagne rested in a pail filled with ice. Sam grabbed for the bottle as Andrew escorted her to one of the seats. His brother popped the cork and poured them each a little of the fizzy alcohol. He raised his glass.

"To my brother and the choice to live again," he said, his joviality tempered for a moment by a serious tone.

Lysandra looked at Andrew from the corner of her eye. He seemed very serious, and his jaw was clenched in frustration or anger.

The lights in the opera house lowered and Sam took his seat next to Andrew as the curtain rose and the music began. Lysandra settled back and watched as the beautifully dressed singers floated onto the stage to sing in Italian about love and loss, death and birth. She wanted to lose herself in the music, but she couldn't help but send a few glances toward Andrew from time to time. Although he was determined to keep his heart, his past, his life a secret from her, tonight she was learning more and more. And with every hint at his pain, she felt a stronger urge to help him. To heal him, as Vivien told her she could.

Even if he resisted her attempts.

*A*ndrew wasn't looking forward to intermission, when he would be forced to go into the hallways and chat with those in attendance, but there was no avoiding it when the lights lifted midway through the show. He turned toward Lysandra with a forced smile.

"Are you enjoying the opera?" he asked.

She nodded, her face still filled with rapt pleasure. A rather arousing expression, actually, for it reminded him of that moment when she reached climax.

"The soprano's voice is wonderful," she said with a happy sigh. "I've always wanted to go to the opera. I had heard such wonderful things and they were all true. Thank you for including me in tonight."

Andrew saw his brother jerk his gaze to Lysandra, and then he looked at Andrew with questioning. Andrew frowned. He had informed Sam that Lysandra was his mistress, but not that the situation was temporary or that Lysandra was really no better than an innocent. Now his brother seemed confused, and he was certain he would be bombarded with questions as soon as she was out of earshot.

"Come, let us join the throng out in the vestibule, shall we?" he said, shooting his brother a look over her head that told him to leave it alone. Not that it would help. Sam was a bulldog.

Lysandra tensed but took his arm with as much calm as she could muster. He had to admire her grit. She was afraid, that was clear, and unsure of herself in this situation. And why shouldn't she be?

She was from a middle-class family, and one with little money, if things she'd said and the situation she currently found herself in were any indication. She had never been to the opera or to a fancy ball. She'd never rubbed elbows with the elite of the *ton* and had them all know that she was the lover of someone in their midst.

And yet, despite all that, she kept her chin up. She might tremble, but she didn't break. And that took some courage.

He squeezed her hand gently and leaned down closer as they joined the throng in the entrance hall. "You are doing very well."

"I shouldn't have asked your brother about his fiancée," she said with a small sigh. "It was too bold."

He shook his head. "It was a friendly gesture and one made honestly. Don't trouble yourself over it."

She glanced up at him, her eyes wide and filled with so many emotions he could scarcely separate them all. She straightened her spine and looked out over the crowded floor, but then her eyes lit up.

"There is Vivien," she said, indicating a place across the room.

Andrew followed her motion and found the celebrated courtesan holding court over a handful of men. She looked utterly bored and Andrew had no idea why the men were trying. Everyone knew she no longer took protectors or even lovers beyond the occasional one-night pleasure.

"I would like to say hello," Lysandra said. "May I?"

Andrew blinked. "You needn't ask my permission. Please, say hello to your friend. And pass on my regards, as well."

She smiled at him, then slipped into the crowd. Andrew couldn't help but notice that several men followed her with their eyes as she joined Vivien. He frowned at their attentions, although that was exactly what he wanted, wasn't it? To help her become more attractive to the right kind of man. One who would take care of her for more than a few weeks and treat her well. Many of the men who leered were exactly the kind she should endeavor to "catch".

"She is a most beautiful woman," Sam said.

Andrew shook his head. He had all but forgotten that his brother was with him.

"And very. . .*interesting*," his brother continued.

Andrew remained silent, but that didn't deter Sam.

"I admit, I was surprised when you told me you were bringing a woman, your new mistress, with you to the opera. Not unhappy, though, just surprised. And once I met her…"

He trailed off, and Andrew pursed his lips. "I hope you aren't implying something disparaging about Lysandra with what you say."

Sam shook his head. "No, on the contrary I very much like her. But she is not like most women who take on that role, is she? She seems a bit out of place."

Of course his brother would point out the obvious. Sam had never been able to turn away from an issue that provoked his curiosity.

"How did you meet?" Sam pushed. He looked at Lysandra, who had made her way to Vivien's side. "Through Vivien?"

"Yes," Andrew said through clenched teeth.

Sam tilted his head and thought about that for a long moment. "I suppose she is the best source for such things, but I didn't know you were seeking a mistress. I thought you had written off all such activities. You decided to live a pious life, punishing yourself in the countryside, didn't you? That was the last I'd heard."

Andrew clenched his fists at his sides. "Leave it alone."

Sam flinched at his tone but ignored the order behind it. "No, I'm afraid I want to know. How is it that you came to be around Vivien in the first place, let alone in a position where you might seek a mistress so different from any you have taken on in the past?"

Andrew shut his eyes. There was no one he trusted more than his brother, but talking to him about anything seemed to bring up most painful emotions and subjects he would rather see closed. However, since Sam seemed to be in no mood to drop the topic, it seemed he had no choice but to explain himself and the strange situation he found himself in.

"Lysandra has never been a mistress before," he sighed in surrender. "She is…*almost* completely innocent. Vivien called on me to ask me the favor of introducing her to the lifestyle, albeit temporarily."

"How temporarily?" Sam pressed.

Leave it to his brother to focus on that part of the statement. "A month at most. I told Vivien that I could do no longer, as I intend to return to the countryside once my business with Father is completed."

His brother's eyes widened. "So your relationship with this woman is charitable?"

"No," Andrew snapped, then tempered his tone. "Of course not. You've seen the woman. How could one not enjoy her company and all that this...this arrangement entails?"

Sam lifted his brows slightly. "And yet you insist it shall be temporary."

"It can't be more." Andrew shrugged. "Nothing has changed in my life."

His brother's frown deepened. "Bollocks."

Andrew's eyes went wide. His brother's voice did not carry, but that still wasn't the sort of thing you said in mixed company at the opera.

"I beg your pardon?" he asked.

"You heard me. Damn it, Drew, how long are you going to lock yourself away from your family, your life, in that gloomy estate? How long are you going to punish yourself?" Sam shook his head. "I hoped that when you told me about Lysandra that it meant you were choosing to live again, but this is worse. You give yourself a taste of pleasure only to snatch it away."

"I'm helping her, as I said," Andrew said, turning away.

"No, that would be noble. What you're *really* doing is continuing to torture yourself and you're using her to do it." Sam sighed. "Rebecca is dead, Drew. You've been trying to climb into the grave with her for three years, but it has to stop. God damn it, I never want to—"

His brother would have continued, but behind them there was a clearing of a throat. They turned to find Lysandra standing there. She was pale, her gaze focused on Andrew and he flinched, suddenly exposed in a way he had been trying to avoid for months, years. How long had she been standing there?

"I'm sorry to intrude," she said, her voice slightly unsteady. "But the lights are flashing and most of the others have gone back inside. I believe intermission is over."

Andrew looked around. Indeed, the lobby was almost empty except for a few gawkers who seemed more interested in the exchange between the three of them than in returning for the final act of the night.

He scowled as he took Lysandra's arm and began to move toward his box.

"Yes," he said over his shoulder for his brother's benefit. "*This* is over."

CHAPTER 14

*L*ysandra had never experienced a more awkward time than the carriage ride home with Andrew. He stared straight ahead as the vehicle rumbled through the dark and quiet streets of the city, unspeaking, unmoving and apparently unseeing.

He had been cold like this for hours. Since his private time with his brother when she went to talk to Vivien. She hadn't meant to eavesdrop on their conversation, but she knew they had talked about Andrew's dead wife…and her.

Her mind turned to Vivien. She had said that Lysandra could help Andrew, but from Sam and Andrew's conversation, it didn't sound like she was doing that. Unless she could help him forget, help him surrender to pleasure instead of dance around the edges of it, then she never would.

"Andrew?" she said softly.

He jolted and then looked at her. "Yes."

"Why did your brother say you were using me to hurt yourself?" she asked.

He turned his face. "Do not ask such bold questions."

She shook her head. "I would not, except that this one has very much to do with me and our arrangement."

There was a long hesitation. "Sam spoke out of turn."

"Not if the look on your face was any indication," she said softly. "When he made that accusation, when he spoke of your wife, you looked...*broken*, Andrew. If that is what our time together does..."

Before she could finish the sentence, he caught her arm and hauled her across the carriage and across his lap. He dropped his mouth to hers, angry and heated, driving his tongue between her lips with punishing pressure. And yet the assault on her lips did nothing to make her recoil. If anything, her body reacted of its own accord.

It was amazing how weak this man could make her. A few days before, she hadn't even pictured making love; now it took only one touch and she panted for him inside of her.

He obliged her silent desire with little preamble, hiking her delicate skirts up over her thighs and pressing his hand between them. She wore nothing beneath, partly because of the fit of the gown and partly on the suggestion of her maid, who had given her a knowing look and said something about "surprises".

Now she was happy she had listened, especially when Andrew glided two fingers into her sheath and stroked her gently.

She arched against him, helpless against the tide of desire and pleasure.

"Don't you understand?" he growled against her ear. "This is all I want. All I can have."

She flinched at his angry, pain-filled words, so at odds with his touch deep within her.

"I want to help you," she murmured in response.

She was challenging him, yes, and she couldn't believe how boldly she did so. But she had to. There was a drive within her to heal this pain he tried to hide, as deep as the drive to join with him.

"You can't," he said, but his voice cracked. "No one can."

She opened her mouth to say more, but he cut her off with another angry kiss, and her words and thoughts melted away. She clung to him, pulling him closer as he maneuvered her to straddle over his lap. He reached between them, opening his trousers and then lowered her onto his waiting, ready cock.

They sighed in time at the joining and she began to move. Being over top of him gave her the power he refused to relinquish in any other facet of their arrangement, and she clung to that, rolling her hips in a circle, reaching for pleasure and forcing it on him at the same time.

He lifted beneath her, his breath harsh and heavy in the close confines of the carriage. She felt him losing control and rode faster, her body quaking with the sudden burst of release that made her clench her pussy, milking him with her inner muscles as she pumped her hips faster and faster in rhythm to her orgasm.

He crushed her against him with a sudden roar and then he burst, his hot seed flowing within her for the first time in their affair. They stayed that way for a moment, staring at each other in the dim lights from outside the carriage windows. Then he shook his head and set her aside gently.

"You had best fix yourself," he said without looking at her. "We're almost home."

Lysandra shivered as she smoothed her dress in place and fixed her hair. Home. That word made it sound so warm, so welcoming... but the house he had given her wasn't a home. There was love in a home. Family. And with him, it was clear there would never be either of those things.

*a*ndrew said nothing as he escorted Lysandra into her foyer. He could think of nothing to say that wasn't angry, accusatory...and far too revealing of his feelings. She had used their physical connection to obtain something he hadn't wanted to share. His emotion. He had said too much, felt too much, and now he wanted desperately to take it back.

"We need to talk about what a man expects from his mistress," he snapped as they made their way into the parlor.

Carlsworth had been approaching them to take their wraps but immediately turned around and left the foyer. Lysandra flinched, her cheeks bright with color, and Andrew stifled a curse. Yet again, high emotion made him lose control.

He expected Lysandra to say something or even cry in the face of this new humiliation, but instead, she motioned toward the parlor in silence. He followed her inside and watched as she shut the door behind them to block out their conversation from the servants. She paced to the fire without speaking and stood there, arms folded.

"I agree," she said, simply and very calmly. For the first time, she looked the cool and collected role of an experienced mistress.

Andrew wasn't certain he liked that.

"Your job, my dear, is to pleasure me. That is all. It isn't to search my feelings or intrude upon my past," he said, hating how harsh and ugly his tone was.

But Lysandra didn't react in any way to the implied emotion in his voice. "That isn't true."

He stared. Was she tutoring *him* now? "What?"

"A mistress's duty is to provide comfort that a gentleman does not acquire elsewhere," she said softly. "Physical comfort, yes. Making love is certainly a great part of what my role will be with whatever man I end up with. But you cannot tell me that is my only role. If it is, then a gentleman could just as easily hire a light skirt for the night. That would be far less expensive and have far less potential for long-term complications."

He frowned. Damn if she wasn't right. A fact that frustrated him even further.

"Lysandra," he said on a sigh.

She shook her head. "I may be inexperienced, but I'm not a fool."

He paced away, running a hand through his hair before he looked at her again. Her new gown was wrinkled, yes, and her hair mussed from sex, and she had never been more beautiful. A temptation he could never fully surrender to.

Perhaps his brother was correct that he had entered into this affair as some kind of punishment. Except when he touched her, it felt like a reward.

"Lysandra," he whispered. "A mistress's duty is to offer her protector the arrangement he desires. You are right that for most that will involve some kind of…emotional connection. For me, it cannot. I am asking you to be in my bed for pleasure and on my arm for companionship during this brief time we share. Beyond that, I can do no more. If you need training on the emotional aspects of being a mistress, you'll have to ask someone else."

She looked at him and to his horror, pity lit up in her eyes. Pity and understanding, like she had just broken a code of some kind.

"Very well," she said without breaking her stare. "I will honor your request."

He nodded, though this victory felt somehow hollow. But no. It was what he wanted, needed. He straightened his shoulders.

"Did Madame Bertrande say when your new gowns will be ready?" he asked, desperate to change the subject.

She turned her face, but not before he saw guilt there. Guilt he didn't understand.

"My gown will be ready tomorrow," she said without looking at him.

Andrew tilted his head in confusion. "Your first gown, good. What about the rest?"

She swallowed. "There aren't any others."

"What?" he asked, the frustration he felt just below the surface surging again. "I made it clear to that woman that you needed a new wardrobe. Honestly, if she cannot make the time after the extra money I paid—"

"Andrew," Lysandra interrupted as she grasped his arm. "It isn't her fault. I-I told her only to make me one other dress."

Andrew stopped and stared at her. "I'm sorry, I don't understand."

"I only need a gown to replace the older one that was torn," she explained, her voice small. She released his arm and paced away. "Any more is far too extravagant a purchase."

He squeezed his eyes shut. This training was far more complicated than he had ever expected.

"Lysandra, I thought we discussed this. The money is in the account for this purpose."

"You said it was there for any purpose," she argued, continuing to stare at the flames. "That it was my money. I couldn't justify spending it on gowns."

He stared at her. Her back was trembling as she looked at the fire.

"Did you spend the money on something else?" he asked, tempering his tone.

She hesitated for a moment and then nodded once.

He reached for her, but stopped himself. If he touched her, she might recoil. And he very much wanted to know the answer to his next question.

"What did you spend it on?"

She stiffened and then turned to face him. "Nothing immoral, I assure you."

He held her gaze. "What did you spend it on?"

She swallowed. "My mother," she whispered. "I had to help her or else…"

Andrew stepped back. She had mentioned her mother the first night they made love, citing her as a reason for her decision to pursue this life. He hadn't pressed her then, there were too many other issues to resolve, and to be honest he hadn't taken her all that seriously. But now…

"I think it's time we talked a bit about your family, Lysandra," he said, taking a seat in front of the fire.

She spun on him. "You refuse to speak to me about anything personal and yet you demand I do the same?"

He pursed his lips. She wasn't wrong. "The difference is that I can actually help you, Lysandra."

She shook her head. "No, you can't."

"I have other ways of finding out the truth," he said with a shrug. "If you don't want to tell me yourself."

She folded her arms. "You would do that? Spy on me?"

He nodded. "Yes, and so will any other man who becomes your protector."

Lysandra sucked in a breath and took a step back. "What do you mean?"

"There have been men who were very powerful who have been dragged through the mud thanks to bad mistresses or mistresses with some kind of secret. The relationship may not be as permanent as that of a wife, but it can be just as damning. But you are changing the subject. I want to know about your family." He held her gaze. "Please."

Lysandra paced away from the fire, away from him, to the window that overlooked the dark street below. She was quiet for a long time, but Andrew could see by the way that her shoulders slumped that she would tell him what he needed to know. So he didn't push her, as much as his instinct was to demand.

"My father was a good man," she said, looking at him over her shoulder. "I want to make that clear. He loved us. He was a merchant, but not one of the richest. And he wanted that. He wanted more, more, always more. He bought anything he could to provide the image of a prosperous man, all the while he made bad investment after bad investment and sunk deeper and deeper into debt. Of course my mother and I knew nothing of this until he dropped dead of an apoplexy when I was seventeen."

Andrew watched her. Her shoulders trembled, but her voice was strong. She was such an odd and alluring combination of fragility and strength.

"How did you find out what he had been doing?" he asked when she was silent for a long time.

She shook her head. "When the creditors came. When they began taking our things, when our servants began to leave and claim they hadn't been paid in weeks, months. When we lost our home. It took a few years for everything to fall apart, but little by little, our lives were chipped away to nothing and we were on the street."

"Did you have no family who could help you?" he asked.

118

She shrugged. "Most on my father's side were in little better position than we were. That whole family was never able to handle itself. And my mother had married my father against her family's wishes. Most hadn't spoken to her in years. The only people who would take her in were my cousins. So I took a position in a Society household as a ladies maid and she went to live with them. I sent half my wages each month to cover her expenses and care and for a while I thought we would survive."

"Half your wages?" Andrew repeated in disbelief. "Your cousins *charged* you for her care?"

She shrugged. "At first it was a reasonable amount, but each month the rate seemed to increase. And then I was let go and now... now he wants more. So much more."

She shivered, and Andrew jolted to his feet as her expression grew sickened. "*You?*"

Her silence and the way she turned her face made clear the answer to his question. He fisted his hands at his sides.

"Bastard," he spat.

"In more ways than one. I've seen..." She stopped and for the first time her voice broke and tears filled her eyes. "I've seen bruises on my mother's arms. I fear he may be abusing her. That's why I had to give him more money. To keep her safe."

Andrew spun on his heel and walked to the fire where she had been standing a few moments before. He drew in several long breaths, trying to calm himself before he spoke again, but his rage boiled and bubbled within him.

This woman had lived a hellish last few years. So had he, but he had a father and a brother who cared for him. And he had money and privilege. He never had to think about the issues that plagued every waking moment of Lysandra's life. She was utterly alone in her pain and her fears.

Or she had been. But not anymore.

"Lysandra," he said softly. "I'm sorry. I had no idea."

"Why should you?" she asked. "Andrew, my duty as mistress is to make your life more interesting, more passionate. It isn't to tell you sad stories."

"My job as protector is to make sure you have few sad stories," he countered.

They looked at each other, separated by the room's distance. And yet he felt remarkably close to her now that he knew something of the woman she was and how she had become that woman.

"It is good to say these things aloud," Lysandra finally admitted.

He nodded. He could well imagine it might be after years of suffering in silence.

"So now you know my secret," Lysandra said. "I'm sorry I didn't spend the money in the way you wished me to."

He waved his hand. "It was your money to spend as you liked."

Of course he would quickly remedy her decision, but that was not a discussion for now. For now he just wanted to touch her. To comfort her.

He reached out a hand toward her. She smiled as she closed the distance between them and took it. He stared at their intertwined fingers for a moment before he shook his head. This connection was exactly what he was trying to avoid.

Without warning, he tugged her hand. She stumbled against his chest and he dropped his mouth to hers in a passionate kiss. That was all he could do to break the spell between them. Sex was what they shared. Nothing more.

"Let's go to your chamber," he said. "And continue your training."

Lysandra drew back, examining his face for a moment so long that Andrew shifted with discomfort, but then she nodded, took his hand and led him from the parlor and up to her room.

*L*ysandra shivered as she stepped from the last of her clothes and stared at Andrew. He too had undressed and was standing before her bed, watching her. She thrilled at the idea that they would make love again, but there was also a nagging sensation of trouble in her mind.

Sex had always been the one thing that bound them, but tonight she felt Andrew pull away from her. Use sex as a way to separate himself, not mold himself to her.

And yet she couldn't resist the draw of passion that was a constant force when she was near this man.

He motioned her forward, his eyes burning into her as she took each step closer. She found herself sashaying her hips a bit more, lifting her breasts, all for his pleasure. This man brought out something utterly wicked in her.

"What will you teach me tonight, Andrew?" she asked as she pressed her body to his and lifted her lips for a searing kiss.

He drove his tongue into her, stroking over and over like it was his cock buried inside of her. She moaned against the assault, clinging to him as her knees went weak and her body wet.

He stared down at her in the firelight, his eyes dark with desire.

"You may not be ready yet for all I have to teach," he murmured.

She laughed. "If I'm not ready now, when will I be?" She lifted on her tiptoes to kiss him. "Andrew, if you want something from me that will give you pleasure, then show me. I want to learn."

He pushed her toward the bed and lowered her against the pillows. "If I do something you don't want, tell me to stop."

She felt her eyes go wide. What did he have in mind that would require such a precursor? But as she stared up at him, so intense in his focus on her, she couldn't help but believe that he would not do anything to hurt her. What he had in mind was pleasure, not pain.

"I-I trust you," she said, the words difficult to find after so many years of being disappointed by men she was meant to trust. But they were true about this man. He might be gruff, but he was not cruel. He was honorable.

His expression turned to one of disbelief, pain. He so rarely showed her any emotion beyond desire and she reveled in the moments where he did. Probably more than she should.

"I won't betray your trust," he said softly.

He pressed his lips to hers, this time gently, and slowly glided his mouth down her throat. She relaxed into the touch. It was becoming familiar, and she anticipated all the pleasure that would come when he sucked her nipple or kissed her intimately.

He did just that, swirling his tongue around her nipple in slow, languid licks and nips. She shivered as sensations so powerful and focused that they made her weak echoed through her body. How could his touch at her breast resonate so loudly at her pussy? How could his kiss make her legs shake and her sheath clench? It was amazing.

He drifted lower, brushing his rough cheek against the smooth skin of her belly and teasing a trail with his tongue even lower. She parted her legs as invitation and he nuzzled her pussy gently before he stroked his tongue along the wet, heated entrance.

"So sweet," he murmured against her body. His words reverberated against her heated flesh and she arched helplessly as he used his thumbs to open her and began to lick and suck in earnest. He was driving her toward release, that was obvious. Even more obvious was that she couldn't fight that drive, nor did she wish to do so.

She thrashed against the pillows, fisting the coverlet and twisting as pleasure built, built and then exploded in a crescendo that put the night's earlier opera to shame.

He continued to lick her through her release until the tremors of her body had eased and finally subsided, then he kissed her inner thigh.

"Now roll over," he said softly.

She leaned up on her elbows, panting as she stared at him in question. Roll over?

Her thoughts turned to the time she'd spent at Vivien's house. She had watched the major take Annalisa from behind. It had been an animalistic display, but the other woman seemed to enjoy it.

She shifted to her stomach and peeked at him over her shoulder. "Like this?"

"Arch your back. So I can see you," he explained as he put a hand beneath her hips and moved her into position so that her backside was raised and her head resting on the pillow, supported by her arms.

Lysandra blushed. She was so exposed in this position. She had been on display for him before, of course, but now it felt even more so.

"I know you like when I lick you here," he said, smoothing his fingers over her still-damp sex.

She jolted as sensation that had just faded lurched back into focus. "Yes," she gasped.

He rubbed his fingers in a gentle, circular fashion, wetting them with her juices. She arched back toward him, pushing into them so they slipped inside of her a little farther.

"Indeed you do," he mused with laughter in his voice.

He slipped his fingers free and slipped them higher until he circled the rosette of her bottom with them.

Lysandra gasped at this new taboo and lurched away from him out of pure instinct.

"What—?" she began.

He stared at her, patient as she looked at him over her shoulder, trembling.

"When I first kissed you where you now so enjoy my tongue, was that not foreign?" he asked.

She nodded. She had been shocked by what he did, frightened even. But the rewards for the act had been great indeed, and now she dreamed of his mouth on her.

"This is foreign to you too. But it will feel good. I promise you, I will make sure of it," he whispered as he caught her hips and dragged her closer.

She trembled as she put herself back in the position he had showed her and closed her eyes as he pressed his wet fingers back against her bottom. Now that the shock had faded, she had to admit that this foreign touch was not unpleasant. His fingers were warm at her entrance, gentle as he stroked the tiny hole in little circles.

She gasped despite herself as he pressed harder and a sudden, unexpected jolt of pleasure rocked her. It was different than when she orgasmed, but just as powerful.

"Very nice," he practically purred as he pressed harder, letting the tip of his finger enter that forbidden channel.

Lysandra shivered, pressing her face into the pillow and squeezing her eyes shut as she focused merely on sensation. His touch on her skin, then inside her inch by inch, to the first knuckle of his finger, then the second.

"How does it feel?" he asked, his voice tense.

She turned her head to the side. "Full. A—a little pain, but still...*good*, somehow."

"Dancing on the edge of pain almost always feels good," he said. "Some people take it much further, though I doubt Vivien would ever arrange for you to match with someone with such proclivities. Not until you were far more experienced, that is."

Lysandra's eyes went wide. Pain as pleasure? Even more pain than this tingling sensation at her backside? How could that be? And yet the thought of it made her body even wetter.

She turned her face back into the pillow to keep her reaction from Andrew. It seemed indecent to like this touch so much.

But she jerked her head up almost as quickly as she pressed it to the pillow when she felt the head of his cock slide against her entrance even as he pushed his finger deeper into her bottom.

"Andrew," she gasped.

"Shhh," he said softly. "Some men put their cock into the place where my finger is, but I don't think you're ready. Although it is so tight and hot that it makes me want to spend just thinking of it. I'll settle for filling you in every way. Like this."

Lysandra gasped as he drove his cock deep within her. With his finger inside her too, she felt desperately full and aching with pleasure and pain mixed at just the right consistency.

"I'll go slowly," he groaned. "As long as I can. Tell me to stop if I hurt you."

She bit her lip, ready for more. Aching for more, though she didn't dare ask for it. She might not be an innocent in any way anymore, but she wasn't bold enough to demand what she desired. Not this.

He thrust with his cock and at the same time withdrew his finger a fraction. Lysandra cried out at the friction of his finger and his cock rubbing against each other through the thin barrier between the two entrances.

He grunted. "Should...I...stop?"

She shook her head. "No, no please. Don't stop."

He laughed low and then thrust again, keeping the motion of this cock and his finger at opposing directions. Lysandra found herself driving backward, rolling her hips in a circle and clenching against his invading body as he took her in every way. Her orgasm hit her, doubled in intensity by the fact that he was inside of her so completely.

His strokes quickened as she arched and cried out through her crisis and then he joined her in release, pulling from her body to splash his seed across her bare back before he flopped down on her bed and pulled her against him, panting.

She stared up at him in the dimness. He had never ended a love-making session by holding her. He'd made it clear, so many times, that he couldn't and wouldn't ever allow her so close.

She snuggled into the crook of his shoulder and slipped her arm around his bare, sweaty chest. In a few moments, a few hours, he would remember why he pulled away from her and go. But until then, she was going to enjoy this closeness and try not to think about what would happen when it was over once and for all.

CHAPTER 15

*a*ndrew wasn't feeling particularly good about himself as he sat in the carriage rumbling across London as a cold rain streaked down the windows outside. In fact, he was feeling quite like a shit.

After a night where Lysandra had given herself in every way he asked, he had slipped from her bed as soon as she fell asleep and left without a word of goodbye. No doubt, that departure would wound her. It seemed that was all he was capable of doing, but how could he talk to her after what they had shared? Emotionally, as well as physically.

He had never wanted a woman more. He kept thinking that, though he never said it out loud. And every time the thought wedged its way into his mind, he hated himself for it.

Shouldn't he have wanted Rebecca the most? Didn't he owe her that, alive or dead, after everything she had sacrificed to marry him and give him what he desired?

And yet, he didn't. He didn't honor her. Truth be told, he had hardly thought of her since touching Lysandra.

Not that he could ever allow Lysandra to know that. He kept that wall between them, refusing to let her near, refusing to give her anything. All he could do was take. Take her body and take her story, as he had last night when he all but forced her to tell him about her family. It had hurt her to talk about them, to spill the painful details he would wager she had kept secret for years.

He knew a little about that.

And yet now the carriage stopped in front of a middle-class home in a neighborhood he had never visited before. He stepped down before the driver could assist and looked up with a sniff of disdain.

There was one thing he *could* do for her.

"Wait for me here," he said. "I won't be long."

"Yes, sir," his drive said with a smart bow, standing at the wait beside the horse's head.

Andrew straightened his jacket and strode up the door. He rapped and smiled when a servant opened it and stepped back in surprise and respect even before he gave over his card.

"M-may I help you...my lord?" the servant said, guessing correctly that he was titled.

There were few times when Andrew enjoyed throwing the weight of his family name and fortune about. Normally it only brought him attention he did not seek and gossip he did not desire. Today, however, he loved every moment of it.

"Indeed. Tell your master that Viscount Callis is here to see him." He pushed into the foyer. "*Now.*"

The servant stammered as he took one of Andrew's gold foil-trimmed cards. "Yes. I shall. Immediately, my lord. Allow me to show you to a parlor to wait for Mr. Ingram."

Andrew followed the servant into the room and as the door shut behind him, he looked around. The parlor was the gaudiest display of new money he had ever seen. From the gold-trimmed everything to the overly stuffed chairs to the mismatched "art" on the walls, it was all designed to scream *rich*. In the end it failed. All Andrew saw was a lack of taste and decorum.

And he liked the man he had never met even less for it, if that was possible.

Within moments, the parlor reopened and a fat, sweaty man

burst through the door.

"Lord Callis," he said, reaching out a hand with a disturbingly wet palm that Andrew ignored. The man stammered and then lowered his hand. His face got even redder. "I beg your pardon for making you wait. Damn servants."

Andrew pursed his lips at the idea that August Ingram would blame a poor footman for the very brief wait. It only made him angrier and angrier.

"It was nothing," he said as he took a seat and glowered up at the man.

"What an honor it is to have a man of such importance in our home," the man continued to gush as he staggered into his own seat. "Though I don't know what I could have done to earn the honor. Have you heard of my shop?"

Andrew shook his head. In the research he had done into the man since the night before, he had learned he owned a somewhat successful bookshop in the same neighborhood where he lived. Nothing spectacular, but he did a decent number of sales each month. Enough to live more than comfortably.

Without Lysandra's pittance coming in for her mother.

"Your shop is none of my concern," he drawled evenly. "In fact, *you* are none of my concern, sir."

The other man cleared his throat in discomfort and shifted his fat frame in the overstuffed chair. "I see." He hesitated and then shook his head. "No, I don't see. What—what do you want of me, then, my lord?"

"I'm here about Lysandra Keates and her mother," Andrew snapped.

To his great pleasure, Ingram swallowed hard and dug into his pocket for an embroidered handkerchief with which to mop his sweaty brow.

"My aunt," he said. "And her daughter, yes. My dear aunt lives with us, we took the poor thing in after some great misfortunes in her family. A pleasure for us, I assure you."

"A pleasure," Andrew repeated, clenching his fists. "I see. A pleasure, you say. Is that why you charge her daughter an exorbitant amount of money each month for your *dear aunt's* room and board?"

Now Ingram began to struggle to get to his feet, but Andrew was much faster. When he rose to his full height, Ingram stopped making the attempt to stand and sank back into his chair with a meek shiver.

"See here, my lord. You know nothing of the circumstances," he argued, though his tone was quite weak. "I only want to cover my expenses when it comes to my aunt. She is unwell. You cannot imagine what a burden that is. One we take willingly, of course, but should we not be compensated for all we do? Now may I ask you, what do you know of my cousin and our arrangement that you would come barging into my home with such an attitude?"

"I'm a friend of Miss Keates'," Andrew said coolly. "And I'm here because I will be removing your aunt from your home today and moving her into a better situation. And I will expect you to return all monies given to you for her care by Miss Keates. Do you understand what I'm saying? *All monies.* With interest."

"Interest for what?" Ingram sputtered.

"For being a bastard," Andrew responded. "And a pig."

Now Ingram managed to get himself to his feet. "I don't have to put up with this, sir. Not in my own home. I can see now how Lysandra has convinced you to act on her behalf. She must be repaying you on her back, but—"

He didn't get to finish. Andrew swung on him, hitting him squarely on the jaw and sending him staggering back over the top of the chair he had just vacated and sprawling across the living room floor as gaudy trinkets that had been set along a side table shattered around him.

"Say anything disparaging about Lysandra again and I will do much worse than hit you," Andrew said softly. "Mr. Ingram, I can destroy your business within moments if I choose to do so. Your livelihood, your life, could trail down the drain as easily as piss does on the street outside."

Ingram crouched on the floor, clutching his already-bruising jaw and nodded. "Yes. Yes, my lord."

"You will now have your servants pack Mrs. Keates' things. They will be ready in an hour and they will be packed with as much care as if they were *my* possessions, because if Mrs. Keates is missing anything or any of her belongings are broken, I will destroy you."

The fat man clutched at the toppled chair and got to his feet. "Yes, my lord."

"As for the money, you may send it to my solicitor, Mr. James Gladwell, under Lysandra's name. It will arrive within a week, or I will destroy you. Do you see the pattern here, Mr. Ingram?"

Ingram nodded, blinking at what Andrew realized were tears. "Yes. Yes, my lord."

"Good, now run along to make the arrangements." He waved off the other man, dismissing him like he would dismiss a disliked servant. "And send in Mrs. Keates. I will see her now."

*L*ysandra stepped from the carriage and wrinkled her brow. Another vehicle was parked in front of her cousin's home, half-blocking the drive. She shrugged as she moved to the front door and knocked.

As she waited for a servant to answer, she sighed. This was the first time she would see her mother since she had begun her affair with Andrew. Her mother knew her better than anyone. Would she sense a change in Lysandra? And if she ever found out what lengths she had gone to, would her mother still love her?

She shivered and then stared at the door. It had been a very long moment since she knocked and no answer. She rapped again, this time harder. Inside she heard a rushing of feet and the door flew open to reveal her cousin's manservant, Clarence. His jacket was cockeyed and his brow sweaty.

"What?" he bellowed, the cockney accent he normally was forced to cover bursting through in whatever upset he was experiencing. Then he shook his head and corrected himself back into a more normal tone and accent.

"Miss Keates. It's *you.*"

His voice was cold, and he actually glared at her. Not that he was ever nice to her, but he had never been so outwardly hateful, either.

Behind him, Lysandra saw flashes of servants running up and down stairs and heard muffled shouts and conversations.

"Yes, it's me," she said with a shake of her head. "What in the world is going on in there?"

He motioned her inside. "Come with me."

She followed him down the hall, still utterly confused by his behavior, the fact that every servant in the house seemed to be in an uproar and that all of them stared at her as she passed by.

He opened the door to her cousin's office. August was sitting at his desk, jacket tossed on the floor, cravat loosened at his neck. He was sweating profusely and leaning over a register making furious notes and swearing under his breath.

"Mr. Ingram, Miss Keates." The servant all but spat her name.

Her cousin froze and then slowly looked up from his papers. Lysandra tensed. She had no idea what was going on, but it clearly had something to do with her. She braced for the worst, but was surprised when he came around the desk and grabbed her hand.

"Call him off, Lysandra," he said, squeezing tight to her fingers until she could scarcely feel them anymore. "Tell him not to destroy me."

She shook her head as she yanked her hand free. She rubbed the feeling back into it as she said, "What are you talking about, August? What in the world is going on here?"

"You must know!" her cousin sputtered. "He's here. He hit me—"

Lysandra drew back. Her cousin *did* have a rather ugly-looking bruise on the side of his jaw. She almost smiled, but was still too confused to enjoy his pain even in the slightest.

"*Who* hit you?" she asked.

"And he said if I didn't give you back the money you just gave me, he'd make sure everything was taken from me," her cousin rambled, utterly ignoring her question.

Lysandra froze. Give back the money? Only one person knew that she had just given her cousin a large sum of money.

She swallowed, her hands shaking. "Are you saying that Andrew...Lord Callis came here?"

Her cousin nodded swiftly. "He's still here, Lysandra. Waiting to take your mother away. He's in the parlor. Call him off, Lys—"

She spun away without letting him finish his plea and rushed down the hallway toward the parlor. Blood rushed in her ears and made her dizzy. Andrew was here? With her mother? This was a travesty!

She burst into the parlor and skidded to a stop. Andrew and her mother sat at the small table in the corner of the parlor with a pot of tea and a plate of cakes between them. They were smiling and turned to see who had intruded when she entered the room.

Andrew got to his feet when he saw it was her, and his smile increased. Like he belonged here! Like she should be pleased to see him like this.

"Lysandra. I was just enjoying your mother's most delightful company."

She stared, unable to look away. Her mother looked very...light. Like she had shed ten years away since the last time Lysandra had seen her. Her smile was real and the light in her eyes was bright.

"Mama," she whispered.

"Hello, my dear," her mother said. "How nice that you could join us. Lord Callis said nothing about that."

"He didn't know," Lysandra said, glaring at him.

Andrew tilted his head, with the gall to look confused at her pointed stare. "Are you well, Lysandra?"

She motioned him to come across the room with a jerk of her hand. "Excuse us, Mama," she managed through clenched teeth. "I have something of importance to discuss with Lord Callis on the terrace."

When he was close enough, she grabbed his arm and stormed out the terrace doors. Once she had closed them, she spun on him.

"What the hell are you doing?" she asked, forcing herself to keep her voice low so that her mother wouldn't hear her inside.

He shook his head. "Having tea with your mother."

She folded her arms. "What are you doing here, Andrew? Why did you punch my cousin? What is this nonsense about money and taking my mother away?"

Her head spun as she asked each successive question. Saying the words out loud made her realize what a tenuous position she was in.

Andrew patted her hand. "Calm yourself. I will explain everything once I have your mother off to her new destination. Now, take a deep breath, and let's rejoin your mother before she begins to ask questions, since it is clear she has no idea of our relationship."

Lysandra's mouth dropped open. "Of course she has no idea of our relationship—"

But he was already heading toward the house.

"Andrew," she called after him, rushing after him. "Andrew—"

He opened the door, and Lysandra shut her mouth. She followed him in, seething, and forced a smile at her mother.

"My dear, when were you going to tell me that you had gone into Lord Callis's employ?" her mother asked.

Lysandra squeezed her eyes shut. Was that how Andrew had explained this? She supposed, in a way, it was true. Though she was hardly cleaning his parlors.

"I was just coming to tell you," Lysandra said with a shrug. "I am surprised that Lord Callis would come all this way to tell you himself."

She glared at him, but he ignored her. "Of course," he said. "After all, you have such an important role in my household. And since we're arranging for your mother to be moved to her own home..."

"Such a surprise," her mother said with a wide smile. "Of course I appreciate my nephew and his wife's generosity, but I have intruded long enough, I think. How lovely that your position will allow me a place of my own, Lysandra."

Lysandra stared at her. She looked so alive, so relaxed. What kind of hell had she been going through that she was so happy to have a new home, or that she could be blind to the fact that the arrangement Andrew was describing made no sense? Why would a woman hired to work in a gentleman's home inspire him to visit her mother?

It was ridiculous.

"Yes, Mama," she said, surrendering to the foolish story they were all pretending was real. "It was kind of his lordship to arrange for your move."

There was a light knock at the parlor door and it swung open to reveal August. He bowed slightly.

"Lord Callis, the carriage is loaded with Mrs. Keates' things, as you requested."

"Good," Andrew said, offering his arm to Lysandra's mother. "Then we shall be off."

August stepped into the hall to allow them to pass, and her mother hesitated. "Thank you for your hospitality, nephew. And thank you wife, as well."

He pursed his lips, and Lysandra could see he wanted to say something nasty. Yet Andrew's presence kept his fat mouth shut. And for the first time, she actually enjoyed this moment.

"It was our pleasure, Aunt. I hope you will call on us soon, as we will all miss your company."

Her mother's eyebrows lifted in disbelief, but she said nothing as they passed through the hall and outside.

"Two carriages?" her mother said as they exited onto the drive.

Lysandra shot Andrew a look. How would he explain this?

"Ah, yes," he said. "One was for your things, Mrs. Keates. We will ride in Lys—in the other carriage."

He motioned for the drivers and spoke to them softly before he opened the door to Lysandra's smaller rig and helped first her mother and then Lysandra inside.

Lysandra clenched her fists at her sides. There was no way she could have this out with Andrew in the carriage with her mother sitting beside her, smiling like she had just escaped a prison. But this wasn't over.

CHAPTER 16

"Your mother likes the new home," Andrew said as he settled back against the carriage seat and sighed.

It had been a long day, helping Mrs. Keates acquaint herself with her two servants and settling her into her new home, a small, tidy place in a middle class neighborhood not far from the far more extravagant home he'd bought for Lysandra.

Regina Keates' happiness and utter friendliness had made it all worthwhile.

"How could you do this?" Lysandra burst out.

Andrew stared at her. She had been bubbling with tension since she arrived at her cousin's home hours ago, but he hadn't expected this explosion within moments of being alone in his carriage. Hadn't she seen how happy her mother was? Couldn't she understand that Andrew had freed her mother from the ugliness of the Ingram home in order to *help* Lysandra?

"Give your mother a place to stay that doesn't require you to give up threequarters of your purse and keeps her from being abused?" he asked softly. "Yes, I am a ghoul, I know."

Lysandra shook her head. "How could you insert yourself into my life? Do you know what kind of explanations I shall have to make?"

He shrugged. "Your mother seemed to accept the story that you have come to work for me and part of our arrangement was that I would help you procure this little home for her."

Lysandra rolled her eyes. "She accepts it now because she is thrilled to be away from my bastard of a cousin. But after a few weeks, as her elation fades, do you not think she will begin to question this? She is not a fool, you know."

"Honestly, Lysandra, I thought you might have told her your grand plans to save her," Andrew said. "I had no idea she thought you continued to work for your old employer or that you were a ladies maid."

Lysandra snorted out a laugh that had no humor or warmth to it. "Why would I tell my mother that I was whoring myself to escape her husband's sins? To save her? To save myself?"

Andrew flinched. "Is that what you call it? Whoring yourself?"

She shook her head. "I don't know. When I'm with you, it doesn't feel that way. But when you give me money, a home not only for me but for my mother, clothing... I cannot be able to repay you in any way. Save one." She sighed. "And even in that element, I'll fall short. Perhaps I *am* nothing more than a whore, dressed up as something more."

Andrew cupped her chin and lifted her face so she was forced to look at him. She seemed defeated and he hated himself for it. He had made her feel this way, after all. Despite his good intentions.

"I watched you today with your mother, Lysandra," he said softly. "How patient you were, how you made her laugh. Today you were no man's mistress. You were just a good and decent woman trying to do right by her mother."

She blinked, tears sparkling in her eyes as the late-afternoon light streamed around the curtain covering the carriage window.

"But I didn't do right by her. You did. You brought her away from my cousin's home and into her own. But what about when you are finished with me? How will I afford that place?"

He leaned down and kissed her lips gently. "We'll work it out, Lysandra. I promise you."

She pulled away and stared at him. "Tell me one thing, Andrew. Why did you do this for her?"

"It wasn't for her," he admitted, knowing he shouldn't say those words, but doing so despite the consequences. "I did this for you."

She stared at him in the quiet of the carriage, and he realized he was holding his breath. Waiting for her to respond to his revelation. Finally, she pushed away and moved to the opposite side of the carriage.

"Please don't," she whispered.

He tilted his head. "Don't?"

"Don't pretend you care for me even in the slightest way when you leave as soon as you're finished slaking your desire," she said, her voice trembling.

"I care more than you know and more than I wish I did," he snapped back and then sucked in his breath.

Why the fuck had he said that?

She stared at him, then opened her mouth, and he lunged for her, desperate to stop this conversation in the one way he knew how. He dragged her across the carriage against him and kissed her hard. To his surprise, she responded with just as much passion and anger as he did. She ripped at his shirt, opening it to slide her hands in against his chest with a hiss of breath that merged with his.

She straddled him, hiking up her skirts around her thighs just as she had the last time they made love in this very vehicle. As she kissed him, she began to writhe over him, rubbing herself against his clothed cock until it pressed against the fabric and ached deliciously.

He cupped the back of her head to kiss her again, but she pulled away and shook her head. He held back, no matter how hard it was, and watched her. He expected her to mount him or undress herself, or anything but what she did next.

She dropped to her knees on the floor before him and extracted his aching cock from his trousers. With one quick glance up at him, she drew him into her mouth.

He arched against the seat, thrusting into her mouth as he lost a fraction of control. If his motion bothered her, she didn't protest. In fact, she made a low moan of pleasure in her throat that reverberated up his cock and through his entire body.

"Jesus, Lysandra," he gasped as she swirled her tongue around him in a slow circle and lit him on fire with pleasure.

She didn't slow her pace, but began thrusting her mouth over him again and again with vigor and passion. He squeezed his eyes shut as wave after wave of pleasure built in him and finally crashed over him. He tried to pull away as he came, but she held tight to the base of his cock and took every drop.

The carriage pulled to a stop as she wiped her mouth and returned to the seat across from his. Andrew hurried to cover himself and only just managed to do so as the driver opened the door and helped Lysandra down. She turned and held up her hand when he moved to leave.

"I find I have a bit of a headache, my lord," she said softly. "So I will bid you good night."

She didn't wait for him to respond, but turned on her heel and strode into her house without so much as a backward glance.

Andrew blinked after her in disbelief. So she would do something so wildly passionate and then just...leave? It felt like a rejection. It felt like he'd been used. It felt like...

Exactly like he made her feel every time he walked away from her.

He shook his head as he motioned for his driver to take him home. Somehow this supposedly brief affair had transformed into something far more than he had ever anticipated. And now he had no idea what to do about it.

"Miss, may I help you?" Lysandra's maid asked as she peeked her head into her chamber.

Lysandra stopped pacing long enough to give the girl a cursory smile. "No, Faith. I'll undress myself tonight."

The maid's eyes went wide at the odd request, but then she

nodded before she bobbed out of the room and left Lysandra alone. She immediately went back to pacing.

Yes, she knew it was foolish not to let the maid attend to her, but seeing the girl only reminded Lysandra that Andrew had paid for both the maid, and for her. And since he had paid, he could now demand anything he wanted. Whether that be her body or her secrets or entry into a life she would rather keep separate from this one.

Yes, she appreciated that her mother was safe now. Comfortable. But how could he not understand how precarious a position that put her in? What if her next protector refused to keep her mother in that place? What if she never found another protector after Andrew discarded her? She would be far worse off and her mother would likely end up on the street after Andrew's heavy-handedness with August.

Not that she hadn't enjoyed that little exchange, but still. The temporary pleasure at August's fear and humiliation could easily transform into long-term problems. But Andrew didn't have to think about that. In his mind and in his world, he took what he wanted and that was that.

But tonight she had turned the tables on him.

She stopped pacing as she thought of the feel of him in her mouth. The way she had stolen control from him in some small way. It had been an act of revenge...and an act of pleasure. He had been shocked by it, shocked by her, that had been clear by the way he reacted to her and her dismissal of him.

Would it backfire on her? Perhaps. But at least, for the first time in a long time, she had taken control of her life. She had refused to bow to someone else's demands, someone else's rules.

And that, as much as Andrew's cock, had been a great pleasure, indeed.

CHAPTER 17

*A*fter a restless night tossing and turning, living and reliving Lysandra's passionate possession and ultimate rejection of him, Andrew was in no mood to do anything but sit in his office and brood. In fact, he was still just waking up when his servant knocked on his door.

"Come," he growled, loath for the interruption when his head hurt and his mind was so unfocused.

"I'm sorry to interrupt your work, my lord, but your father is here to see you," the footman said as he opened the door a fraction. He arched a brow. "I did mention you were working, but he is quite insistent."

Andrew wrinkled his brow. "The earl is here?"

The footman nodded, just once, and from the drawn look on his face, Andrew could see just how "insistent" his father had been.

He groaned. Today was not the day to face his father's judgments and suggestions, but what could he do? Turn the man away? That would certainly cause a most interesting reaction. But not one he wished to face at present.

"Bring him here," he said as he reached for the bottle on the corner of his desk and poured himself a strong drink.

The footman bowed his way out. Andrew got to his feet as he

took a sip of gin. He straightened his jacket and prayed his father wouldn't be able to see his distraction.

The door opened, and the earl walked in, owning this room as he had owned every room he had ever inhabited, probably since birth. Andrew had always admired that quality about his father, worked to create such presence in himself. But it also caused his stomach to tie in knots.

The earl frowned as Andrew came around the desk and held out a hand.

"Father," he said. "I didn't expect you today."

His father shook his hand and looked him up and down as he did so. His perusal was in no way subtle and from the looks of it, there would be no avoiding his father's thoughts on what he saw.

"I hadn't seen you in a few days, Callis," the old man said. "Wondered if I should worry about you, especially after all the talk I've been hearing."

Andrew returned to his seat behind the desk and motioned his father into the opposite. "Would you like a drink?"

His father eyed the bottle with a frown. "A bit early for me. And for you."

Andrew pushed his glass aside slowly. "You say there is talk? What could you mean by that?"

"It's all over Town that you've taken a new mistress," his father said.

Andrew was glad he hadn't been drinking, for he would have spit the alcohol across the room. He cleared his throat.

"Blunt, as always, Father."

The older man smiled slightly. "Well, I've always believed in getting right to the point. No use dilly-dallying around a subject, eh?"

Andrew lifted his brows slightly. "No, I suppose not. But why call this particular rumor to my attention? After all, most men in our circles have mistresses. In fact, I have had them myself in the past, and they never caught your notice."

His father nodded. "That is true. And honestly, when I heard this story, I admit I was actually pleased. I've been telling you for years that you should find a woman to get you out of this funk of yours. But then I heard a bit more about this...this *person* you have involved yourself with."

Any humor Andrew might have found in the situation vanished in a second at that statement and his father's tone of voice as he said it.

"Person," he repeated slowly.

His father nodded. "Yes. Lysandra Keates is her name, is it not?"

"What do you know of Lysandra?" he asked, trying to keep his own tone calm and unreadable.

His father observed his expression carefully. "Do you know she was a servant?"

"And?" Andrew asked, probably more sharply than he should have.

His father leaned back in his chair, but there was nothing nonchalant about the action or his next statement. "A servant for my friend, the Earl of Culpepper?"

Andrew leaned forward. "Culpepper?" he repeated in disbelief.

He had never asked Lysandra about her prior employer. She had seemed loath to discuss the particulars beyond that the man had crossed a line with her. In truth, Andrew hadn't wanted to press her on the subject, not when he drove her so hard on so many other topics and "lessons".

But now that he knew... Culpepper was almost exactly in between his age and his father's. Andrew had never liked him. He was a pompous man with a quick temper, but Andrew did...or *had*...respected him.

He shook his head. There was no use getting into all of that with his father. Not since he still wasn't entirely sure of the earl's motives.

"What of it?" he pressed. "Many a woman has begun as a servant and turned to the more lucrative life of a mistress or courtesan. Especially when she is as young and attractive as Lysandra is."

"Do you know why she left his employ?" his father asked softly.

Andrew pressed his lips together. He wasn't going to spill secrets that weren't his to tell. "No."

"She made a blatant attempt to seduce Culpepper," his father said, disdain dripping from every word. "And then she demanded an exorbitant sum of money to keep her mouth shut about the affair."

Andrew clenched his hands into fists on his desk and drew a few deep breaths. So that was what Culpepper was saying? An interesting lie considering that Andrew knew Lysandra was a virgin. Or she had been. But such statements, said by such a powerful man... no wonder she had been unable to find work as a servant.

The bastard had destroyed her.

And Andrew felt a strong desire to return the favor.

"More to the point, you look at her history... Her father had terrible debts, her mother lives with her cousin and he's as shady a merchant as has ever lived." His father shook his head. "Her entire family is uncouth and greedy and it seems her apple has fallen firmly beneath their tree."

Andrew fought to maintain calm in both his voice and demeanor. "I see you've done your research, my lord."

"I had no choice once I started hearing the gossip over the past few days and Culpepper approached me with his concerns." His father shrugged.

Andrew opened his mouth to argue but shut it again. He knew his father too well to expect him to apologize for prying. It was in his nature.

"I appreciate your concern—" Andrew began.

"Concern?" his father interrupted with a snort. "I'd call it more than that. At four different parties this week alone I was approached by the gossips. Mothers wondering if this delicate situation meant you were thinking of coming back on the mart, men warning me that Culpepper had spoken to them of the situation as well. Hell, some of your old cronies even approached your brother."

"And how do you know that?" Andrew asked.

His father shrugged again. "He spoke to me about it."

"Sam met her," Andrew insisted. "He liked her."

His father laughed. "Well, your brother likes everyone. He can afford to like everyone. He has no responsibilities in life as long as you fulfill your requirements to produce an heir."

Andrew flinched.

"This is a pointless argument." His father waved his hand. "The reason I'm approaching you about this is to tell you that this girl is after your purse. You may be too enamored to see it, but a bad mistress can ruin a man. Look at Baird."

Andrew shook his head. Recently Viscount Joseph Baird had lost a great lump of his fortune and the entirety of the respect he once had because of an obsession with a woman of highly ill repute, Winifred Birch.

"Lysandra is nothing like that," Andrew snapped. "And I'm certainly nothing like Baird."

Except on that count, he might be wrong. Baird had shown up at the woman's house at all hours of the night, loudly demanding to see her long after she had bled his accounts to nothing. Andrew could almost see himself doing the same. Certainly, one day away from Lysandra and he longed to touch her again, consequences be damned.

"I'm certain Baird thought the same thing." His father sniffed. "That the Birch woman was all goodness and light because of whatever tricks she could do in his bed. But when a man is mesmerized by a woman's body, he sometimes does foolish things."

"And that's what you think of me," Andrew said, still barely hanging on to respectful calm.

His father shrugged. "It's been a long time since you were with a woman, and I'm sure a woman of her type offers certain...advantages when it comes to pleasure."

Now Andrew pushed out of his seat and left it rocking behind him.

"Enough," he barked, slamming his hands on the desk. "Do *not* speak of her in such a fashion again."

The earl drew back at the tone and was silent for a long time, staring at him with the same expression of appraisal he had had when he first entered the room. Finally, he shook his head.

"You should end this affair, son."

Andrew flinched. His father never referred to him as anything but Callis. He must be truly concerned.

"Why?" he asked dully, retaking his seat.

"Because you are addled by it." His father shrugged. "Find another woman. Or do as the *ton* has been demanding and put yourself back on the marriage market. If anything has been proven by this mistake you're making, it's that you are most eligible. I've never seen chaperones quiver with such delight at the notion that a man might be available."

Andrew downed the drink he had set aside in one slug. "No," he said when he was finished. "I'm not ending anything and I'm certainly not headed back to the marriage mart."

Now it was his father's turn to jump to his feet, anger and frustration plain in his eyes. "I've been patient throughout this foolishness, but it is clear you are not capable of rational thought. I demand you end this."

Andrew shook his head. "No," he repeated, as clear and calm as he could be under the jarring circumstances. "And now I will have to ask you to leave, Father, as this conversation is pointless and will lead to nothing constructive."

The earl stared, mouth dropped open. Andrew might have laughed had the circumstances been different, for he had never seen his father shocked into silence before. Certainly, *he* had never performed that feat.

Slowly, his father rose and offered a stiff bow. "This conversation is not over, Callis," he said, his tone cool and not at all reflective of any strong emotions. "I will not see you destroyed again."

Then his father turned and strode from the room, slamming the door behind him. Andrew flinched but didn't follow the earl. He stayed in his seat, staring at the empty glass in front of him.

In the thirty years he had been on this earth, Andrew had never defied his father so directly. Even in the years he ran wild, he had checked himself when his father suggested he do so. He respected the earl too much to question his unquestionable authority.

But now he had done so. And over a woman who Andrew supposedly only intended to keep around a few weeks more at the most. More baffling, even to him, was that he could have told his father that. The earl might not have agreed with his tutoring of Lysandra, it might not have changed his mind about her motives, but his father was a reasonable man. Andrew had no doubt that if he had been told that the affair was always meant to be limited, he would have accepted that and backed away from the subject.

But Andrew *hadn't* confessed that. He hadn't even hinted at it. And the reasons why he hadn't... Well, he didn't want to consider them overly long. They made him ponder far too much. Question far too much.

That was one thing he could ill afford to do when it came to an affair that was supposed to be about nothing but sin, yet had transformed to something more despite his best intentions.

*L*ysandra lay in her bed, a book drooping from her fingers as her eyes fluttered shut and then popped back open. She had been lying here for almost an hour, trying to find the sleep that seemed to elude her thanks to her tangled thoughts and heated memories, and it finally was about to come.

She was ready to snuff out her candle and try to find slumber for the fourth time that night when there was a knock on her chamber door. She sat bolt upright, awake in an instant as she glanced at the clock beside her candle. It was one in the morning. Far too late for any interruption that didn't mean something terrible had happened.

She threw back the coverlet and rushed to the door, throwing it open to whatever servant had been sent up here to tell her the news of accident or death. But to her surprise, it was Andrew standing on the other side. A very haggard Andrew, who smelled faintly of bourbon.

"Andrew?" she asked in confusion and then blinked. "Is my mother all right?"

He stared at her and then nodded. "Yes."

She went weak, grabbing for the doorjamb with one shaking hand. "Thank God. I thought..." She shook her head. "I'm sorry. My mother came into my room in the middle of the night when my father died."

"I'm sorry. I shouldn't have come so late."

He weaved a little and she stepped back. "Come in."

After a fraction of hesitation, he did so, stepping into her chamber and looking around as if he'd never seen it before. His eyes were bleary from whatever he'd been drinking and they reflected more emotion than he had ever allowed himself to share. There was no mistaking the upset that surrounded him like a cloud. Or the anger.

Lysandra flinched. The thoughts that had been keeping her awake for two nights straight were of her actions in Andrew's carriage after they had settled her mother in her new home. She had been bold, too bold. She had used her body as a weapon in a war between them.

Was he here because of that? Angry because of what she had done and how she had behaved in her own anger and frustration?

He looked at her closely. "I'm sorry."

"You already said that," she whispered as she motioned to a chair. "Here, sit before you fall over. How much have you had to drink, Andrew?"

He ignored her request and her question. "No, Lysandra. Not sorry about coming here so late. I'm—I'm sorry about how I've treated you."

She blinked and sat down hard in the chair she had been offering him. This was the last thing she had expected.

"Why—why would you apologize?" she asked, examining his face. It was lined with pain he normally kept in check. Pain that went far deeper than this apology directed at her.

He shifted, the alcohol not stealing all his normal hesitation after all. Then he said, "I have not done...*this*...been close to a woman, for a long time. I forget how to do it. And my discomfort sometimes makes me blunt. I know I am confusing. And I'm sorry."

Once he had said the words, he sat down in the chair opposite hers with a *thunk* and stared at her. She moved toward him, sinking to her knees and reaching up to cup his face.

"You are drunk, so I don't know if you'll remember this tomorrow," she said softly. "But Andrew, since you met me, you have been a patient tutor. And a friend to me. You helped move my mother to safety, you forced me to accept gifts I can never repay. If my duty is to give you what you need, then you do not need to apologize. It is I who have not met my part of the bargain."

He blinked and her words hung between them for a long moment before he whispered, "I don't know what I need."

She stroked his cheek. There was every chance that he would reject her when she said her next words. That he would crush her hopes. But she said them anyway.

"Tonight I think you need to be taken care of. Comfort. Will you allow that?"

CHAPTER 18

*L*ysandra held her breath, waiting for Andrew to respond to her question, her plea to allow her to help.

He swallowed hard, then nodded, and her heart swelled both with relief and tender feelings. She leaned up on her knees, drawing his face to hers, and kissed him. He tilted his head to grant greater access and let out a shivering sigh that moved through her as deeply and powerfully as any time he'd ever touched her intimately.

Their tongues touched, gently at first, probing and tasting like it was the first time they kissed. But as Lysandra's body began to react to the kiss, she lost some control over it. Her mouth moved more fervently, she tasted Andrew more deeply as she clung to his arms and lifted herself closer, closer.

He groaned against her lips and his fingers tightened against the arms of the chair. She drew back. Even in an inebriated state, he clung to an attempt to hold back. To keep her at arm's length.

And tonight that would not do. She pushed to her feet and held out a hand. He stared at it for a moment before he took her offer and let her pull him to his feet. She backed toward the bed and when her thighs hit the high edge, she pulled him closer. She reversed their positions so that his back was to the mattress and then gently shoved.

Andrew sat down without any argument and stared at her. It was only then that she realized what he must see. The fire was right behind her and in her thin shift, the light passed through, revealing the outline of her body beneath.

"Do you like to look at me?" she whispered, lifting her arms and arching her back slightly.

He nodded, silent, but his eyes spoke volumes. He devoured her with his stare, his hands trembling as he clenched them on the bed. When he looked at her that way, he made her feel beautiful. Desirable.

Wicked.

She slipped her fingers beneath the thin straps of her night rail and slowly peeled the fabric away. She took her time, showing him only an inch of flesh at a time. He leaned forward, staring, his eyes growing wide as the fabric fell away from her breasts to bunch at her waist. She shimmied her hips and the gown crumpled at her feet.

"Jesus," he breathed, almost reverent as he reached for her. He cupped her hips and pulled her closer. She waited for him to take over, to sweep her away despite her attempts to comfort him with her touch. Instead, he looked up at her, then rested his cheek on her bare belly.

She stroked his hair gently as she stared down at him. Something had happened since their last encounter. Something troubled him. And she knew only one way to ease his pain. Make him forget.

She pressed her hands into his shoulders and urged him back against the bed. He lay down without resistance, but drew her over him. Her hair, only loosely bound during her preparations for bed, fell from its confines and cascaded over and between their bodies. She pushed it aside and leaned over him for another deep kiss.

As their mouths moved against each other, Lysandra began to undress Andrew. His cravat was already gone, so his shirt was easily removed with a few flicks of her wrist. She peeled the expensive fabric away and leaned back for a good look at him.

She had admired him before, but had never really been in control enough or daring enough to truly explore all the beauty of his form. He was muscular, far more so than the average gentleman she had seen. There was nothing soft or pampered about him. She reached out and traced the muscles of his chest, letting her nail drag across his nipple.

He let out a hiss and jerked into a sitting position. He shrugged out of his shirt, cupped the back of her neck and kissed her hard and hot. She arched her back, brushing her own hard nipples against the rough hair that peppered his chest. The rough texture made her hiss out her breath as she broke their kiss once more to begin working on his trousers. He toed off his boots as she unfastened one button after the other, ready and waiting for the hard cock beneath. It sprang free, already fully ready for her.

She smiled. What a difference a few days made. She had gone from nervous and uncertain of what to call his cock, let alone what to do with it, to eager and ready to suck, stroke and let that same cock fill her in any way. She leaned over him and her hair fell around her face once more, brushing the head of his member. He tensed, sucking in a great gasp of breath.

She jerked her gaze to his and then smiled. She tilted her head, letting her hair brush back and forth over him. His breath hissed in and out and he squeezed his eyes shut as pleasure softened his angular face.

Power surged through her. Oh yes. She could make him forget his troubles.

She leaned over him and caught his cock in her hand. She stroked him once, twice, watching how he swelled even harder at her touch. She wanted to feel him everywhere. To mold herself to him.

With a smile, she began to crawl up his body. Her breast rubbed his penis, and he grunted out pleasure that made her stop. Here was an interesting discovery.

She rubbed her nipple against the length of him a second time, reveling in how the touch of skin on velvety skin sent a wave of pleasure jolting through her body and had him gripping the bedsheets for purchase as he moaned. She repeated the action, sliding her breasts against him in a smooth, rhythmic motion. He squeezed his eyes shut with a muffled curse, then reached down to press her breasts together as he shifted to slide his erection through the valley between them.

Lysandra looked down and darted out her tongue to lick the head of his cock as it plunged out between her breasts, once, twice, three times.

Andrew groaned and then released her breasts, grabbing for her wrists to yank her over top of him.

"I'll spray everywhere if I keep doing that," he panted. "And I want you over me, around me, when that happens."

Lysandra shivered as she spread her legs and maneuvered herself into position over him. Her pussy was slick with anticipation and pleasure as she glided him against the entrance to her body in a few readying strokes. He lifted his hips and half his length disappeared within her, stretching her deliciously as she arched her back against a wave of pleasure. She shifted and took the rest of his length inside of her, then held still as she utterly enjoyed the feel of their two bodies merged as one aroused entity.

She leaned back against her arms and watched his face as she began to ride him in long, slow stokes. She stroked against him, rubbing her pelvis in small circles and gasping as her clit pulsed and throbbed in reaction.

He opened his eyes and stared, so she gave him the best show she could, arching her back so her breasts were on display, biting her lip as she tried to hold back the mounting pleasure that started between her legs and spread like flame to the rest of her body. Her orgasm built with every smooth stroke of her hips, and she slowed down to hold off the explosion as long as she could. She wanted to drag out the pleasure tonight. To make them both pant and sweat and beg.

But pleasure mobbed her, crushing her will and her plans, making her ride ever harder, ever faster. She gasped as the first spasms hit, and careened forward to crush her mouth to his. She sucked his tongue as she came, jerking her hips forward and back with no finesse, no control, nothing but pure ecstasy guiding her heated movements.

"Fuck!" Andrew bellowed and in an instant, he flipped her on her back and drove into her so hard and so fast that the orgasm that had just begun to fade doubled in intensity, until she screamed, until she wept with sweet release.

*A*ndrew strained, his neck tightening as he dug his fingers into her hips. He was probably hurting her, bruising her tender flesh, but at that moment he had no control over his actions. His cock was in control and it beat out one drumbeat of an order:

Claim. Take. Mine.

Pleasure overtook him, and he poured hot seed deep within her clenching sheath. He collapsed on top of her, panting with exertion and utter pleasure. Spent.

She shifted beneath him to wrap her arms around him. When he tried to move, she held him close, smoothing her fingers down his sweaty back.

"I'll crush you," he whispered, fearful to speak at full voice in the dark, as if he might break the spell created by their erotic coupling.

She looked up at him, dark blue eyes shining in the candlelight. "I like your weight."

He stared at her for a moment, her hair tangled around her face, her cheeks flushed. He had never seen another woman so beautiful in all his life. She could stand toe-to-toe in her night rail with any supposed Diamond of the First Water and win the battle of beauty.

He kissed her once and then rolled to his side, moving her with him so that her head rested against his shoulder. She pressed a hand to his chest and began to trace a pattern on the muscles there.

It had been some time, he couldn't have said how long, before she spoke again. "Why?"

He blinked down at her. "Why what?"

"When you came here, you said you hadn't been with a woman in a long time. Why?"

He closed his eyes briefly. He'd still been tipsy when he arrived. Liquor had loosened his tongue before passion sobered him. Once again, he had said too much. But now that it was out there, he couldn't exactly take it back, especially since he had no desire to push her away and leave. Not tonight.

"I was once a..." He hesitated as he tried to think of a description. "...a different man. I was wild. I was a rake."

She smiled, but there was no mocking in the expression, even when she said, "Vivien said that to me once. But you are so somber now, it is hard for me to picture you as a rogue. Though the image I do have is most interesting." She tilted her head. "What changed?"

"I got married," he said, his tone flat and emotionless, although his mind was anything but. On the contrary, it was a tangled mass of thoughts he normally tried to suppress.

She continued to stare at him, her expression unreadable, though he could well imagine her thoughts. He never spoke of his wife; she had to be curious.

"The fact that they are married stops few men from pursuing their pleasure, it seems," she said softly.

Andrew sent her a side-glance, wondering if she was thinking of the unwanted advances of Lord Culpepper, a married man of the utmost respectability. At the very least, he hoped she did not compare him to that bastard.

"I loved her," he found himself admitting, perhaps for the first time to anyone but Rebecca herself. "I changed for her. When she died... I didn't know what kind of man to be."

There was a long moment of quiet and he held his breath. This was the point where most people would remind him that Rebecca had been gone for far past the usual mourning period and suggest he fuck a courtesan or marry a chit ten years his junior and move on with the life everyone expected him to lead. His grief, his continued struggle, made them all uncomfortable and they wanted it to stop.

But Lysandra simply touched his cheek. "She has only been gone a few years, yes?"

He nodded but did not speak. He didn't trust himself to do so.

She smiled. "I can understand that it would take a long time to recover from such a loss. To re-establish yourself as a man, as a person."

He drew back at that reaction. No one else had ever put it so succinctly. Even his brother, who gave him the most leeway in his grief, had never been able to fully understand his reaction and was forever trying to gently prod him toward a return to his "normal" life.

"You are the only one who thinks so," he said softly.

He shook his head, thinking of his father that afternoon. The old man would have his way by one means or another if they remained together. He would find a way to take this affair from Andrew in the name of his "own good" since Andrew wouldn't surrender Lysandra willingly.

Suddenly, he sat up on his elbow and looked at her as a thought struck him. "Lysandra, we should go to the country."

She drew back at his sudden change of tone and subject. "The country?"

He nodded, excitement for this notion building with every word he spoke.

"Yes. My estate is only a day and a half's travel from London, and there is a pleasant inn along the road that would be suitable for a stop. We could conclude your training there."

She wrinkled her brow, a look of continuing confusion on her face. "Why?"

"There will be no distractions there," he explained, again thinking of his father, of the Society that had apparently taken a new interest in him, even of his brother and the happy union he was building. He was finished with it all. At least for a little while.

"There is great privacy so I can tutor you even further," he continued as he shoved those thoughts aside.

God, what he could do to her there, when he had her in his home, in his bed. He could possess her in every way and surely *that* would purge this desire he continued to feel for her. And at home, his *real* home, he would feel more himself.

Lysandra nodded slowly. "Now that my mother is safe and happy away from my cousin and his moods, I see no reason why I couldn't leave the city for a time. I will go to her tomorrow and make some excuse about my disappearance."

He smiled. "Then you will come with me?"

She nodded, but he sensed a hesitation that he chose to ignore. Instead, he leaned over her and kissed her, deep and hot and heavy. She relaxed at the onslaught of his passion and he lowered her back onto the pillows.

"After you talk to her," he whispered, "we'll depart. In two days we will be there. And everything will be different."

But as he let his fingers travel down to the place where her legs met and began to gently stroke her, he tried to ignore the loud, insistent voice in his head. The one that told him he was running. The one that said he could never truly make anything different.

Not even with this woman.

CHAPTER 19

*L*ysandra sat perched on the edge of a pretty little settee, preparing tea as she waited for her mother to join her. She looked around with a contented sigh. The house was small but perfect for her mother. The rooms were pretty, the servants were kind. For the first time, she felt like everything she was doing, everything she had sacrificed, was worth it.

The door to the parlor opened, and she stood as her mother stepped into the room.

"Dearest," she said, pressing two kisses to Lysandra's cheeks. She looked at her, and Lysandra shifted.

Her new gowns had been delivered that morning. Not one, as she had requested, but five. Andrew had intervened with Madame Bertrande and chosen the fabric himself.

They were beautiful gowns, ranging from everyday outfits to riding frocks, and of course her gorgeous evening gown that was probably being packed up by her servants as she stood here.

What they were not, however, were the gowns of a servant. Even a high ranking one, as Andrew had explained to her mother that she was.

"Sit down, Lysandra," her mother said, her tone soft. "We'll share tea."

She nodded. "How do you like your new home?"

Her mother smiled. "It is lovely. I've actually had friends to visit in the last week. Imagine, actually seeing a friend without having to ask permission."

Lysandra shut he eyes. "I'm so sorry, Mama. I didn't fully realize how terrible a situation it was for you at August and Marta's home. If I could have taken you away sooner—"

Her mother shook her head and covered her hand briefly. "Lysandra, you did not create this situation. You must stop blaming yourself for it and taking responsibility for fixing it. Your father made bad choices. Perhaps I should have been more aware of those choices. But it was never your duty to save me."

"I didn't do a good job of it, even if it was. I plopped you in the middle of a home where there was no warmth or care for you." Lysandra sighed. "But you are out of there now."

"At what seems to be a high cost," her mother said, looking at her gown again.

Lysandra gripped her hands at her sides and then ignored the comment. "This will have to be a very quick tea," she explained. "I came to tell you I'm leaving Town for a little while."

Her mother hesitated before she drew a cup toward herself. "I see. Where are you going?"

Lysandra cleared her throat and took a sip of tea to wet her suddenly dry throat.

"Lord Callis has decided to return to his country home for a short time. And so he's packing up his household."

"And bringing the servants with him?" her mother asked. "I would have thought he'd have a whole other set of them awaiting him in the countryside."

Lysandra hesitated. Blast! In her excitement to leave London and escape to the country with Andrew, she hadn't actually thought that part of her story out so very well.

"S-since I'm so new," she began. "I think he thought I needed training—"

"There are no servants in London who could train you here?" her mother pressed.

Now she was holding Lysandra's gaze evenly, her grey eyes filled with the same stern quality that they had held when Lysandra was a naughty child.

"You see—that is—" she stammered.

"Please stop, Lysandra," her mother said on a sigh. "It is evident you are lying. Your cheeks have those two spots they always have gotten when you told a falsehood."

Lysandra dropped her gaze to the hands clenched in her lap. "I-I'm not lying."

"How long have you been Lord Callis's lover?" her mother asked.

Lysandra jerked her gaze toward her mother. In the past few years, Regina Keates had grown withdrawn, almost fragile, but looking at her now was like looking back in time to the woman she had been before her husband's death. Before she lost everything. Her arms were folded, her jaw set, and grim determination lined her mouth.

"Only a fortnight," Lysandra said softly.

"I see." Her mother shook her head. "And what are the intentions of this relationship? I assume he does not plan to marry you, or you two wouldn't have gone to the lengths to lie to me about you being a servant. Are you his mistress?"

"I'm not comfortable talking about this, Mama," Lysandra said, rising to her feet and pacing to the window. Her mother had a beautiful view from her bay window of the park across the street. Out there men and women strolled arm-inarm, and Lysandra flinched at how open they could be with their intentions and affections.

"You had a good position in the Culpepper house," her mother pressed. "How did things become so desperate?"

Lysandra turned to look at her mother. She seemed…disappointed, and that broke Lysandra's heart. Anger she could have borne. Sadness would have been better. But disappointed…that was the worst.

"Culpepper tried to take something from me," she explained.

"When I refused to give it, he let me go and proceeded to ruin any chance I had of obtaining another post. I tried to find other work, Mama. I was too 'high-class' for the lower establishments. Culpepper had poisoned the higher."

Her mother gripped the arm of her chair as pain ricocheted all over her face. Finally, she nodded. "I see. Of course."

"I never would have thought to do this, to become a man's mistress, if the situation had not been dire." Lysandra sighed. "August demanded more and more money and favors to keep you in the house and I had no funds left."

Her mother stared at her. "Why didn't you come to me? At the very least, I would have been someone to share your troubles. And perhaps we could have thought of some alternative solution."

Lysandra sat down again with a thud. "I suppose that would have been best, but I didn't want to trouble you with my problems. Not when you were still so sad, so devastated by everything that had happened."

She stopped before saying more. She had treated her mother exactly as Andrew described his family treating him in his grief. As if they knew better what and how he should be. Like he was glass.

"I'm sorry," she added. "I realize now that I took this problem, which belonged to both of us, and made it my own."

"I'm sorry you had to shoulder the burden without anyone to talk to," her mother said, tears glimmering in her eyes. "Is there not any other way?"

Lysandra shook her head. "Even if there once was, it is gone. I'm on this path now, Mama." She blushed. "Things have been done that cannot be taken back. And to be truthful, it hasn't been as terrible as I once imagined. Lord Callis...Andrew... is a kind man."

Her mother nodded. "Yes. He was nothing but kind to me when we met. A true gentleman. At least I know that you have a good protector."

Lysandra bit her lip. Her mother had asked her for honesty. And now that was going to be put to the test.

"Actually, Mama, he isn't going to be a permanent protector for me. I visited a woman—her name is Vivien—and she asked him to... This is indelicate, I apologize... To train me in what a mistress is required to know."

Her mother blushed. "Oh. Oh, I see."

"But he has been nothing but kind and generous," Lysandra hastened to add. "I'm certain he will be helpful in my finding a more permanent protector once this time between us is...over."

She hesitated in saying the last word because it actually hurt her to do so. Over the time they had spent together, the idea that what they shared would end had become a more and more foreign and a less and less pleasant concept. How could she be with another man like she had been with Andrew?

Her mother tilted her head. "You care for him."

Lysandra blinked. "No. I mean, of course, I care for him as one person cares for another. He is a friend to me. A good friend. He has shared something with me I could never share with another."

"With every sentence you come closer to admitting you love him," her mother said with a smile that was sad rather than pleased.

Lysandra shoved to her feet a second time. "No. I don't love him. There are not many rules a mistress must follow, but that is one. Falling in love with a protector would be...foolish at best. And what Andrew and I share will be over in another few weeks. I will return to London where Vivien will match me with a man." Lysandra looked at her mother. "Andrew has said that he will ensure you are still allowed to stay here, though. You'll never be forced to return to that awful house again."

Her mother's face softened with relief, but then she said, "A lot of trouble for him to go through for a woman he has no intentions of keeping."

Lysandra shrugged. "Perhaps, but that is just the kind of man he is."

There was a long silence between them and then her mother said, "So he is taking you away to the country, then?"

She nodded. "Yes. For a short time. I will write to you so that you will know I'm well and settled in. And the servants here have our direction there, so you may write to me, or if there are any emergencies. Oh, and Andrew has promised me that August will not be welcomed here by the servants, unless you choose to allow him entry."

Her mother laughed. "Ah, I'm sure August was very unhappy with all this."

Lysandra laughed too. "You should have seen his face. Andrew *hit* him and he looked like a schoolchild racing around trying to cow to 'his lordship's' orders."

For a moment, they shared a giggle at the idea. Then Lysandra moved toward the door.

"Andrew is waiting for me, though. I should go."

Her mother stood and followed her to the foyer. At the door, they embraced and as they parted her mother said, "Dearest, do be careful. I don't have any experience in the world you have been forced to join, but I do know that physical...*attachment* can lead to love. And if that is the only rule you should not break, then I worry for you."

Lysandra touched her face. "I do love you, Mama. Enjoy your new home and I'll write to you as soon as we have settled in the country."

She turned toward her carriage at the bottom of the drive. But as she got inside and Wilkes shut the door behind her, her smile fell.

Her mother was treading far closer to the truth than she would have liked to admit. There were many rules meant to be broken in life, but she feared that if she broke this one it would be the end of her.

CHAPTER 20

*L*ysandra had always been impressed by Andrew's London home. Unlike her cousin, who depended on gaudy trinkets to shout to the world about his wealth, Andrew was more subtle. But his country home... It took her breath away as they rounded a corner and entered the gate.

The house was situated on a hill overlooking a massive lake and wide, green expanses of hill and valley. Marble columns supported the structure. It was something out of a fairy tale. Or one of those books by the anonymous author that were all the rage these days.

"What do you think of Rutholm Park?" Andrew asked, leaning over her shoulder to see the same view she was.

"It's wonderful," she breathed. "Andrew, it's beautiful."

He smiled as he leaned back. "It's been in the family for hundreds of years and was a favorite spot of mine as a child. When I took on the title of Viscount at my majority, I was thrilled that my father offered me this estate as my own. But I suppose, knowing my love for the place, that was why he did it."

Lysandra glanced at him from the corner of her eye. Already she was learning much more about Andrew than he ever would have shared in London. And in the last few hours, he had begun to be... relaxed. As if a weight was lifted from him.

"Ah, looks as if the staff is ready for us," he said as he glanced out the window again.

Lysandra followed his line of vision and tensed. At least ten servants were lined up at the staircase as the carriage pulled to a stop.

"Oh, Andrew," she said, squeezing back against the carriage wall as if that would make her disappear. "I wasn't expecting an audience for my arrival. What will they think of me?"

He frowned as he looked at her. "Think of you? They'll think you are a lovely woman who is my guest."

He stepped from the carriage and offered her a hand out, but as she took it, Lysandra couldn't help but marvel at the disconnect Andrew truly had from the servants. She had been one not so very long ago. They always talked and judged belowstairs.

And it underscored how very different her world was from his.

She forced a smile as he approached the staircase and began to greet the servants. He introduced her only as Miss Keates with no other explanation for her arrival. They must have known she was accompanying him, for Lysandra saw no hint of surprise or reaction on their faces as they welcomed her.

Slowly, as she relaxed, she began to watch their faces not for their response to her, but to Andrew. All of them smiled widely as they said hello, welcoming him home and saying how much they had missed his presence. And, to her surprise, their response seemed utterly real. There was no doubt that the staff adored their master. But of course, they would. He had proven again and again to be a decent man with a generosity of spirit.

But there was something else, too. Once he had passed by a servant, often their gaze followed him for a fraction too long. They seemed concerned, worried...*afraid*, just as she had thought that Sam seemed afraid at the opera. Again she wondered what could cause that kind of deep emotion.

Eventually, they reached the top of the stairs where a butler was awaiting them. He was a middle-aged man with dark hair that had a touch of grey about the temples. He was dressed smartly and had a no-nonsense way about him that wasn't unfriendly, but very calm. He didn't seem the kind of man who would suffer fools lightly.

In short, the perfect fit for a servant for Andrew.

"Ah, Berges," he said with a wide smile. "I trust everything has been right during my absence."

"Welcome home, my lord. And yes. Everything has been right as rain."

"This is Miss Keates." Andrew motioned toward her, and the servant nodded with just the right level of deference. Unlike the other servants before him, he took a slightly longer look at her, though Lysandra couldn't tell if he was judging her or not.

"The bags are already being taken to your chamber, my lord," the butler said. "May I offer you refreshment of any kind?"

"No, we had tea in Crosswater at Mrs. Tate's," Andrew said with a smile.

"Ah, yes. She does a lovely tea there at the inn," the butler said with a brief nod.

Lysandra's eyes went wide as she watched them talk. They were so friendly with each other. There was respect there, yes, but also something deeper. But perhaps that was what happened once a household had gone through a tragedy like the death of Rebecca Callis.

"I believe Miss Keates and I will take a walk around the grounds, have a bit of air after that carriage ride," Andrew said. "The weather is meant to be fair only a day or so longer, and I would hate her not to see the estate once the rain begins."

"Of course. Your supper will be ready at seven." The butler now turned to her. "Welcome to Rutholm Park, miss. If there is anything you need during your stay, please don't hesitate to ask me or anyone on the staff. We are at your disposal."

Andrew took her arm as the butler gave a stiff bow and disappeared back into the house.

He smiled at her. "You see, no judgments."

She shrugged. "Belowstairs reactions and abovestairs are often very different. But your staff seems very nice, and I'm certain they'll never let me know whatever they are saying about me behind my back."

Andrew shook his head. "I cannot believe that is true."

She laughed. "That is because you've never truly been below-stairs, *my lord*. It's a whole different society than the Society you are a part of. But just as ruthless."

"I am fascinated that this is what is going on beneath my very nose," Andrew said with his own chuckle as they walked out onto the lawn toward the lake she'd seen from the carriage. "I would love to be a fly on the wall then."

"Probably not," she said. "They might talk about *you*. In fact, I'm certain they do."

The smile fell from his face and his pace slowed. "I can only imagine what they would say."

She glanced at him from the corner of her eye and it was obvious that the very idea troubled him.

"I think it mostly has to do with which female servants think you have a nice backside," she teased gently. "And I'm certain the answer is all of them."

His eyes went wide with shock and for a moment Lysandra thought she had gone too far in her joking. But then he burst out laughing.

"I never would have expected you to be so cheeky, my dear," he said as he wiped his eyes. "I think I like this side of you that comes out in the countryside. But I must know one thing."

She tilted her head. "Anything."

He arched a brow. "Oh, I'll follow up on that later, but my question for now is, what side of the backside issue do *you* fall on?"

She slipped her arm free from his and looked around at his bottom as if to judge its worth.

"I likely know the backside in question a bit better than the servants do." She locked eyes with him. "Don't I? There aren't any chambermaids waiting to scratch my eyes out are there?"

He shook his head. "Most definitely not."

She sighed in mock relief. "Excellent. Well, if I were to be invited into the discussions belowstairs I would say that the backside in question is very fine, indeed."

"My relief is palpable," he said with another laugh that warmed her to her very core. Then he caught her hand and drew her against his chest. "Though at this particular moment, your opinion is the only one that matters to me. Perhaps you would care to explore the issue further?"

"Here?" she asked, surprised at his ardor.

He nodded.

She looked around. They had crested a small hill and were now walking along a laughing brook. She could not see the road, nor the house. They were utterly secluded.

She was reminded of the wicked feeling of watching Annalisa and her major at Vivien's home. Except this time, there was the chance that *she* would be the one being watched. An unexpected thrill worked through her at the idea.

She lifted on her tiptoes and kissed Andrew as her reply. Immediately his arms tightened around her waist, his hands drifted until he found her backside and lifted her against him. She felt his cock, half-hard already, nudging at her stomach, and shivered with the knowledge that he would soon be inside of her.

Without speaking, they began to undress each other, pausing only to exchange kisses as more and more skin was exposed. Finally, he stood before her, utterly naked, and she only in her thin chemise. She looked around herself nervously a second time. The idea of this was thrilling, but...

"No one will see us," Andrew reassured her. He reached down for his jacket and laid it out on the grass so that the silk-lined interior would be a bed for them, then he pulled her against him and lowered her to the ground.

"The sunlight on your skin," he growled as he opened her legs and laid his hand there, just resting it to tease, not stroking yet. "We should do this every afternoon."

She laughed, though it was slightly shrill from nervousness and high emotion. "What if it rains?"

"Then I shall lick every bit of moisture from your skin," he whispered, his voice low and gravelly against her throat. "I should practice."

He pressed his mouth to her throat and began to suck there, nibbling at her flesh as he glided lower, lower. She arched as he crested over her breasts, hesitating to lick each one through the silky chemise. Feeling his heat through the wet fabric only made her body ache all the more. Once her nipples were hard against the damp silk, he moved lower, pushing her chemise up to reveal her sex.

He opened her legs wider and looked at her pussy.

"Sometimes I wake up thinking I taste you on my tongue," he said, stroking a finger along the slick entrance. "I dream of making you come over and over, until you beg for more, for less."

She jolted as he leaned down and blew a gust of hot air against her trembling sex. Her clit throbbed, aching for more. More she knew was coming. Except that wasn't enough. She wanted to receive the gift of his mouth, his tongue, his fingers. But she wanted to give one in return, as well.

"H-have you ever seen the wallpaper in Vivien's parlor?" she gasped as he licked her once, twice.

He lifted his head and looked at her. "Oh yes. Those dirty little pictures she had designed into an innocent red wallpaper. What about it?"

"There is one where the image is of two people...pleasuring each other with their mouths. At the same time," she said with a dark blush. "I want that. Now."

He let out a low sound of possessive pleasure deep in his chest and then tugged her to a sitting position.

"The best way for us to achieve that," he said with a wicked smile. "Is for you to straddle my mouth while you suck me."

He lay down on the makeshift blanket she had abandoned and pulled her down for a kiss. She could taste her own earthy essence on his tongue and it sent wet desire and heat to her already-soaking pussy.

He caught her hips and helped her to turn so that her sex hovered over his mouth and she stared down at his rock-hard cock. She licked her lips before she took him in hand and stroked him.

He was right. With the natural sunlight on their skin, she could see everything so differently. The shadows moved, the light glistened over the bubbling water that was the soundtrack to their passion.

All thoughts cleared her mind as he opened her outer lips and began to lick her in earnest. She arched her back, thrusting her hips helplessly against his tongue as pleasure built deep within her loins. Her vision blurred and she gasped and moaned at the feel of him beneath her, inside of her, piercing her with his wicked tongue.

But she had her own duties to perform. She stared at his hard cock and lowered her mouth to it, just rubbing it against her closed lips and reveling in the velvety steel of it. He hissed out a breath against her sex, and she quivered as the steamy air filled her. But he didn't hesitate long, he returned to tasting and teasing her.

She drew him between her lips, licking just the head of his cock with a few teasing darts of her tongue. When he moaned against her a second time, she went to work in earnest. She drew him in as far as she could take him and swirled her tongue around the length of him. He bucked beneath her and his mouth began to work harder in response.

Lysandra took the unspoken challenge, and they each quickened their pace. She pumped her mouth over him in long, languid strokes, using her tongue to increase his pleasure each time she took him deep within her throat. And he sucked her clit, adding two fingers to her aching slit. It was a race now, who would come first? Who would win by making the other explode with pleasure?

Lysandra knew she was losing the war. Almost from the first moment Andrew pressed his lips to her sex, she had been on the edge of orgasm. Her entire sheath quivered each time he stroked his tongue against it. And her clit was already pulsing, making her dizzy with the impending wave of pleasure ready to break on her shore.

When it did, she arched her back, her cries muffled as she continued to work his shaft with her tongue. He groaned beneath her, and the hot saltiness of his seed flooded her mouth at the same moment that her hips jerked out of control against him. He continued to lick her long after his own pleasure had ended and her orgasm went on, dragged out by his talented tongue and lips until she collapsed, weak, against his thigh.

He shifted, lifting her and maneuvering her so that she lay against his chest. They panted in the silence for a long while, for there was nothing to say. Nothing to describe what they had done out in the sun-kissed lawns. Lysandra only knew it had been perfect.

But it seemed everything about this affair was perfect. Except that very soon it would be over.

CHAPTER 21

*L*ysandra pulled her wrap a bit tighter around her shoulders and stepped into yet another long hallway. After supper Andrew had been called to meet with his estate manager about the goings-on since he had been in London. He had told her to look around the house, and that was exactly what she was doing.

The estate was as beautiful inside the walls of its mansion as it was out. Each room enchanted her more. From the pretty yet comfortable parlors to a massive library built for a bibliophile, to a music room with a grand piano worthy of the finest musician, which Lysandra was most definitely not.

Down the corridor, she passed more rooms for gathering. There was a tall, ornately carved door at the end that piqued her interest. It was heavy and took effort to push open into what she had thought was another room, but was instead another long hall. But this one was lit by dozens of glowing lamps. The walls were covered with portraits.

"Oh," she murmured. "That family gallery."

She had heard of such things when she was in service of Lord and Lady Culpepper. Some of the servants had talked about the gallery her former master had kept at his country estate. Apparently there were some terribly ugly members of his family, ones the upper level servants giggled about when the topic came up below stairs.

Andrew's family, on the other hand, didn't seem to have an ugly member in the bunch. Lysandra moved down the hallway slowly, looking at each portrait. His most handsome features were reflected on the faces of his ancestors. His nose on one man, his full lips on a lady. They were stern portraits, of course. It seemed that was the rage. But there were moments where she saw a flash of kindness in a man's eyes or the hint of a smile on a lady's face.

She rather liked his family history. The older paintings often included children or dogs or in one instance a very large, fluffy black-and-white cat perched on the back of a velvet settee behind a lady posed in a stiff green gown with a huge collar. The artist had captured a twinkle in her eyes, despite her posture.

She smiled at the image and continued. Now she was getting closer to the more modern pictures. There was one of a family, and she stopped to draw in a breath. The man and woman were not familiar to her, but the two boys in the picture, standing beside each other, were most definitely Sam and Andrew.

She stared at this image reflective of Andrew's youth. He had a mischievous expression, like he knew some kind of secret. Not an unpleasant one, but something silly or frivolous that his serious parents might not approve of. There was none of the hint of sadness he carried with him now.

Of course, she knew why. Something terrible had happened to him in the interim. Something had changed him.

She shivered and moved on, but the next portrait on the wall did nothing to clear her mind. It was of a woman. She didn't look like the other women in the family portraits. Her black hair was done up in a fancy style, and her eyes were a stunning shade of blue that almost seemed unreal, it was so bright and vibrant.

And then there was her gown. Lysandra gasped. It was a wedding gown. Could this be...?

Her gaze moved to the next portrait, and her guess was confirmed. The same woman sat on a chair. Andrew stood behind her, his hand resting on her shoulder while her opposite hand covered his.

This was the woman who had changed Andrew's life forever. Whose *death* had changed his life forever. The woman Lysandra had wondered over and even secretly been jealous of since she first learned of Andrew's existence.

This was Rebecca Callis.

She leaned in closer to the image of the bride on her wedding day. Rebecca had been a beautiful woman, there was no discounting that. She had high cheekbones and fine features that seemed to be carved from the most delicate porcelain.

"Rebecca..." Lysandra breathed, just to hear her name out loud.

"Yes."

Lysandra spun at the sharp female voice that interrupted her very personal reverie. A tall, thin woman stood at the entrance to the hallway. She wore a heavy dark blue gown, her dark hair pulled back in a tight bun away from her face. Her expression was one of sadness as she stared at the same portrait that had so fascinated Lysandra.

"I didn't know you had come in," Lysandra said, hand on her pounding heart.

The other woman glanced at her "I didn't mean to frighten you. I sometimes come in just to look at her ladyship's picture."

"I see," Lysandra said softly.

With another brief glance at Rebecca's portrait, the woman smiled at her. "I'm Hester Eversley. I was personal maid to Lady Callis."

"Oh. *Oh.*" Lysandra shifted uncomfortably.

Here she stood, the temporary lover of the master of this house, with the former maid of his wife. A woman who, by all rights, should have moved on to another post after the lady's death.

Hester smiled at her silence. "You must wonder why I'm still here. Everyone does. Lord Callis kept me on. Shifted my duties to other matters."

Lysandra stepped forward. "Oh no. It isn't that. I'm certain you are a most important member of the household. I would never question why someone was here or not."

The last thing she wanted was for a hoity-toity attitude to follow her belowstairs. That was how one's soup got spit in.

"Thank you," Hester said.

They turned and silently looked at Rebecca's picture together.

"She was lovely," Lysandra said softly.

"Yes. Beautiful," Hester agreed with a sigh. "Both inside and out."

Lysandra glanced at her from the corner of her eye. This was a most rare opportunity. She had questions about Rebecca, ones that Andrew would certainly never answer, he had made that abundantly clear. But Hester had known Rebecca very well. And she might be able to offer some insight into the dead woman...and that, in turn, offered insight into Andrew.

"Can you—" Lysandra broke off, well aware of how suspicious her question might sound. "Can you tell me more about her?"

Hester kept her gaze on the portrait for a long moment and then her dark eyes moved to Lysandra with caution.

"I realize it must seem an odd question given our..." Lysandra sighed. There was no use pretending the servants didn't know exactly what she was. "...our situation. But there is so much implied about Lady Callis and so little said. I cannot help but be curious since she is clearly such a big influence on Lord Callis."

"Indeed she is." Hester shook her head sadly. "Perhaps too much of one after all these years."

Lysandra wrinkled her brow, for she didn't understand that statement. Hester didn't explain, though, she only kept speaking.

"She was the daughter of a duke, but I never saw her put on airs like some of their ilk. She loved her family. I've never seen a lady so thrilled that she would soon be a mother."

Lysandra sucked in a breath and stared once more at the image of Rebecca. A mother?

"Hester."

Both women turned to find Andrew standing at the entrance to the gallery. He was half in shadow, but Lysandra could see his jaw was set and his hands were clenched at his sides. But his voice was calm and even kind.

"You may go," he said.

Hester lowered her head as she walked away from Lysandra. At the door, she paused to look at Andrew. He reached out to pat her shoulder in a silent expression of support, then she left them alone.

Lysandra stayed silent as Andrew moved toward her. He took his time, looking up at each portrait as he passed. He seemed to be in no hurry to reach Lysandra, to discuss what had been said.

She stared at him and finally stepped forward where he would not.

"Andrew," she whispered. "A child?"

He stopped moving, though he continued staring at a picture of a man who was probably his father. Slowly, he turned his steady, emotionless gaze on her.

"I want to make this very clear to you, Lysandra," he said softly. "I brought you here to escape this very type of intrusion. My wife and…"

He stopped and for a moment his entire face transformed with a grief so powerful that it broke Lysandra's heart. In that fraction of a moment she saw all his loss, all his anguish, all his guilt, and then it was gone. Replaced by his normal calm and cool expression.

"The subject is closed," he said quietly. Then he reached out and took her hand. "Please."

She stood still, pondering her options as she looked at their intertwined fingers. She could push him, but what right did she have? She was a lover, not a love. Doing so would likely only result in her being sent home. Or she could let the subject rest, as he asked. That answer was uncomfortable and unpleasant, but wasn't it his right to keep his secrets from his mistress?

"Very well," she finally said.

"Now—" He lifted her hand to his lips. "I have finished with my work for the evening and I find myself very tired after this long day. You have two choices. You can retire to your own chamber or…"

He drew a breath like what he was about to say was difficult.

"You could join me in my bedroom. For the remainder of your stay."

Lysandra stared at him. Though he had come to her bed and stayed for hours before, he had never spent a night with her. The idea of waking in his arms was a bewitching one.

She stepped closer and wrapped her arms around his neck.

"Your bed sounds warmer and more comfortable." She kissed him. "If I am welcome there, that is my choice."

"Then follow me," he said against her lips. "We have much training still to be done."

*A*ndrew felt many things as he stepped into his bedchamber with Lysandra at his side. There was excitement since he had not shared this bed for many years. There was guilt because the last woman who had slept here had been his wife. But the overwhelming feeling he experienced was a lack of control.

Lysandra and the questions she had posed to Hester had unearthed memories and feelings he had long squashed. Thoughts of his wife and unborn child that he kept buried deep inside. He hadn't wanted Lysandra to know about them. Except he had brought her here, which almost guaranteed she would find out about his past.

He shook his head as she looked around the chamber. He wanted control back. And he knew one way to get it that could also be called "training".

She turned on him with a smile. "It is lovely. Your whole house is a thing of beauty. I can see why you don't like to leave."

He forced his own smile in return. The fact that he loved his home was only a very small part of why he locked himself away here. But he wasn't going to tell her that.

Even if he ached for confession in a way he'd never felt before.

"Did you know that some men like to exert control over their lovers?" he asked.

She glanced at him, still distracted by her explorations of the room. "All men control their lovers," she said with a light laugh.

He frowned. "I suppose that is somewhat true. But this is different."

She lifted her brows. "How so?"

"Undress," he ordered without answering her question.

She hesitated and there was a nervousness to her expression he hadn't seen since the first time he touched her.

He smiled. "Please."

That additional word seemed to help. She nodded and lifted trembling fingers to the buttons along the front of her gown. He forced himself to look away from the show of her removal of clothing and instead moved into his dressing chamber. He opened a long-neglected, almost forgotten lower drawer of his bureau and withdrew a pair of velvet restraints.

He stared at them. He hadn't used these since a lover he'd had many years ago, one who liked her sexual encounters to be rough and overpowering. It had thrilled him to be utterly in control, to watch her squirm. But the moment he was finished touching her, he inevitably forgot about her until their next encounter.

With Lysandra it would be different.

It always was.

He moved back into the room and stopped in the doorway between the two connected chambers. Lysandra stood waiting for him, utterly naked. Her back was to the fire, and the light outlined her form to perfection. Her breasts were trembling, nipples already hard, and with her hands clenched at her stomach, they made a perfect arrow to the soft triangle of curls that covered her sex.

He resisted the urge to throw aside the restraints and simple fuck her hard and fast against the nearest wall, but only barely. Instead, he moved toward her.

"You should remain naked the entire time you're here," he said with a soft chuckle. "At my utter command and for my pleasure."

She laughed, though the way her cheeks darkened and she shifted, he could see the suggestion aroused her.

"What would the servants say, my lord?" she teased.

He arched a brow. "They could watch for all I care."

She shivered and he smiled. Oh yes, he had guessed her little voyeuristic secret. Whatever she had seen while at Vivien's had made her long to watch and be watched. He rather liked that very wicked streak in an otherwise upstanding young woman.

He was about to introduce her to another.

"Lie down," he encouraged.

She smiled and took a place on his bed, propped up on his pillows so she could watch him as he moved around the room. He moved toward the bed and leaned over her, pressed a hard and fast kiss to her lips.

She jolted in surprise at the forceful embrace but melted into him. Her hand fluttered as she began to lift it to cup the back of his head, but Andrew didn't allow that. Instead he slipped the restraint first around her wrist and then around the subtle hidden hooks built into his bed.

Lysandra yanked her head back and stared, first at him, then at her bound wrist.

"What are you doing?" she asked, her voice a little shrill with surprise. She reached to remove the bind with her free hand, but he caught it.

"*This* is what I mean by control," he said, massaging her palm gently. "And you may want to learn how to accept being dominated, for your lover may wish to do so."

Her eyes went wide, clear with fear.

He shook his head. "I won't hurt you. I promise you that this will feel very good. For a very long time."

She shivered, but shook her head. "And how do I know whoever is my permanent protector will not take advantage of me in this position?"

He flinched. He hated to think of any future protector in Lysandra's life.

"I-I'm certain Vivien will think of someone who would never be anything but mindful of your pleasure. No matter how he obtains it."

A series of heated images bombarded Andrew. Of Lysandra spread out for another man, some libertine who would tap into her secret pool of wickedness. Of that man tasting her, taking her, tying her, feeding her desires and introducing her to new ones. The pictures in his head were both troubling and utterly arousing.

She stared at him. "You have a very dark look in your eyes."

He smiled as he restrained her opposite wrist. "I have very dark intentions."

CHAPTER 22

*L*ysandra opened her mouth, unsure of how to respond. The idea of being at this man's utter mercy was a highly arousing one. And terrifying. In truth, she had been at his mercy from the first moment she saw him. But this...

This would take that control to its very end. What if she lost herself entirely? What if she broke every rule she was meant to keep?

"You will do as I ask," he said, interrupting her thoughts with equally disconcerting words. "You will not argue. You will put all of your faith in me. And I will offer, in exchange, pleasure."

She swallowed. She was tied now. There was no going back. And he was right that another man might demand this. At least she trusted Andrew to take her to this place without taking advantage of her weakness.

"Yes," she whispered.

He grinned and for a moment she had a flash of the rake he claimed he had once been. What a specimen he must have been then. Any woman would have begged to take her place.

But *she* was here and that gave her a bit more confidence than she had felt a moment before.

"I'm going to pleasure you," he explained as he moved over her.

"And you are going to say nothing. The moment you speak, I stop. The moment you moan, I stop. The moment you cry out, I stop. Do you understand? Your pleasure is mine and I will tell you when it's time to release it."

She bit her lip and opened her mouth to speak, but he held up a hand. "Starting now."

She snapped her jaw shut and glared at him. Then she nodded, wordless.

He climbed onto the bed and straddled her, trapping her in with a hand on either side of her head. He was still dressed as he loomed over her, emphasizing his control in this situation and her decided lack of the same.

He leaned over her with another heated smile. She arched as far as the binds would allow, leaning up to accept his kiss, but he dodged her.

"Tsk, tsk," he purred against her ear. "You are not in control. Just surrender, Lysandra. Surrender and let this happen in its own way."

She stared at him. He couldn't understand what the idea of "surrender" fully meant to her. There was more at stake for her than her body. Her heart was involved in this relationship now. Her mother was right. She was in love with this man. And surrender meant fully accepting that and all its consequences, as well as his body.

And yet she said nothing as he nuzzled her neck, nibbling her skin gently as he moved toward her ear. He nipped there, a touch harder and a mix of pleasure-pain whooshed through her body, settling between her legs to make her clit throb and her pussy wet. She gasped and he pulled back.

"No sound, Lysandra."

She bit her lip as the truth of what he wanted to do settled in. This was to be torture by pleasure. And she shivered at the very idea.

He moved down her body inch by slow inch as he tasted every part of her. He sucked her neck once again until the burn of pleasure bordered pain, but this time she only arched slightly. She managed to swallow back her cry of pleasure.

He smiled against her skin. "You're learning. Very good."

When she didn't respond, his smile turned to a chuckle as he traced her collarbone with his tongue. She tensed again. Had she always been so sensitive there? There was no answer to the question, though. Andrew was already dragging his mouth lower, lower until he positioned himself between her breasts.

He licked her there and her sex squeezed in response, almost like his tongue had found a home between her legs instead.

He took his time at her breasts, teasing a trail along the swell of one but not quite sucking the nipple, and then retreating to repeat the action on the opposite breast. She squeezed her eyes shut as she fought not to beg him to do more. That would only result in punishment. Withdrawal of his mouth entirely. And at this point, that seemed akin to much greater pain.

He leaned up to look at her.

"You so desperately want to moan, don't you?" he whispered. "For me to suck your nipples."

She nodded as a response to both questions.

"None of the first," he reminded her. "And for being such a good mistress…"

He trailed off and drew one hard nipple between his lips. She shuddered in relief and pleasure as he sucked, sucked harder. Sucked hard enough that her hips bucked and the shadow tremors of an orgasm rippled through her pussy.

Her eyes flew open and she couldn't help her gasp at the sensation. How could she be so close to coming from just his mouth on her breast?

He lifted his head and met her eyes. "So responsive, Lysandra. And normally I like that so much about you. I like hearing you purr and moan. Beg and gasp. When I slide inside of you, there is nothing better than the way you exhale in such pleasure."

She arched toward his words, so sensual. So revealing. She never thought much of her reaction while they made love, but now that she had to temper it, she was fully aware of how often she wanted to cry out, to gasp her breath, to moan with pleasure. She was fully aware of what he did to her that made her do those things.

Now that the power had been taken from her, she wanted it all the more.

He lowered his mouth back to her breast, and her mind emptied. She shut her eyes and simply thrilled at the way he licked her, swirled his tongue around and around her taut nipple, sucked her with pressure meant to tease and please in equal measure.

Then, just as suddenly as he had tasted her, he removed his mouth and glided lower. He licked a trail down her belly, dipping the tip of his tongue into her navel as if it were her slit. She felt him nuzzle her thigh and tensed as she waited for him to taste her pussy.

But he didn't. She opened her eyes as he glided his mouth down lower, nibbling and kissing behind her knee, against her calf, even along her bare foot. Every touch was electric against her skin, sending jolts of pleasure through her entire body. She ached like she'd never ached before. She longed for him to touch her in new ways, to take her body and claim it.

But instead he sat up on his knees, still fully dressed and stared down at her. She leaned toward him, almost against her will, until her arms strained at the binds and her wrists ached from the velvet cutting into her flesh. It took everything in her to remain silent, submissive, but she did it so that he wouldn't take away whatever release she had already earned.

Slowly he lifted his hands and tugged his shirt open. He tossed it on the floor and went to work on his breeches. She stared as his flesh was revealed and realized she'd never really watched the entire show of his undressing. They were always touching, or she was distracted by his kiss. But now she could watch him get naked for her.

And it was amazing. To see that body revealed inch by inch and know it was hers, at least for a while, was a heady thing. He shoved the breeches toward the bottom of the bed and she stared, unwavering, at his penis. It was hard already from his teasing, thrusting against his belly in perfect readiness for her flesh. She lifted her hips toward him in a mute request for him.

He laughed and crawled forward on his knees until he was positioned right between her legs. He cupped her backside and lifted her until her hips rested on his thighs, then speared her with his cock in one long, languid thrust.

She bit her lip until she tasted blood, fighting to keep herself from crying out at the ultimate pleasure of this heated joining. He pulled back, dragging his cock through her heated channel with maddening and utterly satisfying slowness. She felt all of his length so keenly, and she wanted more and more. She wanted him fast and hard, until she couldn't control the thrust of her own hips, until their sweat and their orgasms merged into one like their bodies were merged at present.

Of course that was not the path he took. He held tight to her elevated hips and continued his slow and steady thrusts, building her by inches, rather than by bounds, toward release. When she tried to lift toward him, to force the pace, he held her firm and merely shook his head with a *tsk, tsk* sound in his throat.

"Submit to me," he whispered. "Surrender fully."

She fisted her hands in their bindings. This was her last chance to protect herself, her heart.

She didn't take it. With a shiver, she released all the tension in her body and gave herself over to him. Her body. Her soul. And her love. Her love for him washed over her just as her orgasm did, sweeping her through a pleasure so powerful that it overwhelmed and threatened to destroy her.

And she didn't care. She would rather burn in the fire of her love than to drown without him. Even though this would soon end. Even though he would never, *could* never love her in return. This moment was enough.

He must have felt the surrender and the orgasm that rattled through her because his thrusts grew harder as he guided her through the pleasure.

"Now, Lysandra," he said through clenched teeth. "Let go. Let me hear everything you've held back."

She cried out, louder than ever after keeping quiet for the entire evening. Her body shook from the power of release both bodily and vocally. And when her orgasm was over, she went limp against the pillows, her arms dangling above her in her bonds as Andrew poured his seed deep within her with a cry so loud that it seemed to shake the very room around them.

*A*ndrew rubbed the slight red marks that indicated where the bonds had bitten into Lysandra's skin. She smiled as he kissed each wrist.

"I'm sorry," he murmured. "My intention wasn't to hurt."

She opened her eyes and looked at him through a hooded stare. "I hurt myself," she whispered, and for a moment it seemed like she wasn't only talking about her wrists. "You didn't hurt me."

He pressed her hand against his bare chest and rested his head on the pillow with a contented sigh.

"Why would a man of your kind of power want more control?" Lysandra asked as she smoothed her palm over his chest over and over.

He glanced down at her. "What do you mean?"

She leaned her chin on the top of her hand and said, "I mean that you spend all day running estates, taking your seat in the House of Lords, dictating to servants and tenants, whatever else it is you do..."

He chuckled but allowed her to continue.

"It seems to me that you might not *want* to then continue that utter and complete control in the bedroom with a lover."

"An interesting question," he said, pondering what his answer would be. "Perhaps it is *because* people see men of power as being so in control that we exert it. After all, yes, I spend a great deal of time and energy dictating the way things should happen. And in many cases, it is an exercise in futility. At least when we demand control in a bedroom, it ends with pleasure and not angry words or frustration."

Lysandra seemed to consider that for a moment.

"But wouldn't it be just as much a relief to give over your control to a woman? To let her please you and not have to dictate the terms?"

Andrew wrinkled is brow as he looked at her. Was she suggesting...

She lifted herself slightly and took his wrist. She kissed the inside of it gently and then lifted it toward the bindings that still dangled from the bed. Her gaze held his with every moment and only flitted away when she slipped his hand through the loop and tightened the first binding with a tug.

Andrew stiffened. The idea of surrendering was...odd. Not entirely unpleasant when he thought of how utterly in control Lysandra would be. And wasn't this just as much a part of her training? What if a future lover wanted her to take control? Andrew would be remiss if he never allowed her to try.

He was silent as she moved his opposite hand to the binding and tied him down. He lay there, thinking about how he felt: Out of control. At her mercy. Utterly aroused.

She smiled as she glanced down at his cock slowly easing back to attention.

"How do I put this..." she murmured as she moved to kneel and placed a hand on each thigh. "Come before I give you permission and I shall leave you here all night long and force you to watch me pleasure myself until you are ready to burst."

Andrew's eyes went wide at her unexpected forcefulness.

"Lysandra, you little minx," he laughed.

She didn't join in and it was in that moment he realized she was utterly serious. His cock throbbed even harder at the idea that she would be so...so *bold*.

With a smile of pure wickedness, she pressed her nails against his thighs and gently dragged them downward. Not hard enough to hurt or to mar his flesh, but a sizzle of erotic heat followed in their wake as Andrew's hips lifted.

She looked at him in wonder. "Did I do that?"

He gritted his teeth. Her innocence mingled with her wickedness was something that could make a man burst on its own.

"That and much more," he said, his voice strained. "As you can see, I'm already ready for you once more. It's like I'm a randy schoolboy with his first lover."

Her smile turned soft and shy. "Because of me. Truly?"

He laughed. "How else can I show you that is true except to tell you to finish what you've started. If you are going to steal my control, Miss Keates, please do it."

She looked at him for a long, charged moment and then leaned down to cup his cheeks. She kissed him, pouring every ounce of passion into his body, like she could revive him in some way. Truth be told, she *was* reviving him, bringing him back to life with every touch, every kiss. It might be against his will, but it was happening nonetheless.

She pulled back and smiled as she straddled his lap. His cock nudged her entrance, and she sighed as she reached between them to position him properly. She leaned back as he slid home in her sheath and shivered from head to toe.

He wanted so badly to reach for her. To guide her strokes, to lick and kiss her while she fucked him to oblivion. His tied hands prevented that and kept her in control. To his surprise, he rather liked it. All he could do was feel in this moment. So he leaned back and enjoyed just that.

Lysandra leaned back, pressing her hands on either side of his legs as she stroked over him again and again. Her head dipped back as she groaned and moaned with pleasure. Her throat constricted as she neared climax, the fine veins there becoming far more noticeable as she edged toward release.

And then he felt her pulse around him as she thrashed out pleasure with long, heavy thrusts of her hips. She dragged the sensation over his cock until he could take no more of the magnificent torture. He came a second time with a grunt of pleasure and smiled as she fell against his chest.

She reached up without looking at him and released his wrists so that he could wrap his arms around her. Their bodies were still molded together, their breathing slowing to one shared breath. In the semi-darkness of the chamber, he held her. Something had shifted since their arrival in the country. Something that changed everything.

But he wasn't going to think about that. Not now.

CHAPTER 23

*L*ysandra sighed as she pushed away her plate from a well-earned late breakfast. She had spent three days of utter bliss with Andrew, giving and receiving such pleasures that her body seemed to constantly hum with desire and release.

Best of all, and perhaps most dangerously of all as well, was that unlike in London, where Andrew had put up walls all around himself, here he was open with her. They spent nights talking about any manner of books, music, diversions of all kinds. No topic was taboo, save one.

She didn't even try to ask questions about Andrew's past anymore. Hester's words about Rebecca and an unborn child hung between them during their happiest moments, silently mocking Lysandra with her questions and fears.

But she held them back. For him. Because he had asked her to do so. And since she had admitted to herself that she loved him the first night they arrived, she had come to accept that fact. She loved him and this was what he needed.

Now if only she could ignore how much that hurt.

A young maid swept into the room to clear her plates away. She smiled up at the girl.

"Thank you...Polly, isn't it?"

The girl blushed with pleasure at her recognition. "Yes, miss. You have a good memory for the servants. We've all commented on it."

The blush that stained the girl's cheeks was now mirrored on Lysandra's at the compliment.

"I once worked at a house, though not so great as this," she admitted, for she had decided not to hide or be embarrassed by who she was or who she had been. Andrew's opinion of her was all that mattered at any rate.

The girl lifted both eyebrows in surprise. "Then you do know."

Lysandra laughed despite her discomfort. "Oh yes. *I* know."

The young woman set the tray she was holding aside and edged closer, apparently encouraged by Lysandra's friendliness or perhaps that fact that she had no rank and had once served just like this girl.

"Miss," she said, looking over her shoulder with a guilty glance. "I-I wanted to say something to you. Something we all say below-stairs, but no one has told you."

Lysandra stiffened. She wasn't certain she *wanted* to know what the servants were saying about her passionate, and often *loud*, love affair with their master.

"Yes?" she asked on the barest of whispers.

"I grew up here, you see, in this estate. My mama is one of the senior maids. When I came of age, Lord Callis hired me so that I wouldn't have to leave her side or my home."

Lysandra nodded. That kindness seemed exactly like something Andrew would do. But what it had to do with her, she had no idea.

"What I'm saying is that I've known him since before...and after the—*the tragedy.*" The girl blinked as if simply saying those words made tears sting her eyes. "And he seems happier now, with you here, than he has in an age."

Lysandra bit her lip. She had been nervous at the idea of servant gossip because she was certain it would be about her affair with Andrew. Or her history. Or her clothing. Or a dozen other things she'd heard servants pick apart like vultures as soon as the doors were closed.

This she had not been expecting.

"Oh, I see," she whispered.

The girl nodded, swiped at the tears that had now begun to roll down her cheeks, and continued, "We were all so worried about him after Lady Callis's death. Especially when he tried to—"

The door to the dining room opened and Berges burst in. His face was red and his eyes dark with something very close to anger.

"Polly, cease your wagging tongue," he snapped out in a dark, no-nonsense tone that made even Lysandra flinch like she'd done something wrong.

The girl sucked in her breath through her teeth, grabbed her forgotten tray and rushed from the room with a clatter of plates and silverware.

Lysandra flopped back in her chair with an exasperated sigh. Once again, she had been effectively shut out of the truth about Andrew's wife and his past. All she got were tantalizing bits and hints, but no resolution.

"I apologize, miss," Berges said, still standing in the doorway. "Polly is a young, boisterous woman and often speaks out of turn. She should not have been so bold with you, and she will be reminded of such from both her mother and from me as soon as I have a moment."

Lysandra got to her feet. "Oh Berges, don't be too hard on her. She's a friendly girl, that is all. And because I was once…in a similar position to hers, I think she felt a kinship to me. That might have loosened her tongue a bit more than if she were speaking to a lady far above her."

He pursed his lips. "Yes, but in the future she may wag her tongue at someone far less understanding and that could cause problems not only for the household, but for Lord Callis. Most of the women who will visit here will be ladies."

Lysandra flinched, and Berges dropped his head. "I'm sorry, miss, I didn't mean to offend."

Lysandra waved off the comment. "I know you didn't. And you're right. Ladies will visit here far often than women like me. Samuel Callis's future wife or…or even someone Lord Callis, himself woos in the future with a mind to marriage. Someone more like his late wife."

The butler lifted his gaze and held hers evenly. From the expression on his face, he knew where she was going with this.

"Yes, miss," he said softly.

"What happened?" Lysandra asked quietly. When he turned his face, she continued swiftly. "Please tell me. If I knew, it might enable me to help Lord Callis more while I remain here."

Berges was silent for more than a minute, pondering what she had asked of him. Then he shook his head.

"There is part of me that would like to tell you, miss," he said with a sad sigh. "Because I think somehow you *could* help him. But a servant of my rank only has one thing to recommend him and that is the trust of his master. If I betrayed that, I would betray everything I am. Everything I promise to be. It isn't my place."

Lysandra smiled at him. She liked this man a great deal and while his denial frustrated her, after serving in a household herself, she also understood his reasoning.

"I do apologize," he said.

She shook her head. "No need to do so, Berges, I shouldn't have put you in such an awkward position. The fact is that if I want to know something about Lord Callis, I suppose I must demand that knowledge from him. Anything else is unfair to everyone."

He looked at her, and she realized it was probably more directly than he had ever looked at a houseguest in the time he'd been a servant. "You are a good woman, Miss Keates," he said softly. "A fine *lady*."

She smiled, knowing this was his way of showing her respect. Something she appreciated greatly. "Thank you."

"Miss, I truly hope you find the answers you're looking for." He nodded his head slightly and then left the room.

Lysandra paced to the window. After two days of rain, she and Andrew were to share a walk together in just a few moments and once they were alone, she was going to finally push him on the subjects he avoided. It was time for the truth to come out and those answers Berges had spoken of to be found.

It was past time that Lysandra stopped being a warm body to fill Andrew's bed and started being a true mistress and partner to him.

One thing Andrew had come to appreciate about his relationship with Lysandra since their arrival at Rutholm Park was that they could share a comfortable silence as easily as a passionate kiss. Except today, as they strolled arm and arm through the rose garden, Andrew didn't feel comfort in the silence between them.

He felt anxiety from Lysandra in the way she held herself, in the way she shot him side glances every few seconds. There was something going on with her, something she hesitated to tell or ask him.

And that just wouldn't do.

He stopped and motioned to a secluded bench at the back of the garden. The trees around them and the trimmed bushes that walled in the garden itself, both offered them some privacy in case a gardener or some other servant approached.

"Shall we sit for a moment?" he asked.

She hesitated and then nodded. "Yes, that might be best."

Once she had taken her place beside him and smoothed her skirts, he reached out to take her hand.

"Something is obviously troubling you, Lysandra," he said, smoothing his thumb along her hand until she shivered. He smiled. So utterly responsive.

But this wasn't about making her shiver, it was about determining what made her so nervous. Had someone in his household said something to her? Or had a letter from her mother upset her? He needed to know so he could deal with that. Help her.

"Andrew," she said softly. "Since my arrival here...no, it was before that."

She bit her lip and he leaned in closer. "You can tell me anything.

Did someone say something to you? Has your cousin bothered you or your mother?"

"No, this isn't about me," she breathed. "If it were, I think it would be easier. You would be open with me about that. You would assist me, whether I asked you to do so or not. But when it comes to you..."

She trailed off and he frowned as he pulled his hands away from hers slowly. "Me? What about me?"

Lysandra reached out and caught his fingers, drawing his hands back into her lap and holding them gently. "Andrew, from the first moment I met you, I was struck by not only your handsomeness, not only the fact that you make me weak to you...but that you carry a grief with you no one can touch."

He flinched and tried to pull away, but she held tight and forced him to remain by her side.

"Please, let me say this," she encouraged. "Not only that, but it is clear that others who love you see your pain, as well. It hurts them, just as it hurts me, to see how much you hold that grief in your heart. But there's more. What you feel, it also *frightens* them."

"Ridiculous," Andrew interrupted and yanked himself away from Lysandra to pace a few steps away. He couldn't be close to her when she was violating his request that she refrain from broaching these personal topics.

She followed his pacing with her stare for a moment and then shook her head.

"No, it isn't ridiculous. Your brother had not just pity or pain, but *fear* in his eyes when he looked at you that night at the opera. And I've seen it again with your servants here." She grasped her hands together in her lap. "Andrew, I've heard a tiny bit from you and even more from the servants."

"You shouldn't pry," he snapped as he turned on her.

"I didn't," she retorted, and finally the heat of her voice matched his. "Damn it, *you* brought me here. You brought me to this place you shared with Rebecca. To a place where I would see her pictures and interact with her servants. You brought me here and you must have known that being here would give me more information and more questions all at once. I think you did that on purpose so that these secrets you carry so heavy in your heart would finally be purged."

Andrew glared at her. "What could you be going on about? I don't want to speak about this, why would I purposefully expose you to it and hope that you would ask me?"

"Perhaps you don't *want* to speak of it."

Lysandra stepped toward him, slowly like she was moving on a skittish horse. Slowly, she lifted her hand to his cheek. The warmth of her touch moved through him, soothing him in ways he didn't like to consider.

"Andrew, I think you *need* to talk about it. With someone who wasn't there during the worst time of your life. With someone who is here for your pleasure and for your pain. A mistress. Me."

He stared at her, horrified by the fact that her accusations, which he tried so hard to deny, might actually be true. Had he brought her here on some deep, secret level, in order to confess his soul? To use her to heal in a way he denied he required? Was it possible?

"So please tell me, *why* is there fear in the eyes of those who love you?" she whispered. "Why do the servants whisper of a child your wife looked forward to bearing? Why do they speak of something you tried to do that horrified them?"

Andrew couldn't move. He couldn't speak. Images bombarded him. Memories long sunk away so deeply that he prayed he would never feel their effects again.

"You can trust me," Lysandra said, smoothing his cheek as she looked up at him with eyes so dark blue that he could lose himself forever. He *could* trust her. He had been denying he wanted to for weeks, but there it was. She was here, for him. And he suddenly wanted to confess the things he had buried deep inside.

"She was pregnant," he said, choking on the words. "Rebecca was almost six months along the night..." He stopped because the words were impossible. "We argued. It was over something foolish."

"What?" Lysandra asked softly.

He shut his eyes. "When she told me she was with child, I panicked. I had given up the life of a libertine to be with her and I knew that a child would change even more between us. Change *me* even more. I had gone out a few nights in a row with old friends who were visiting the shire. She wanted me to stay with her. I wanted to, that's the worst part. But we argued about my 'freedom'. I left and within an hour a servant rushed to find me, to tell me that my wife was gravely ill. I came home to discover she had begun bleeding. The baby was coming, far too early, and there was nothing the doctor could do to stop it."

She shut her eyes. "Oh, Andrew, but that wasn't your fault."

He shook his head. "Wasn't it? She asked me to stay. Perhaps if I had, I could have done something. Or perhaps she would have been calmer and she never would have become ill."

Lysandra's pity was written all over her face. The same pity he hated from everyone else who looked at him that way. He didn't deserve it. He deserved their hate. Their judgment.

"The baby didn't survive?" she whispered.

He shook his head. "My son didn't even cry. He was gone before he even had a chance to take his first breath. And my wife's bleeding couldn't be stopped. She died alongside him within half an hour of his birth."

Lysandra finally moved on him, reaching to take his hand. He pulled it away. He didn't deserve to be comforted.

"Andrew," she whispered. "These things sometimes happen. For no reason. With no fault, as much as we want to find someone to blame."

"She needed me, and I let her down," he said, his tone filled with the pain he had kept inside for three years. "I knew it. I felt it in my very soul. I dreamed of her for years afterward, and I felt her hatred toward me in those dreams. And so I—"

He broke off. He had never said this out loud. Not to anyone.

"What did you do?" she whispered.

"The reason that those who love me look at me with fear is that two and a half years ago, I tried to end my life."

He let out a long breath. To his surprise, it was almost a relief to say it. Oh, others had tried to talk to him about what he had done. The physician. His brother. His father. His friends. But he had always put them off, not fully denying the attempt, but never admitting it either.

"Andrew!" she cried out, taking a staggering step backward as her face twisted in horror. "What did you do?"

"Drank myself nearly to death." He swallowed hard. "And then took a pistol and fired it at my head. Only, a drunk is a bad shot. I winged myself, nothing more."

He lifted up a section of hair to reveal the white scar that marred his scalp near his temple. Lysandra swallowed and tears began to sparkle in her eyes as she looked at the evidence of the depth of his despair that night.

"I would have shot again, finished the job, but Berges, who was meant to have the night off, had actually come home earlier than I thought. He heard the shot, wrestled the gun from my hands and had a footman call for the doctor while he sat on my chest to keep me from getting to the weapon again."

Lysandra's eyes were wide as saucers, not that he blamed her. What he described had been quite a scene, indeed. He remembered chaos, blood, screaming...

"And what did you feel about that?" she pressed. "Him saving you?"

He blinked. No one had ever asked him that question before. Everyone talked to him about what he should or shouldn't have done. They told him he was lucky to have lived at all, which was true. But no one had ever asked how the thwarting of his attempt on his life felt to him that terrible night.

"I was angry for almost six months," he admitted slowly. "I almost sacked Berges a handful of times for his interference. He refused to leave."

Although the tears still ran down her cheeks, Lysandra actually smiled. "And then?"

He sighed as he retook his seat with a thump. "I realized that had

I succeeded, all I would have done was hurt my family even more than they were already hurt by the loss of Rebecca and the baby. It was a selfish inclination that capped off a life filled with selfish inclinations."

Lysandra made a face as if she didn't entirely agree with that assessment and then said, "And there is the fact that your life has value and shouldn't be wasted."

"Yes. I suppose there is that, too." He shrugged. He still wasn't entirely certain that her reason existed.

She wiped her tears away and then stared at him for a long, appraising moment.

"I am glad you did not succeed," she said softly. "And you don't wish to do such a thing again, do you?"

"No. Not anymore." He was surprised that those words were true. He had said them before, of course, to others, even to himself. But never had they been truer than when he looked at this woman.

She smiled at him and his heart stuttered. He turned away and stared at the flowers again. He recognized this feeling growing inside of him. He had felt it once before. It had driven him to change everything about himself. It had made him a better man, albeit utterly briefly.

It was love.

He had sworn never to love anyone ever again and he'd meant it. Even if he hadn't, a man didn't love his mistress. Well, some men did, though it inevitably led to problems with second families and scandal.

Certainly, *he* didn't love a mistress. Especially a temporary one like Lysandra. She would leave him in a short time, move on to another man who she would likely be bonded to for years. He had to let her go for her own good, as well as his.

He turned back and offered her both an arm and a false smile. "Come, let's go back up to the house. I find myself tired."

She nodded, but as she slipped her hand into the crook of his elbow, she leaned up to kiss his cheek. "Andrew, I'm happy you told me. I know it was difficult, but I'm glad you trusted me to enough to share this with me today."

He nodded, though he didn't have enough confidence in himself to speak. Slowly, he led her back to the house. Once inside, he pressed a kiss to her cheek.

"I need to take up an issue with Berges. Will you excuse me for a while?"

She looked at him, uncertainty on her face. "Are you angry with me?"

He touched her face. "No. Far from it."

She nodded, though her eyes said she didn't fully believe him. "Perhaps I'll read for a while up in our chamber."

He nodded and watched as she moved up the stairs and down the hallway. Once she was gone, he walked to the little set of stairs that led down to the area below the kitchen and main living area of the estate.

He found the butler in the small room that he called an office. A cramped, but highly organized space Andrew had always admired. From here, his servant ruled the house like a mini-king.

"Hello, my lord," the servant said, removing his spectacles and rising to his feet when Andrew entered. "I wasn't informed you had returned from your walk with Miss Keates. I apologize that you had to come searching for me."

Andrew waved off the apology and shifted uncomfortably.

"Had I heard that Miles...er, the Marquis Weatherfield was visiting his brother in the shire?"

The butler's brow wrinkled, and Andrew didn't blame him for the confusion. Weatherfield was one of his old cronies from the days before his marriage. His younger brother owned a stretch of land in the shire, which was how they had met. But the man hadn't darkened his doors for years because he had been one of the friends Andrew went out with the night his wife died.

"Yes," Berges said slowly. "I heard something to that effect through gossip."

Andrew nodded. There was no relief that what he'd heard was true. And yet he pressed on.

"I see. Send word to him, will you? I'd like to see him tomorrow, if possible."

The butler nodded, his motions once again slowed with confusion. "Yes, sir. Of course, sir. I will send a message to their manor right away. Is anything...*wrong*, my lord?"

Andrew hesitated. Everything was wrong. What he was about to do was wrong. But it was the only answer.

"No," he said as he turned from the door. "Nothing. Let me know when you have a response from him. Good day, Berges."

Then he left the servant and went to find Lysandra. Tired or not, he wanted to spend every moment he could with her. Before everything changed.

CHAPTER 24

*L*ysandra was seated at the dressing table in the room adjacent to the bedroom. She was staring at her reflection, but not with seeing eyes. Her mind drifted to everything Andrew had said to her that day. Every emotion that had darkened his eyes and his mood.

And then there was the confession of his desperate suicide attempt.

She shivered. The very idea of it made her sick. Sad. And so desperate to save him, even though he didn't seem to want to be saved. He wallowed in his pain, his grief. He tortured himself, just as his brother had said at the opera that night that seemed a hundred years ago.

And now she knew why.

Suddenly, Andrew strode in, slammed the door behind him and crossed the room, his eyes boring into her. She got to her feet in an instant, ready to greet him, though she had no idea what to expect from him with that expression on his face.

"And—"

She didn't get any further. His mouth crushed against her, his arms came around her, and he dragged her up and against him with so much force that she could scarcely breathe. His mouth assaulted her, his tongue driving hard between her lips, his lips bruising. But she opened to him, as she always did and gave herself over to the hard, demanding kiss. There was something so passionate in it, so...desperate.

She drew back with a start. That was it. There was desperation to his kiss, to his expression as they stared at each other in the firelight.

"Andrew?" she whispered.

He shook his head and began unbuttoning her gown. "We've talked enough, Lysandra."

She stared at him as he worked on her dress, his gaze focused entirely on his task. Something had happened since they returned to the house. But what? Or was he simply digesting what had happened between them in the short time they'd been apart and was panicked by it?

She opened her mouth to speak again, but he cupped her face for another heated kiss. This time he was gentler, but it took an effort for him to be so. All that desperation was still present in his kiss, along with all his desire for her, all his attempts to give her as much pleasure as he could.

He had done as she asked and told her the truth. If a heated coupling was what he needed in response to that then she wasn't going to deny him. In truth, denying him was impossible, so she relaxed against him in utter surrender.

At that, he pulled away, slipped his hands beneath the opening in her gown and stripped it from her shoulders. Her chemise followed and soon the entire contraption of her dress was on the floor, leaving her only in her stockings and slippers.

She moved to remove them, but he shook his head.

"No, I like you like this," he murmured before he began removing his own shirt. She reached up to help him and soon he was as naked as she was. As ready as she was.

He kissed her once more, and as he drove his tongue into her, he lifted her up, cupping her against him as he carried her backward toward the wall next to the fire. Her back hit the hard surface, and she wrapped her arms around his shoulders for balance.

They were eye to eye now, and he held her gaze as he lifted his hips and glided into her waiting body.

Lysandra's eyes went wide. She had never considered that sex might be possible like this. But it felt like heaven. Wicked heaven filled with utterly fallen angels, but heaven nonetheless.

He pressed one very gentle, almost chaste kiss to her lips and then began to drive, pounding her against the wall with fast, hard thrusts of his hips. He pushed her toward orgasm with a drive, a desperation and a violence she'd never felt before. She couldn't fight it. Not when he was hitting her clit with every thrust of his hips, not when his hard, heavy cock slid inside her so perfectly.

She came within moments of his first thrust, but he didn't slow his pace, not even as she cried out her release. If anything, her orgasm seemed to encourage him. He cupped her tighter, gasping each time he thrust into her, the muscles in his neck grew tight, his face reddened, and then he cried out.

"Fuck!"

His come splashed hard and hot into her, sizzling across her overly sensitized flesh and making her pussy ripple with the last echoes of pleasure. He tipped his head forward, resting his forehead against the wall beside her, as his panting breaths slowed to normal.

"Andrew?" she whispered.

He glanced at her briefly, then carried her, their bodies still tangled together, to the bed. He laid her down there, covering her with his warmth and began to kiss her again with just as much abandon as if he had never fucked her against the wall in an animal display of lust.

Lysandra knew she should stop him. She should demand why a few moments apart had inspired him to such a desperate, heated display of passion. But she couldn't. Not when he was beginning to move inside her a second time, not when he was holding her so tightly she could believe it would last forever.

Instead, she kissed him back, pouring her passion and love into him and hoping it would be enough to fix whatever was broken inside of him.

*a*ndrew rubbed his eyes before he began to pace his office a second time. After a night of pure passion with Lysandra, one where he had made love to her again and again and yet still hadn't purged the desire to do so from his body, he was exhausted. Yet he had to be his best, his most awake, because Weatherfield would be arriving any moment.

What was he doing? Why had he invited a long-former friend to his home? The idea, which had seemed so right the day before, now seemed more and more idiotic with each passing moment.

But it was too late to stop the tide. There was a rap on his door, and Berges appeared.

"Lord Weatherfield, my lord," he said as he opened the door a fraction to reveal his old friend.

Miles was a handsome man. Tall, with dark hair and darker eyes that Andrew had heard women swoon over endlessly. The two men had been friends since their teenage years, rampaging through the countryside looking for girls to debauch and trouble to cause. They had even shared a woman or two during steamy nights of passion.

"Callis," his friend said as he stepped into the room, hand outstretched. "Good to see you, friend."

Andrew swallowed hard and took the offering. "Yes, good to see you, as well. Here, sit. Would you like a drink?"

His friend lifted both eyebrows. "No. Not of whiskey, at any rate."

Andrew shrugged. "Tea, then? Or coffee?"

"No." Miles leaned back in his seat to stare at Andrew. "You look well. Better than the last time I saw you."

Andrew wrinkled his brow. "When was that?"

"Passing by in London probably two years ago. You didn't see me, that was clear. Hell, I don't think you saw anything around you." His friend shook his head. "Dark times."

Andrew shifted. His old friends had all been permanently ousted from his life after the death of his wife. He hadn't realized any of them gave a damn anymore.

"Well, it was a long time ago."

"I hear a woman may be part of the change," his friend said with a teasing smile. "If that's true, I would damn sure like to meet her. She sounds like a miracle worker."

Andrew shifted. He wasn't about to get into the subject of Lysandra, not yet. The very idea that anyone was talking about her... talking about *them*, gave him great pause.

"Thank you for coming on such short notice," he said instead, as a way to change the subject.

Not very subtle, as Miles gave a slight, knowing smile.

"Well, I do love my brother, but he and his wife are utter bores. And to be honest, I was quite curious when I received a message on your behalf."

Andrew tilted his head. "Curious?"

"Oh yes." Weatherfield leaned forward. "You must know why, Callis. After all, you haven't spoken to me since...well, since Rebecca's death. Then you made it very clear that you wanted nothing to do with me or any of our old friends."

Andrew shifted. He *had* lashed out at anyone close to him in the weeks following her death. Especially the friends he had been drinking with the night of her death. Like Miles.

"I apologize for that," he said softly.

His friend shrugged. "You weren't yourself, and for good reason," he said. "But to have you suddenly reach out to me, ask that I come see you, I couldn't resist that mystery."

"You've obviously heard I have a new mistress," Andrew said, shifting.

"Oh yes," Miles laughed. "It's all the talk. The questions abound. Will you return to your old ways? Who is this girl who tempted you back to wickedness? Why is your father stomping around in a rage about it at every party?"

Andrew squeezed his eyes shut. Yes, those were the very questions he had hoped to avoid. And yet now he was the center of a mild scandal.

"She isn't permanent," he said softly, but he couldn't help but think of Lysandra, naked on his bed. Lysandra, holding his hand as they strolled through the gardens. Lysandra, talking to him long into the night about books or the current state of the middle class in London. All those things felt very permanent.

His friend tilted his head. "I-I don't understand."

Andrew sighed. "It's a long story. Let me tell it to you."

*L*ysandra took a moment to check her reflection in the mirror in the hallway before she went to Andrew's office. She hadn't expected to be called to see him after he claimed he had work to take care of in the morning. But the fact that he had demanded she join him made her think that perhaps a passionate little interlude was in order.

She smoothed her hair and her gown with a smile, then continued up the hallway to knock on his door.

"Enter," came his voice, but she frowned at the tone of it. Very serious.

She walked inside with a smile meant just for him, but skidded to a stop. Two men were inside waiting for her. One was Andrew, but the other man who stood up from the seats before the fire and turned to look at her was one she didn't recognize. He was devilishly handsome, though, and he looked her up and down as if appraising a sweet treat he was thinking of buying.

She shifted in sudden discomfort.

"I apologize, I didn't realize you had company," she said, then hastily added, "my lord."

Andrew motioned her inside with a pinched expression that seemed as uncomfortable as she, herself, felt. "I wanted you to meet my friend, Lysandra. Come in."

She stared at him for a moment. Although he had taken her to the opera in London and introduced her to his brother, Andrew had made it very clear that she was to be kept separate from most aspects of his life. In all truth, she had always thought he had few friends, spurning the ones he'd had before Rebecca's death and never bothering to make new ones.

"Please," he encouraged quietly.

She reached behind her to shut the door and stepped forward to the two men.

"This is Lysandra Keates," he said to the stranger. "And Lysandra, may I present the Marquis of Weatherfield."

She swallowed as the Marquis held out a strong, ungloved hand.

"Miss Keates," he said softly. "Callis has been telling me a great deal about you. I'm more than pleased to make your acquaintance."

"Th-thank you, my lord," she said, taking the hand he had extended. He pressed a kiss to her knuckles that warmed her hand and felt entirely inappropriate, though not unpleasant.

She shot a glance at Andrew. His jaw was tight and a look of grim determination lined his face.

"Won't you join us, Lysandra?" he asked, motioning to the chair he had vacated.

"Of course," she said, sitting.

Weatherfield took the same place he had had before, in the chair beside hers, but to her surprise, Andrew took one halfway across the room, folded his arms and simply watched them.

"Andrew tells me you are a new convert to opera," Weatherfield said, snagging her gaze with his. It was very focused. Very dark. She could well imagine many a lady had lost herself in it.

She nodded. "Y-yes. I *did* enjoy the show we saw while in London. I can see why it is such a popular diversion."

"There is a great deal of passion in opera," Weatherfield said softly. "Or at least I have always believed that."

Lysandra sent another look Andrew's way. Was another man supposed to talk to her of something so intimate as the subject of passion? It seemed quite bold to do so with her lover sitting not three feet away, watching them. But Andrew said nothing. He did nothing. He just continued to stare with that sour look on his face.

"I-I can see how that point of view would be valid, my lord," she said.

The other man smiled, but she could see that he was searching her face, examining her on a level that went beyond mere interest in a friend's companion. But why?

"You are a very pretty woman," he mused.

Everything became clear in that moment. She jerked her gaze to Andrew, but he wasn't looking at them anymore. His was staring at his hands, clenched in his lap. His hangdog expression told her everything she wanted to know. He had brought his friend here to... to...declare her as open season for a protector. Weatherfield was being groomed for that position and she had been invited to the room to be examined like cattle at a market.

She swallowed hard, then straightened her shoulders and lifted her chin. She would not allow this humiliation to break her.

"Thank you, my lord. I appreciate the compliment." She turned toward Andrew. "Might I see you on the terrace for a moment, Lord Callis?"

Andrew jerked his head up in surprise. "I—"

She turned back to Weatherfield. "You will excuse us, just for a moment, won't you, my lord? I have a sudden need to discuss something of importance with Callis."

Both Weatherfield's eyebrows lifted, but then he chuckled. "Of course, Lysandra. I will wait here patiently for your return."

She got up, snapped her skirts into place and marched past Andrew to the doors out to the terrace. Without waiting for him, she stormed onto the wide stone patio and then turned to watch him follow her. He shut the door and crossed to her.

"What is it?"

"You are selling me off to your friend?" she snapped.

He frowned. "Mind your tone, Lysandra, you'll bring the house down."

"That isn't a damn answer, Andrew," she said, though she did temper her voice. No use letting the other man hear everything she was about to say. "Did you bring this man here in order to offer me up, like you are some kind of...of...mistress matchmaker? Like Vivien? Because I hadn't realized that was a business you were interested in pursuing in your spare time."

Andrew flinched but didn't stop looking at her. "Lysandra, we both know this affair is swiftly coming to an end. I simply want to make sure you are taken care of when our time together is done."

She stepped forward, her hands trembling, her lips trembling. "Why?"

He looked at her in confusion. "I don't understand."

"Why do you feel this sudden drive to foist me off on a new man?" she asked, her voice rising again, despite her attempts to control its level.

He shook his head. "I'm not foisting you off. We both know that I cannot provide what you need." He turned his face. "What you deserve."

Lysandra pursed her lips, but remained silent, too afraid to speak for fear she would reveal far, far too much.

"And I worry about you and your future," Andrew continued. "I've been thinking about it for some time now. I want to be sure you are with a man who will treat you well, who will take care of you and your mother. If that is all I can give you, I want to make sure I do."

She fisted her hands at her sides and tried not to feel the shattering of her heart. Impossible. It ached in every part of her. She had been a foolish mistress and fallen in love with this temporary protector. Now she suffered for it as keenly as if he had stabbed her in the chest without regard for the lifeblood that would spill out on the stone terrace.

"I see," she said, her tone curiously flat when she felt so much high emotion on the subject. "And you think this man, Weatherfield, would be the right man for me."

He shrugged. "As much as he is considered a rake, he is also a decent man. He will think of your comfort and your...your pleasure."

Lysandra squeezed her eyes shut. Were they truly having this conversation? Was this truly what their affair had come to? Or was this all a nightmare?

But when she opened her eyes she was still standing on his terrace, looking at a man who seemed sick with the idea of what he was proposing. However, he made no effort to back away from it.

She nodded. Then this was his choice. Very well.

"I suppose I should thank you for going to all this trouble to ensure my comfort and my *pleasure*." She sighed. "But I think if this is the path we are now taking, I should move out of your chamber into a separate one of my own, as you offered when I first arrived at Rutholm Park."

He tensed. "And what if I want you in my bed?"

She stared at him, filled with disbelief and even more humiliation. "You would continue to take me, even while this other man decides if he wants to...to woo me to him?"

Andrew swallowed. "It isn't entirely uncommon."

"How comforting," Lysandra said, her voice as cold as an icy dawn. "Well, then you can call on me and I will fulfill whatever duties I still owe to you. Will that suit you?"

He folded his arms. "Lysandra—"

"I should go back inside," she said, turning away from him.

"Why?" he asked, his voice cracking.

She looked at him over her shoulder. "If I'm to determine whether I want to put myself in this man's bed for months, perhaps even years, I should put myself to the task. I assume he will only be here for a short time."

With that, she strode back into the office and the man who awaited her there. And left behind the one she loved, the one who refused to keep her.

CHAPTER 25

The supper had seemed like a benign enough idea when Andrew suggested it. But he had underestimated Weatherfield's single-mindedness when it came to his interest in a mistress, and Lysandra's focus when she put her mind to a task was equal to the Marquis'. Now the two sat close together at the small table, talking as if Andrew were not even in the room at all.

"Four horses?" Lysandra burst out with laughter at some silly story Weatherfield had been telling. Andrew hadn't been listening, but he doubted it deserved so much mirth.

"Yes, and I swear that the poor groom must have run five miles that day trying to catch them." Weatherfield chuckled.

"Miles," Lysandra said, wiping her eyes with her napkin. "That poor man!"

Andrew tensed. She had called Weatherfield by his given name, an intimacy that meant a great deal to men of his station who were usually addressed by their title or simply "my lord". Anything more was a privilege.

He fisted his napkin in his hand and shoved back from the table with a screech of his chair. "I think perhaps we should retire to the parlor for drinks," he said with a forced smile that he was certain resembled a grimace more than anything else.

The other two glanced at him like they had forgotten he was even in the room.

"I suppose we have been finished with our meal for some time," Weatherfield laughed. "I had quite lost track thanks to my charming companion."

Lysandra blushed like a schoolgirl, and Andrew's stomach turned. Thank God he hadn't eaten much of that supper to begin with or it would be roiling most unpleasantly.

"Yes, well…" he began, moving around the table toward Lysandra.

"May I escort you?" Miles asked her before Andrew could reach her side.

Andrew shook his head. This was quite enough. "I think I shall take her," he snapped.

Lysandra stared at him, her face pinched with anger and frustration, though he wasn't certain if that was because she so desperately wanted to hold on to Weatherfield's arm or that she was still angry at Andrew. He found himself wishing for the second as he reached out his elbow toward her.

She sent Weatherfield a slightly apologetic glance, then slipped her hand into the crook of Andrew's elbow and let him lead her from the dining room with Weatherfield trailing behind them at a polite distance.

"Seems as though you are no longer so hesitant about the idea of a new protector," Andrew said, his tone tight with emotion.

She refused to look at him as they entered the parlor.

"Just remember that this was *your* idea, Andrew. And who am I to question my betters? After all, once a mistress loses her protector, she must find another. This is what you wish me to do, for you no longer want me." She shrugged as he let him go. "So please keep your judgmental tone to yourself."

Andrew heard the pain in her voice as she turned on her heel and crossed back to Weatherfield at the fire. He had hurt her, as he always seemed to hurt her, but Lysandra was a resourceful woman.

It was all but programmed in her to make the best of the worst situations. Something he admired except for this moment when making the best seemed to mean turning all her considerable wiles on Weatherfield. It was evident the other man was already quite taken with her.

And that meant she would be in Miles's bed, and out of Andrew's life, in record time.

He poured himself a drink and downed half of it before he turned away from the poorboy and found Weatherfield and Lysandra both staring at him. His friend cleared his throat and said, "Miss Keates, it's a lovely night. What do you think about taking a stroll out on the terrace with me to enjoy the moon?"

Lysandra hesitated a fraction, which made Andrew's heart swell with pleasure. At least she was still a little bit torn about what was happening. But the high emotion faded the moment she smiled.

"Yes, I think that would be lovely." She glanced at Andrew. "As long as Lord Callis doesn't mind that we are abandoning him for a short time."

Andrew bit his lip. He could refuse. But that would effectively end Weatherfield's pursuit of Lysandra. A short-term win for him, a long-term loss for her. As much as it pained him, he found himself nodding.

"Y-yes," he choked. "A fine idea, indeed."

Lysandra stared at him for a fraction too long, but then she dipped her chin and took Weatherfield's arm, disappearing out onto the terrace with another man. And all but disappearing to a new life where Andrew would no longer be able to call her his own.

*L*ysandra could hardly keep her breath as the terrace door closed behind her and left her alone with Lord Weatherfield. Not only was she with a man who would possibly be her next protector, but Andrew had sent her here, practically wrapped her as a gift for Miles.

A fact that made her want to cry, even though she didn't do so.

"Ah yes," Miles said as he guided her to the edge of the terrace and leaned against the wall there. "Our moon."

Lysandra glanced up and a bit of her tension faded. It was a beautiful night. The moon was full and big in the sky, casting a glow down on them that was, by all accountings one could make, very romantic.

"Do you want to talk about the real reason I am here?" Miles asked her softly.

Lysandra stared at him for a brief moment, then swallowed hard. "Is that what happens next?"

He nodded. "I think for us, it should. Clearly you know that Callis has asked me here because you will soon be in the market for a new protector. And perhaps I am the man for that most pleasurable job."

Lysandra shifted. Miles was very different from Andrew. Andrew was reserved, almost swept away by desire he did not want. But this man...he was something different. There was an attitude about him of pure confidence. And he didn't seem the kind who would apologize for what he wanted or felt.

"I must let you know," she said on the barest of squeaks, "although I have been...er...*trained* on the subjects of desire, I have little experience. I wouldn't want you to be disappointed once you made a bargain with me or feel that I, or Andrew, tried to trick you into taking something you did not expect."

Miles's eyes grew wide and he edged closer to her. "You are a very unique woman, Lysandra."

She looked at him, framed by moonlight. He was so different from Andrew. Almost his polar opposite in looks, where Andrew was blond and with bright eyes and Miles dark as a more moonless night.

But she couldn't deny Miles was wickedly handsome. And she was, to her shock, attracted to him.

"Is unique a bad thing?" she whispered.

He smiled. "Oh no. Not at all."

He moved closer again and tilted his head as he lowered his lips to hers. Lysandra sucked in her breath as he brushed his lips over hers and then gently probed her lips with his tongue. He tasted of mint and a faint hint of whiskey. A pleasant, masculine combination. But she hadn't expected to be kissing another man on Andrew's terrace, of all places.

She had to admit, though, the experience was not unpleasant, and soon her body took the control her mind could not. She slowly glided her hands to Miles's forearms and held there, as close to an embrace as she could manage in this moment. She tilted her head and granted him greater access to her mouth while she parted her lips and darted her tongue to meet his in an erotic, slow dance.

He made a sound of desire deep in his throat and to her surprise, her body reacted even further. She felt her nipples tighten against the silk of her gown. Her sex grew wet, and a dull, familiar ache began between her legs.

She didn't know if Miles sensed that shift in her desire or if he merely wished to test her willingness to express it, but he moved his hand, which had been resting against her hip, slowly upward until he cupped one breast.

She arched her back at the intimate touch, even as her mind raced with thoughts of Andrew. Andrew doing the same thing, Andrew making love to her sweetly, violently, pleasuring her.

She moaned against Miles's lips and he strummed a thumb against her nipple as she swayed closer to him. When they parted, she looked up at him.

There was no doubt a man like this would give her security and pleasure. Clearly, her body would and did react to his touch. But when she stared at him, she felt none of the complex feelings that Andrew inspired. There wasn't even a twinge of feeling that stirred her soul. She liked him, insofar as she knew him, but that was all.

And perhaps that was what she needed. To forget Andrew. To nurse her broken heart back to something that would never again be so foolish as to love a man who was incapable of returning that feeling.

"What do you think?" Miles asked.

She blinked, clearing her head of the wayward thoughts that troubled her. "Think?"

"You are staring at me with a most appraising gleam in your eyes, I can only guess you are rating my kiss, my touch, and I am more than curious about what your conclusions are. Am I the kind of man you could take as a lover?"

Lysandra swallowed. This frank talk was not something she was yet accustomed to, but this was the life she had chosen and she had to adapt.

"I think it's clear that we could be...good together in very important ways." She blushed, and he chuckled.

"Oh yes, that is *more* than obvious to me." He became more serious. "I know your mother is a part of your life as a mistress. Andrew tells me she has been put up in a home and I will pay for her upkeep, as well as generously provide for your own. If you are interested in leaving your current position, that is."

Lysandra hesitated, then shook her head sadly. "I believe that decision is entirely out of my hands. And I need a protector, so if you are willing to become that to me, I think we would be a good fit."

He leaned down and brushed his lips back and forth against hers a second time, sending shocking desire through her already humming body.

"I look forward to testing that fit very soon, Lysandra," he murmured against her mouth. "But I think for now we should return to the parlor. Andrew and I will have much to settle. I return to London tomorrow. Will you want to travel with me, or wait a few days to..." He trailed off. "Finish your business here?"

Lysandra froze. Tomorrow? So soon? Part of her wanted to cling to this place. To what she had shared here with Andrew. But in truth, wouldn't that hurt even more?

She sucked in a ragged breath and said, "I think I should return with you, Miles. There is no use dragging out the inevitable."

He looked at her for a long, charged moment and then nodded. "Very well, then, Lysandra. I will take care of the arrangements. Now let us go inside."

She took his arm, but as they turned toward the parlor, she couldn't help but blink at tears that stung her eyes. Tears she refused to shed. She couldn't afford the pain they would bring.

*A*ndrew stood at the window, staring out onto the terrace from a darkened room down the hall from his parlor. In the moonlight, he could clearly see everything Lysandra and Miles were doing. And he hated it.

They were talking so close and then the moment he had been dreading happened. Miles kissed her.

Andrew leaned closer to the glass, his breath short as he watched their kiss deepen and its passion intensify. He jolted as he realized that this moment of voyeurism wasn't only inspiring anger, as he expected, but something more. He was growing hard as he watched the woman he had bedded so many times that he'd lost count become aroused by another man.

A thousand questions rolled through his head. Was she wet with desire? When Miles glided his hand up to cup her breast, did her gasp sound like it did when he did the same thing?

Worst of all, was she thinking of *him* as they gently ground together in a precursor to a bedding? He wanted to go out onto the terrace and touch her as Miles kissed her. To physically imprint himself on their relationship so that he would always be a part of it.

But although he and Miles had shared women before, often during very drunken nights half a dozen years before, he didn't think he could manage that now. Not with Lysandra. Not with someone he cared for so deeply.

They were talking now, their bodies still touching, their heads close together, and the desire Andrew felt faded to nothingness. The passion he could take. That was Lysandra's body. But this intimacy in the way they spoke was proof that he was going to lose her.

Soon.

They turned toward the door and he scurried to get back into the parlor where they'd left him, but his mind was racing.

What would he do when Lysandra was gone?

CHAPTER 26

*A*ndrew could control a great many things about his emotions. He'd had plenty of practice in doing so since the death of his wife. But as Lysandra and Weatherfield walked into the parlor from the terrace, he was fully aware that his expression was of anything but friendliness. He felt angry and he was sure he looked the same.

Not that Lysandra even noticed. She hardly spared him a glance as she wandered, wide-eyed, away from Weatherfield and took a long, bracing sip of brandy from her abandoned glass.

Weatherfield watched her as closely as Andrew did, and with as much concern on his face.

"My dear," the Marquis said before Andrew could speak. "You look tired and with good reason. You've had a most trying night. Why don't you go up to bed? It won't offend us."

Andrew clenched his fists as his sides. Who was fucking Weatherfield to order *his* mistress up to bed?

Lysandra didn't have the same reaction. She sent Andrew the briefest of glances and then nodded. "I am tired. Good night to you both."

She turned on her heel and left the room without a second look at either of them. Andrew stared at her, using all his self-control to keep his jaw from dropping open.

"I have to admit, I'm happy to see you so emotional," Miles said as the door shut behind her and they were left alone. "Even if that emotion is anger toward me."

Andrew glared at him as he picked up Lysandra's abandoned glass and swigged her remaining liquor. He could see the mark where her lips had been and placed his own mouth there as the good-night kiss she had not given him.

"Look at me all you like," Weatherfield said with a shrug. "But it's clear you'd very much like to pound my face into oblivion right now. Though I don't know why."

"Don't you?" Andrew snapped as he slammed the glass down on the table hard enough that a crack splintered up the side of the tumbler.

Both men stared at the broken glass, but then Andrew continued.

"You take *my* mistress out on the terrace, accost her as if I'm not standing just in the next room, and then send her off to bed like she's already yours? How should I react?"

Weatherfield arched an eyebrow slowly. "Is this not why you brought me here? I thought you made that very clear to me today. You told me, point-blank, that you were finished with her and you thought we would make a good fit. Obviously, I must test that notion before I simply accept her as my mistress. We must have attraction. We must have some kind of connection beyond attraction."

Andrew pursed his lips. Very true. Except that didn't matter when they were talking about Lysandra.

"You could have been more discreet," he muttered.

Weatherfield laughed. "A weak argument, indeed. Would you have preferred that I sneak up to her chamber tonight? I could. I heard her tell you to move her out of yours."

Andrew squeezed his eyes shut to keep from seeing only posses-sive, red rage. He liked Miles. Or he had a long time ago. And he *had* called him here to do exactly as he was doing. But at this moment, he could not help but think of all the places he could bury the man's body on his estate.

He rubbed his eyes to clear his thoughts.

"You know me," Weatherfield said softly. "I would never pursue a woman you were truly interested in. I would never take a woman you cared for. So the question is, do you want her or not?"

Andrew stared at his friend. "Yes. *No.*"

Miles sat down and pulled a cigar from his front pocket. "Very clear, my friend." He shrugged. "Look, you have buried yourself out here for years. I don't think you want to bury her, too. You've asked me to offer to be her protector, and I have done so. I will take care of her and her family...if you tell me that is what you want. But make up your mind. I leave for London tomorrow and I'll take her with me."

Andrew flinched. Tomorrow. Dear God, he hadn't thought the end would come so soon. That he would be forced to surrender her within hours.

"Now it's time for me to return to my brother's estate. It was good seeing you. Let me know by tomorrow after luncheon what your decision is." His friend pushed to his feet and moved for the door, pausing only for a brief clap on his shoulder. "One way or another, you have to figure out a way to let this woman go. *If* that is truly what you want."

Andrew grunted something, perhaps goodbye, though he no longer heard his own voice, and Miles slipped from the room. Andrew stared at the fire. Let her go. Yes, that was what he had to do. But she was his for one more night.

And he intended to enjoy that fact.

*L*ysandra sat at the dressing table in her chamber. Not Andrew's chamber where she had spent her time here on his estate. *Her* chamber where her maid had led her when she called for her.

It was very nice. And very lonely. But that was how it had to be. What Andrew very clearly wanted.

She pushed to her feet and began to pace the small chamber. She was exhausted, but her mind raced with images of Andrew. With images of Miles. With images of a foggy future she had allowed herself to hope would include the first man, but now would center around the second.

Funny that if she had begun with Miles, she knew she wouldn't dread a new life with him. But since she had begun with Andrew, loved Andrew, years of passion with another man seemed...*wrong*. And yet that was exactly what Andrew wanted her to do.

"Impossible," she muttered as she rubbed a hand over her tired eyes.

The door behind her opened and she turned, expecting to see her maid back for some reason. But it wasn't her maid standing in her door. It was Andrew, his shirt half open, his breathing heavy, his hair and eyes wild as he gripped both sides of the door and stared at her with heated, angry eyes.

She stepped back and swallowed hard, not because she feared him, but because the sight of him made her love and want him all the more.

"Andrew?" she croaked out.

He stepped inside and slammed her door behind him. "I'm pleased you remember my name at all," he said, his tone ugly.

She refused to flinch. "This is what you wanted, what you demanded," she reminded him softly. "To survive, I must do this. Do not mistake my acceptance as pleasure."

He arched a brow. "There seemed to be a great deal of pleasure when you were kissing *him* on my terrace...letting him fondle you."

She narrowed her gaze even as her heart leapt to her chest. "You were watching us?"

He shifted, but then nodded. "Why shouldn't I? This is my house and you are my mistress."

She hesitated. His anger proved he wasn't any more pleased

about this than she was, but he still was ready to let her go even though he had every power to keep her.

"No." She folded her arms. "I don't think I ever was. From the first moment you touched me, you were preparing to let me go. You have never thought of keeping me beyond a brief affair that you always told me was just for 'training'. I was never yours, Andrew. So you don't have a right to be angry that I will now be someone else's."

He stared at her. Just stared. Almost as if she had spoken some obscure foreign language or danced in the middle of the room like a heathen.

"You were never mine," he repeated, low and dangerous.

She shook her head. "No."

He was across the room before she could even draw her next breath. He caught both her arms and hauled her against his chest. "It certainly felt like you were mine when I did this."

He dropped his mouth to hers for a punishing, passionate kiss. She should have pulled away. After all, she had made an agreement with Miles not an hour before. But she didn't. Andrew's touch, his kiss, the idea that she could love him one last time before she lost him, was too intoxicating. She lifted herself closer, wrapping her arms around his neck, driving her tongue against his in a violent dance of desire.

He shoved her backward until her backside hit the high edge of the bed. Her nightgown tore beneath his fingers, and she was naked in an instant, fabric fluttering around her feet as he unfastened his trousers. His hard cock pushed free and he lifted her, wrapped her legs around his waist as he pushed home deep within her channel.

They cried out in unison, but he gave her no time to adjust. He plowed forward, slamming her against the bed, digging his fingers into her hips to keep her steady as he took and took and took. She writhed against him, reaching for pleasure, stroking her clit against his pelvis until the electric hum of pleasure exploded. She dropped her head back as she cried out his name in the silence of her chamber.

He grunted out his own release, pouring his seed deep inside of her.

They flopped backward on the bed together, his head against her naked breasts, his cock still buried in her twitching sheath. There was nothing but silence between them for a long while. Long enough that Lysandra began to wonder if he had fallen asleep in this awkward position, half on and half off her bed.

"Tomorrow Weatherfield is going to come here and collect you," Andrew said softly.

She blinked as tears stung her eyes. "Yes," she whispered. "I know. We talked about it."

He lifted his head. "You did?"

She nodded and braced herself for renewed anger. Instead, he cupped her face gently. "Come back to my room. Please. Let's spend this last night together, in my chamber."

She hesitated. How lovely that would be. But if she went to his bed, spent a night in his arms... How could she leave?

She shook her head. "No. We probably shouldn't have gone as far as we have already. If I go back to your bed—" She broke off. What was she going to say? That she loved him? There was no point in it. "Well, tomorrow will be much harder. Let us just say good night."

He stared at her, and she could see that he wanted to argue. To demand. Instead, he nodded slowly.

"If that is what you need, I will do my best to give it to you."

He rose to his feet, separating their bodies, and buttoned his fly as she watched him. She sat up and gently cupped his face.

"Andrew, you must know," she whispered, "you always gave me what I needed. I haven't forgotten that. I won't ever forget it."

He stared at her in the firelight, opened his mouth as if to say something and then shook his head. He bent to kiss her one more time, then left the room. Left her.

And she knew it was over. So she curled up on her lonely bed and finally let her tears fall.

. . .

*L*ondon hadn't changed. Lysandra knew that was true. But it felt different. Truth be told, she knew exactly why. *She* was different. She would never go back to being the woman she'd been before she turned to Vivien. Before she found Andrew and fell in love with him. She felt it keenly when she visited her mother, who frowned at her with concern. When she supervised the removal of all her things from the home Andrew had provided for her and almost sobbed as she bid farewell to the servants she had come to know there.

She felt it now as she stood in the parlor of a new home, just as nice as the one she'd been given by Andrew, and waited for Miles. Miles, her soon-to-be new lover and protector.

She swallowed past a suddenly full throat and walked to look outside at the gardens below.

"You can do this, Lysandra," she whispered so that she might start believing it. "You must, so you will."

Behind her, the door opened, and she turned to watch Miles stride into the room. He smiled at her, utterly handsome in his perfectly tailored formal attire. But there was only the barest twinge of appreciation in her heart. Instead, anxiety clutched at her, whispering, "This is it. This is it," over and over until she feared she would go mad from it.

"So you are settled," Miles said as he looked around him with a satisfied expression.

"Yes," she squeaked, then cleared her throat. "Yes. Thank you for all your help in making the arrangements. It went as smoothly as could be expected."

"Excellent," Miles said, though he didn't really seem interested in the subject. It was more polite conversation than a true interest in whether or not her move had been a pleasant one.

"The home is lovely," she said, searching for something to fill the awkward silence between them and perhaps put off the inevitable.

"Yes, it seems to be. My solicitor suggested the neighborhood."

He looked at her, searching her face for what seemed like forever. Then he held out a hand to her.

She hesitated before she moved across the room and took it. She looked up at him, knowing what would happen, knowing her traitorous body would probably enjoy it. Knowing her heart would break during every moment.

He lowered his lips to hers and kissed her. He was gentle, coaxing as he parted his lips and tasted her mouth for what seemed like an eternity. She relaxed, mostly because pleasure was not something she could easily control, and lifted one hand to his chest to fist it there.

He drew back, looking down at her. And then he utterly shocked her by stepping away and releasing her hand.

"Lysandra, there isn't going to be an affair between us," he said softly.

Her breath seemed to stop entirely and her eyes widened until she was sure she resembled some kind of hideous bug as she stared at him.

"What?" she blurted out when she could find enough air to speak.

He tilted his head and smiled, gentle and indulgent, as if she were a child he had to explain something complicated to.

"You and I could never share an affair." He shrugged. "I think I realized it the night we kissed, but tonight... Well, it seals that suspicion."

Lysandra rushed toward him, taking the hand that had held hers a moment before. "No, please, Miles. What can I do to change your mind? What have I done to displease you already?"

He lifted her hand to his lips and held it to his heart. "My dear girl, there is nothing you have done wrong. But there is something you've done. You love someone else. You love a man who was once someone I called my best friend."

She jerked her hand from his and stumbled away from him a step. "N-no," she lied and knew that there was no confidence to her tone or her words. "Don't be ridiculous. Of course I don't love

Andrew. He was my protector, that is all, and for such a short time that it was…it was meaningless."

"You are so pretty when you lie," he laughed. "But you are not particularly good at it. Your honesty reads all over your face."

Lysandra snapped her mouth shut. "Damn," she muttered.

"How long have you loved him?" he asked.

She glanced at him. She didn't feel right talking to this man about Andrew, but who else could she turn to? Who else knew the facts of what had been shared between them?

"A while," she admitted. "But it is folly, surely you know that. He does not love me."

To her surprise, Miles shrugged a shoulder almost as if he took issue with that statement, but said nothing.

"Even if he did *want* me on some level, he made it clear he has no interest in pursuing more with me. That was made clear when he dragged you out to his home and practically shoved me into your carriage."

Miles frowned. "It may appear that way, yes, but I can tell you that Callis took no pleasure in that moment. I thought he might kill me that night when we kissed on his terrace."

Lysandra blushed as she thought of what had happened after Miles left. That angry taking that had been the last time she and Andrew touched. Would be the last time they *ever* touched.

"He does care for you," Miles said softly.

"But not enough," she said with a shake of her head. "And I am left still needing a protector."

He touched her chin and lifted it so that she was forced to look at him. "Perhaps that is true, but it cannot be me. I am many things, but I'm not so cold that I would do that to a friend."

"Even though he asked you to do so?" she pressed, hoping to find something to say to change his mind.

He smiled. "I meant *you*. You, my friend."

She couldn't help but return his smile and reached up to cup his cheek before she turned away with a sigh.

"I suppose I will need to find some other place to stay," Lysandra mused.

At least now she had a few baubles to sell, and Andrew had paid for her mother's home for six months in advance. There would be a good while for her to find another man, and perhaps Vivien would help.

"No," Miles said, interrupting her train of thought. "You will stay here, just as we arranged, until you find another man to move on to. And if that proves difficult, I promise you I will begin telling tales to the right people about how you wear a man out. Coming from me, that will have fifteen prospects banging down your door, demanding you come to them. It will be a bidding war before we're finished."

She laughed, although the thought of being sold off to the highest bidder gave her no pleasure.

"That isn't fair to you, though," she insisted when the moment passed.

"Hmm," he mused. "Well, I would say there is a great deal that isn't fair to *you* in this situation. Let me take a bit of it from you, will you?"

She hesitated and then nodded. "Very well, if you insist that this isn't an inconvenience."

"I do." He leaned down and kissed her once more. It was on the lips, but he no longer urged her to part them, he no longer tasted her. "And I am sorry you are hurt."

She shrugged as she backed away. "I cannot afford to be hurt." She smiled at him.

"You know, my dear, my only regret is that I think we would have been very good together," he said as he offered her an arm to take her to the supper that her servants had prepared.

She smiled. "Yes. I think you might be right. We could have been very good together."

CHAPTER 27

*A*ndrew had spent the past few years hiding away in the country. He had always been comfortable there, wallowing in the place where he had gained and lost so much. Hating himself in peace. But now, with the departure of a woman who never should have been there in the first place, everything was different.

Rutholm Park seemed cavernous, empty and he could find no comfort there anymore. So much so that less than a week after Lysandra's departure in Weatherfield's carriage, he had followed in his own, back to London and a life he hoped he could find there.

A life without her.

He would try not to think about the fact that she was comfortably situated in Weatherfield's house for her now. In *his* life. In *his* bed.

That was why he had come out, after all. To forget. He had been invited to his brother's home in order to meet his fiancée at last, but his ill humor hadn't allowed him to fully participate in the small party of just a few friends. He stood back as his brother chatted with friends and Adela flitted from group to group with a smile and kind word for them all.

It all seemed like it was happening in slow motion, or that he was watching the scene through a glass. Because all he could think about was Lysandra.

Andrew stifled an angry growl and slugged back his drink.

"Are you quite all right?"

He glanced up to find Adela coming across the room toward him with a concerned expression on her pretty face.

"Yes, Lady Adela," he forced. "Of course."

She frowned as she stopped in front of him and slipped a stray lock of blonde curls behind her ear. "It is only that you have a very... stern look on your face. We haven't had much of a chance to speak tonight, I hope that fact doesn't mean you disapprove your brother's choice."

Andrew drew back, partly due to Adela's boldness in approaching the subject so directly, partly out of horror that his attitude could be misconstrued in such a way.

"Oh no, my lady," he insisted. "I promise you that my mood is not caused in any way by a poor reaction to you."

She smiled with a hint of relief, but he could still see her hesitance about him in her eyes. He didn't want that. His brother would marry this woman and his brother was one of the few people Andrew knew he could depend upon in any situation. If Adela didn't like him, or feared he didn't like her, it could affect and change his relationship with Sam...and not in a positive way.

He pushed thoughts of Lysandra as far back into his mind as he could and refocused on the lady before him.

"I have been watching you tonight," he said, "Even if I have been too absorbed in my own little troubles to speak to you at length. In fact, I much approve my brother's choice of bride. You are obviously a fine lady and a good match."

She smiled, though it wasn't an entirely happy smile.

"And there is the fact that I love him," she added gently.

Andrew looked at her closely once again. She was a direct person. He found he rather liked it. In many ways, that quality reminded him of Lysandra.

"Yes," Andrew said softly. "Which could very well be the most important, and most overlooked, quality that recommends you."

She shifted. "You lost your wife, and it was a love match, was it not?"

Andrew clenched his fists. Just a few weeks ago, this question would have ended the conversation. But things had changed for him since then. He slowly nodded, forcing himself to stay.

"Yes," he all but whispered.

"Then you know how rare and valuable love is," Adela said with a long gaze in his brother's direction. There was nothing but utter devotion on her face. True love that, in that instant, Andrew envied. Adela could love Sam, marry Sam, freely.

"I do know," he said. "Cherish it every moment."

"I intend to do so," Adela said with a quick blush and a glance back at him. "I have always been of a mind that if one is so lucky as to find something as rare as love, especially in our class where marriages for money or rank are so valued, one should hold on to it at any cost."

Andrew flinched. He had found love not once, but twice. Once he had lost it. Last week he had thrown it away like it was garbage. And now her words stabbed at his heart and made him hate himself in all new ways.

"Yes," he said slowly. "But what about love that is considered inappropriate?"

She smiled, and it lit up her face. Andrew could see why his brother was so besotted.

"How could love be wrong or inappropriate?" she asked.

He couldn't help a smile of his own. This woman was bright and beautiful, but perhaps a bit naïve. "Come now, my dear, you must realize that it could be. Let us say that I decided to...marry someone utterly inappropriate tomorrow. A woman of no rank. Perhaps a woman with a low reputation due to...circumstances out of her control. Can you truly say that you wouldn't have to reconsider your marriage to my brother since my scandal would affect you and your reputation?"

He blinked. He had just described a marriage to Lysandra, at least on the surface, though he hadn't added that the woman in question was beautiful and funny, kind and sweet, perfect in every way to him and for him. He hadn't mentioned that he loved her with everything in his soul.

Adela stared at him as if he had sprouted a second head, and Andrew's heart sank. For all her grand notions about love, of course she would want to avoid a scandal caused by him.

"I don't even understand the question," she finally said. "Why in the world would I leave the love of my life just because *you* married a woman?"

"The scandal," Andrew repeated. "Would it not run rampant in the circumstances I described?"

Adela pinched her lips, pondering the question he had asked. "Before I answer that, I need more information."

"Very well."

"Firstly, the woman in this scenario, you say she is of no rank, but her low reputation comes from circumstances out of her control." She frowned. "Is she a good woman?"

"Very," he said, his voice growing low. "The very best."

Adela stared at him for a long moment and then nodded slowly. "I see. And is she of intelligence and wit?"

He nodded. "Yes."

"I suppose the most important question comes next. Do you love her?"

"I do," he answered before he realized that they were no longer talking hypothetically.

They looked at each other for a long moment. Adela's brown eyes were soft with understanding as she said, "Then I would say to you, bring on the scandal. It sounds like this woman would be a good friend to have. Someone who has come through heartache and maintains wit and charm is far more interesting than someone who has been kept on a pedestal all her life." Adela touched his arm briefly. "If you love her, don't think of reputation or rank or anything else but your heart, Andrew. Follow that and it will very rarely steer you wrong."

Andrew looked at this woman. She had been protected her entire life, sheltered by a duke for a father, groomed in the ways of Society, and yet she was so much more. She was teaching him a lesson and offering him a strange permission to love Lysandra.

He shook his head. "Well, if she existed, then I suppose I would have to follow your advice."

Adela was quiet for a long moment, and Andrew jolted as he realized that she *knew* about Lysandra. Sam must have told her all about their night at the opera before Andrew took Lysandra to the country and ruined everything. Adela knew exactly what Lysandra was and she still told him to follow his heart.

She smiled. "Well, if we are only having a broad debate on the subject, then you know my stance. And I look forward to these conversations throughout our years as family. I can see you and I will have spirited debates regularly. I shall have to study up on my current political and social matters before we tackle the next one."

Andrew smiled as she squeezed his hand, then his brother approached and the topic mercifully shifted. But even as he attempted to engage himself in the party more fully, he couldn't help but have his thoughts turn back again and again to Lysandra. Until he brought up the topic with Adela, he hadn't fully realized that he didn't want Lysandra as a mistress. He wanted her as a wife.

But he had lost her…given her away, actually. He had no idea if he could win her back, especially now that she was in an arrangement with another man. But he had to try. Only if he was going to do that, he had to come to her at his very best. With all the reasons she would refuse him resolved. And with his heart on his sleeve the way he had avoided for three long years.

In short, he had some work to do.

. . .

*L*ysandra turned the pages in the copy of *Debrett's*, which Vivien had brought over to her the previous day. After a lengthy explanation of what had happened with both Andrew and Miles, during which Lysandra was certain that the courtesan knew she had fallen in love with Andrew, Vivien had agreed to help her find another match. The copy of *Debrett's* was so that Lysandra would know the men who would be coming to a party that very night, men who might be the ones for her. Vivien had even helpfully circled the top candidates and made notes in the margins as an accommodating guide.

Lysandra's head spun and her stomach turned as she read about each gentleman and tried to picture herself surrendering to one of them. Some faceless man with a title who would take her on as a burden in exchange for... Well, she knew exactly what it was in exchange for.

She shivered as she closed the book and paced to look at the fire. Its proximity did nothing to warm her and she was about to return to her distasteful reading assignment when the door to her parlor opened.

She turned to find a man standing there who she did not know and her new butler, Adams, standing behind him.

"I'm sorry, miss," the servant said weakly. "He was insistent."

The stranger turned and glared at her butler. "Get out."

Lysandra froze, and fear gripped her. Not because some stranger had burst into her home, was dismissing her servant and had God only knew what plans for her...but because as soon as he spoke, she knew he wasn't a stranger at all.

Adams scurried from the room, and the man closed the door and turned to glare at her. She straightened her shoulders.

"You must be the Earl of Sutherland."

He arched a brow in surprise. "And how do you know that, chit?"

She shrugged. "You look like your son. You sound a bit like Andrew, as well."

More than a bit on both accounts, actually. The older man had the same blond hair, the same strength to his tone as Andrew did. And, of course, she had seen his picture in Andrew's gallery.

He nodded once. "You are correct, Miss Keates, I am *Lord Callis's* father. I came to the home he purchased you in Bikenbottom Court first and was surprised to hear that you had departed there. But I suppose a woman of your ilk has no thought about moving on to the friend of her once protector."

Lysandra pursed her lips. "I see. And what ilk is that, my lord?"

His eyes grew wider at her question and perhaps the very calm way she delivered it, which made her happier than it should have.

"A whore, Miss Keates."

She shut her eyes briefly, then opened them to look at him evenly. "If that is what I am, and if I am no longer affiliated with your son, then why did you come here?"

"Because ever since Andrew returned to London he has been moping about, mooning over you, apparently. I came to your home there to pay you to leave him be. And once I realized you had left his...*employ*, I came here to tell you to stay away."

Lysandra blinked. Andrew was back in London? Even though he hated the city and had fulfilled his quarterly duty to his father? He was so close and yet so far away...

She shook her head. No use pondering that overly much, nor the bewitching idea that he was actually moping around, mooning after her. His father had to be wrong on that account.

"Lord Sutherland," she said softly, yet succinctly. "I have no idea what you have heard about me, but let me tell you, for my own edification, that I am not a whore. I am a woman whose circumstances have put her in a position she never thought she would be in. I am a daughter, a friend, a woman not unlike any in your own life. I was simply born in the wrong part of the city to belong where you live."

Lord Sutherland blinked, but she seemed to have shocked him into silence, for he didn't try to interrupt. Lysandra continued as quickly as she could so that he wouldn't.

"As for your son, I did not leave him. He no longer wanted me.

So the idea that he is mooning over me is a ridiculous one. And I have no intention of any further pursuit of him. My heart has been broken once, I am not so foolish as to put it out on display to be crushed a second time."

The older man's brow wrinkled. "I see."

"Yes. And now I hate to be rude, but since you have been thus far, I would ask you to please leave. You have nothing to fear from me when it comes to Andrew...Lord Callis, I assure you."

She motioned to the door and tensed as she waited for Lord Sutherland to argue with her further. To scold her for daring to rise to his level and try to put him out. Instead he stared at her for a long moment and then gave a brief bow.

"I apologize, Miss Keates. I thought I understood the situation, but I think I see it far more clearly now. You needn't worry about me darkening your door again. Good day."

He turned and exited the room without another word. Lysandra collapsed into the nearest chair as soon as he was gone. What in the world had just happened?

Actually, she could guess it. He had come here thinking he had to protect his son against her, and realized there was nothing to protect. And the idea broke her heart all the more.

She sniffed back impending tears and shook her head.

"No," she said out loud. "I have cried far more than enough. Tonight I *will* go to Vivien's party and I *will* find a new protector. I may not be able to control anything else in this situation, but I can control how hard I try to make a future for myself and my mother." She sighed as she fiddled with the hem of her gown. "Without Andrew."

CHAPTER 28

*A*ndrew shifted his weight back and forth as he waited for the arrival of his host and was startled when he realized he was behaving just as he'd seen boxers in the underground do for years. He was preparing for battle.

And that was exactly what this was. The first skirmish in a war for Lysandra. One he intended to win or perhaps lose everything trying.

The door opened, and he turned to glare as a man he'd known nearly all his life entered. The Earl of Culpepper was a tall man, intimidating in his finely tailored attire and with an air of controlled sophistication about him.

But Andrew no longer saw that when he looked at the man. He no longer saw a figure he respected. He saw only a person who had hurt Lysandra. Humiliated her. Made it his mission to destroy her, just because he could. Just because she had dared to lift her chin and say no to an offer most women couldn't refuse.

In short, Andrew despised the man to his very core.

"Callis," Culpepper said with a thin smile. "What a pleasure to see you. I thought you had gone back to the country after your quarterly visit."

"I had," Andrew said, carefully controlling his tone as best he could. "But I think you knew that, rather than simply 'thought' it, considering the company I took with me."

Culpepper's smile faltered just a fraction and his eyes grew dark with the beginnings of anger. "Ah. So you have come here not for a friendly visit, but with something more specific in mind."

"Yes."

Culpepper took a seat in one of the chairs and waved for Andrew to take the other. He ignored the request and remained standing.

"I admit, I had heard you had struck up some kind of affair with my former employee. I was horrified to think that that wench had taken advantage of you. But now I have also heard that she is no longer living in a home you provide. So it seems you have dodged quite the dose of heartache."

Andrew ground his teeth. "Shut your fucking mouth."

Culpepper flinched, and Andrew stifled an ugly smile. Good, now he had his attention.

"I beg your pardon?" Culpepper asked, rising to his feet.

"Sit down," Andrew said, moving on him. "I highly suggest it."

Culpepper hesitated, and Andrew could see he was debating the merits of refusing Andrew's "suggestion". But in the end, Andrew was younger and stronger, and Culpepper sat back down and folded his arms in petulant anger.

"Explain yourself," Culpepper snapped.

Andrew leaned in closer. "I know what you have been saying about Lysandra. The lies you have been spreading."

Culpepper shrugged. "They aren't lies. The strumpet seduced me and then demanded I give her exorbitant amounts of money to keep her from spreading tales to my wife and anyone else in Society who would listen."

Andrew could scarcely see past his rage. "Ah, you see, I know you're lying. Not only do I know Lysandra, but when she came to me, she was a virgin."

Culpepper hesitated and Andrew almost laughed. The bastard

could hardly imagine that a woman so beneath him could be virtuous. Or innocent. Or anything but a toy for his pleasure.

"Well, I never said we made love," he offered weakly.

"You never touched her, because when you cornered her with your demands, she refused you. And that angered you so deeply that you not only sacked her without reference, but you made it your mission to destroy her." Andrew placed a hand on either arm of Culpepper's chair and leaned in closer. "Isn't that right?"

There was a very long moment of silence as Culpepper struggled with an answer. Andrew held his gaze the entire time, not allowing him to weasel into a denial.

"Yes," Culpepper said on a scarce whisper. "But what right did she have to say no? We're men of power, and she's nothing but a servant."

"She has every right to determine what and who she is," Andrew growled.

He pushed away from Culpepper's chair, mostly because his emotions were so raw and wild that he feared he might actually kill this man if he was so close for too much longer.

"I am about to tell you what is going to happen," Andrew said. "And you are going to bloody well listen and hear me. You are going to stop talking about Lysandra. If her name crosses your lips anywhere, anytime, I will destroy you in every way that is possible. Do you understand?"

"That whore has you under her spell," Culpepper sneered as he leapt from the chair, as if he'd found his courage. "She must be a hell of a fuck, or why else would you defend her?"

Andrew stormed on him, caught him by the throat and smashed him against the wall with all his might. Culpepper's legs dangled and he sucked at air.

"She's not a whore. If I have it my way, she will be my wife and I will protect her with every fiber of my being. Hurting her will be very unhealthy for you."

He dropped Culpepper and the older man staggered to stay on his feet as Andrew walked away from him.

"Your wife?" he repeated, his voice hoarse from the damage to his throat. "Are you serious? You're going to bring that...that *person* into our circles? No. I won't accept that. I'll do whatever I please and make sure she is never accepted by anyone of good Society."

Andrew stepped forward to charge a second time, but before he could the door between the parlor they were currently in and the one next to it slid open to reveal Culpepper's wife. Lady Culpepper was willowy, and she glided into the room with the dignity of a queen even though her cheeks flamed red and her eyes snapped with anger and humiliation.

"My dear," Culpepper choked as he stared at the adjoining doors. "I did not realize you were in the next chamber."

"I'm sure you didn't," she said, cold as a frozen winter. "But I could hear every word you two said. And all it did was verify what I have long suspected about why we've lost so many good servants over the years. Including Lysandra, who I actually liked a great deal."

She shot Andrew a look, but he couldn't read her intentions.

"You may have the title, my dear," she said to her husband softly. "But the money comes from *my* family and a good deal of it remains in *my* control. So I will add my own threat to the one of Lord Callis: if you attack this girl, in private or in public, I will do something about it. And I have the capability to do so. As for her acceptance..." She turned to Andrew with a sad expression. "I think you know it will be difficult for her. But I will certainly try to make her transition into Society as easy as possible if you truly intend to marry her."

Andrew stared at her. He had barely ever interacted with Lady Culpepper, but here she was, offering to help Lysandra. In that moment, she became one of his favorite people.

"I do, if she'll overlook my many faults and take my hand," he said softly.

She smiled and waved him toward the door. "It seems you have someplace to be." She glared at her husband who was still shifting, opening and shutting his mouth like a fish out of water. "I have this situation under control, I assure you."

240

Andrew bowed toward her, then strode past Culpepper without hesitating and toward the door. But as he moved into the foyer, he skidded to a stop. His father stood there, staring at him.

"I heard you," he said without preamble.

Andrew shook his head. "Apparently Culpepper needs to invest in thicker walls. Why are you here?"

His father shifted. "I saw the girl today. Miss Keates."

That stopped any movement Andrew had been making. He stared at his father. "Where?"

"I looked for her at the place you put her and when I realized she was with Weatherfield, I pursued her to the home he let for her."

Andrew rubbed his face. This was it. Any chance he had with Lysandra had to be dashed if his father had gotten hold of her. The amount of damage he could have done might very well be irreversible.

"What did you do?" he whispered.

His father shrugged. "I went there fully intending to pay her off to leave you be. To make sure that she wouldn't take advantage of you. But what I found when I met her was something quite different from my expectations based on the...well, apparently the lies Culpepper told me."

Andrew tilted his head. "So you did hear everything."

His father nodded. "But it was when I told her that you were wrecked, moping about since your return to London that I realized something."

Andrew flinched. That wasn't exactly how he wanted Lysandra to know that he needed her. "What did you realize?"

"As I heard the words come out of my mouth, I recognized that you must care for this woman, very deeply, to be so hurt by losing her." His father sighed. "And I never thought you would or could care for anyone ever again after you lost Rebecca. This woman gave you a gift, a gift of emotion. Of *living* again, not just looking for a way to die faster. And I suddenly appreciated that a great deal."

Andrew stared in utter shock at his father. "I see."

"I may seem too proper for you, but the truth is that I almost lost

you two and a half years ago, and I hated that moment, that feeling."
His father shook his head. "I'm not certain I approve of the plans I
overheard in the parlor. That you plan to marry this woman. But in
truth, I would rather see you chose to live and be happy than see
you proper and alone and desperate. So I will not interfere. I will
accept her. Because..." His father shifted and Andrew saw his utter
discomfort. "I do love you, boy."

Andrew blinked. His father hadn't said such an intimate thing
since he was a child. He knew it, of course, despite his father's
propensity toward propriety over emotion, Andrew had never
doubted his father's love, but hearing it meant something. Knowing
his father was in his corner in this war meant a great deal more.

"Thank you," he said, clapping his father on the back. "Thank
you."

His father shook his head. "I think you have someplace to go."

"Yes." Andrew grew sober. "Weatherfield's house to try to
convince Lysandra to end her affair with him."

His father cocked his head. "Don't you know? After I met with
her, I had three of my best men do some research. They quickly
discovered that Lysandra has not entered into an affair with Weatherfield. But I do believe that mistress woman...Vivien Manning, I
think her name is, will be presenting her tonight at a soiree."

Andrew's heart leapt and sank in the same moment. Leapt at the
thought that Lysandra had never taken her relationship with his
friend so far. And sank because if she was going to Vivien's, it meant
she continued to seek a permanent protector.

"Then I'd best go now. Before it's too late."

His father smiled. "Don't forget, son, it's never truly too late.
Good luck."

Andrew smiled as he departed the house and bounded to his
carriage below. Luck he would need.

. . .

*L*ysandra's body was standing in the ballroom at Vivien Manning's home, but her heart wasn't in this place at all. It wasn't that the gathering was bad. She had imagined so much when she thought of coming here for a ball and to look for a protector. But the music was good, the punch much stronger than in the few gatherings she had attended or served at in the upper class, and the company was friendly.

Yes, there were some shocking displays of passion in the hallway and on the stair and sounds of them coming from parlor after parlor, but Lysandra could see they were displays enjoyed by both parties, so she could look the other way with a blush and a tingle in her pussy that told her she would have plenty of images to pleasure herself by for weeks to come.

As for the company…it was also pleasant enough. Several gentlemen had approached her for conversation, indicating their interest in her if she was interested in return. None were horrible. Many were actually very handsome men with good humor.

Only none of them were Andrew, and that was the central problem. She couldn't think, she couldn't focus, she couldn't begin to imagine starting an affair with anyone else.

"Stupid girl," she muttered.

"Oh, I wouldn't go so far as to say stupid."

She turned to find Vivien approaching. Her friend slipped a hand about her waist and squeezed. "What can I do to make this easier, for I can see it is tearing you apart?"

Lysandra sighed. "Am I that obvious?"

"Only to someone who is more interested in your well-being than your lovely bosom, my dear." Vivien laughed. "So in other words, none of the men will have even noticed your mood."

Lysandra laughed, though the comment made her shift with discomfort. The idea that these men were judging her on her bosom and didn't give a damn about anything above it was not a particularly comforting one.

"You are distracted," Vivien continued. "Why don't you go onto the terrace for a little while? Get some fresh air, though I would avoid the southwest corner...unless you want to watch Sabrina make love to both Lord Nightengale and Lord Jazby."

Lysandra swallowed. Under any other circumstance, she just might go spy on a woman with two lovers. It sounded quite...bracing. But for now, she couldn't think about something so brash when her mind was racing.

"Yes, I think I shall go outside for a bit. I promise to gather my senses and return as a far more pleasant guest."

Vivien patted her arm, then strolled away into a crowd of men who watched her like she was candy. With a sigh, Lysandra slipped onto the terrace. She sent a longing look toward that wicked southwest corner, but then turned to the north, away from the crowd, away from any wicked activities.

She stared up at the stars let out a sigh. On Andrew's estate, they had taken a walk in the moonlight and made love under stars as pretty as this. Would he think of that night the next time *he* looked at the stars?

She heard the faint closing of the terrace door behind her, but she ignored the sound. She didn't want to be disturbed, so perhaps pretending as if she didn't know someone else was with her would be message enough of that fact.

Footsteps moved toward her, but before she could turn, there was a warm chest pressed to her back and arms came around her. She tensed, knowing she should be afraid. Or at least affronted that a drunken partygoer had pinned her like this.

But she wasn't. There was something comforting about this man's touch.

"I hear," he whispered, his voice odd in the darkness behind her, "that you are seeking a protector."

She shivered. "Yes," she managed to squeak out.

"Hmm," he said, though his arms came around her even tighter. "I'm afraid I am not looking for a mistress."

She frowned. What in the world did this stranger mean? "Then why are you accosting me on the terrace at Vivien Manning's? Don't all men come here looking for a mistress?"

He laughed, and she froze. She knew that laugh. Knew it as well as her own.

"This man isn't seeking that. I am looking for a wife, you see."

She spun around and found Andrew standing before her, holding her ever so gently against his chest. Without demand, but also without releasing her.

"Andrew, what are you doing here?"

He lifted one hand to stroke her cheek. "I have loved two women in my life. I lost one through chance and for three years regretted the way I treated her. The second woman I lost through utter foolishness. Fear. Panic. But I wonder if I might be able to get her...*you*...back."

Lysandra sucked in her breath. "Are you...are you saying you love me?"

He nodded slowly, never breaking their stare. Joy flooded her, overcame her, mobbed her with pleasure so intense it was pain. She sobbed out her breath.

"Andrew, you must know I love you," she admitted and adored how his face lit up with a joy she'd never seen from him before. It was a gift and she cherished it. Only she had to crush it. That was clear. "We couldn't marry."

He shook his head. "Why?"

"I'm not of your rank, I'm not of your class, your father despises me, I would create a scandal for you thanks to my former employer, your brother is getting married and his future wife is too important for me to ruin that, I was a mistress—"

He lifted his hand to cut off her stream of reasons they couldn't ever be together.

"Let me address these before you go on to your secondary list," he laughed. "I do not care about your rank, nor your class. I've learned how empty those labels can be. My father does not hate you. In fact, he blessed my desire to marry you this very afternoon."

She blinked in disbelief. "After he came to me, blustering?"

Andrew laughed. "He does bluster, but I assure you he is a good man. And he was impressed both by the way you handled yourself and by the fact that I love you. He wishes for my happiness, and I think he recognized that you are my only path for that to happen."

Tears stung Lysandra's eyes, but she refused to let their joyful streams fall.

"What of the rest?" she whispered.

He laughed. "Where did we leave off? Oh yes, the scandal created by Culpepper." She gasped and he nodded. "Oh yes, I know who he is. He has already been admonished, first by me and then by his wife, who also said she would accept you if you were mine."

"Lady Culpepper?" Lysandra repeated. "She was always so lovely, but I thought—"

"Oh, she is far stronger and much more aware than perhaps any of us, including her husband, gave her credit for. As is Adela, our future sister-in-law, although she may not know the particulars, she gave me quite a lecture about love. I think she would welcome a scandal if it were for a romantic reason like the fact that I adore you."

He bent and pressed a quick kiss to the tip of her nose. Lysandra gasped at the gentle, intimate and loving gesture. He truly did love her. This wasn't some odd attempt just to win her because he was angry or a desire to win something he felt he had lost. He loved her.

Her!

"And then there is the last point you have made," he said with a somber shake of his head. "That you were a mistress."

She nodded.

He smiled slightly. "It has come to my attention, and caused me great happiness, that you have only ever been *my* mistress. *My* lover. *My* love."

"But no one else will know—"

He covered her lips with his fingertip. "Society can hang. I would be happy to squire you away to my country home and make love to you day in and day out if they won't have us."

Lysandra shivered at the images that created in her wicked mind.

"Now let me ask you again. Will you marry me?"

She closed her eyes. All she wanted was this man's love, this man's company, this man at her side for the rest of her life. She would be a fool to throw it all away for fear and for worry.

With a smile, she looked at him. "Yes," she whispered.

He gathered her to his chest and dropped his mouth to hers in a passionate kiss. She melted, pulling him closer, trying to mold herself to him in every way possible.

He drew back. "On the terrace, my dear?" he chuckled.

She smiled, for the first time in years feeling the weight lifted off of her shoulders and leaving only love of the deepest kind, joy of the brightest variety, hope that only a guaranteed future could bring.

"Oh yes," she whispered as she drew him into the darkness. "If it's good enough for the southwest corner, it's good enough for us."

He laughed, though it was clear he had no idea of the reference she was making. And then he pulled her against him and claimed her as his for once, for all.

Forever.

ALSO BY JESS MICHAELS

THE SCANDAL SHEET

One wicked little paper, six stories of the scandals within.

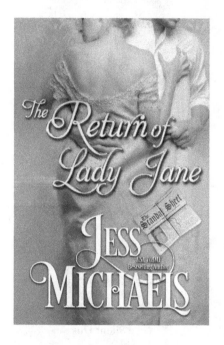

The Return of Lady Jane

Stealing the Duke

Lady No Says Yes

My Fair Viscount (coming July 2019)

Guarding the Countess (coming September 2019)

The House of Pleasure (coming November 2019)

THE 1797 CLUB

For information about the series,
go to www.1797club.com to join the club!

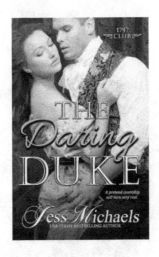

The Daring Duke

Her Favorite Duke

The Broken Duke

The Silent Duke

The Duke of Nothing

The Undercover Duke

The Duke of Hearts

The Duke Who Lied

The Duke of Desire

The Last Duke

SEASONS

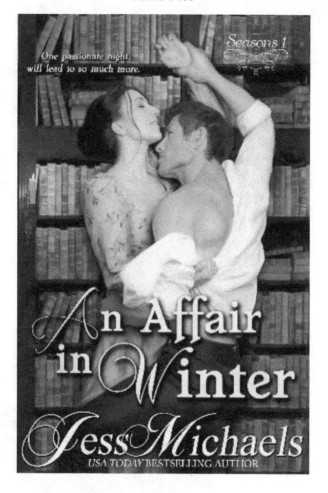

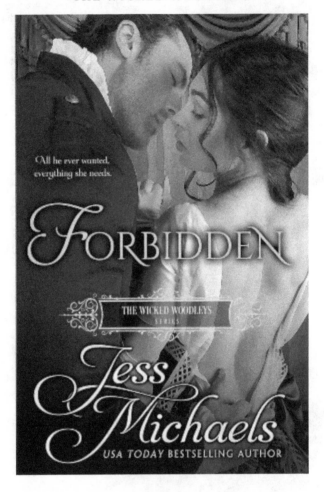

All he ever wanted,
everything she needs.

FORBIDDEN

THE WICKED WOODLEYS
SERIES

Jess
Michaels

USA TODAY BESTSELLING AUTHOR

~

THE NOTORIOUS FLYNNS

The Other Duke
The Scoundrel's Lover
The Widow Wager
No Gentleman for Georgina
A Marquis for Mary

~

THE LADIES BOOK OF PLEASURES

A Matter of Sin
A Moment of Passion
A Measure of Deceit

~

THE PLEASURE WARS SERIES

Taken By the Duke
Pleasuring The Lady
Beauty and the Earl
Beautiful Distraction

~

ABOUT THE AUTHOR

USA Today Bestselling author Jess Michaels likes geeky stuff, Vanilla Coke Zero, anything coconut, cheese, fluffy cats, smooth cats, any cats, many dogs and people who care about the welfare of their fellow humans. She is lucky enough to be married to her favorite person in the world and lives in the heart of Dallas, TX where she's trying to eat all the amazing food in the city.

When she's not obsessively checking her steps on Fitbit or trying out new flavors of Greek yogurt, she writes historical romances with smoking hot alpha males and sassy ladies who do anything but wait to get what they want. She has written for numerous publishers and is now fully indie and loving every moment of it (well, almost every moment).

Jess loves to hear from fans! So please feel free to contact her in any of the following ways (or carrier pigeon):

www.AuthorJessMichaels.com
Email: Jess@AuthorJessMichaels.com

Jess Michaels raffles a gift certificate EVERY month to members of her newsletter, so sign up on her website:
http://www.AuthorJessMichaels.com/

f facebook.com/JessMichaelsBks
🐦 twitter.com/JessMichaelsBks
📷 instagram.com/JessMichaelsBks